THE

GREEN

TUNNEL

Dorothy V. Wilson

The Green Tunnel

ISBN-10: 1530088410

ISBN-13: 978-1530088416

This book is dedicated to the city
of Great Falls, Montana, for the inspiration
I drew from the local panorama, especially
the green tunnel of Third Avenue North
where I lived for twenty-four years.

Dorothy V. Courtnage-Wilson

ACKNOWLEDGMENTS

I wish to thank the Emerald Coast Writer's critique group, past and present members. A special thanks to the most recent members for their support and critique contributions that assisted me to bring THE GREEN TUNNEL to fruition. Without them, this book would not have been written.

And, a particular thanks and appreciation to my gifted editor, Laurie Allen. She patiently worked with my narrative from start to finish and assimilated our ideas to craft the beautiful Green Tunnel cover.

CHAPTER 1

Shadowy storm clouds hugged the Montana horizon as a sliver of sun disappeared, imprinting a Monet sunset of pink and orange across the twilight canvas. A white sedan with a blue and gold seal on the door reading "Great Falls Police Department" pulled in front of the redbrick building. Years of neglect had turned the Becker Apartments, once a prime north side residential address, into a dilapidated eyesore. The glass entry door had missing panes and peeling paint. The trees lining the street had died of Dutch elm disease and the city had not yet replaced them, adding to the decayed ambiance of the area.

Two police officers stepped out of the patrol car, in no particular hurry; it wasn't a crime scene—only a call from a worried neighbor.

Porter Jablonsky scratched his shiny bald head. "Damn, don't like the look of those clouds."

"Yeah, the forecast calls for possible rain and freezing temps," Zach Anzalone said. "Get a load of that chain lightning over the Highwood Mountains."

Porter belched, his double chin rolling like an inbound wave. "That will make for wicked driving tomorrow, and I promised the kids we'd go hunting in the Highwoods. Sure glad this winter's about over. Been a bitch this year."

Zach noted the time and address in his notebook. "Which apartment did dispatch say?"

"The caller lives in 2C, next to our missing person."

Zach opened the squeaky front door. "Check with the super and meet me upstairs." When he knocked on 2C, an attractive woman in her twenties flung the door open. "Finally. I know something is wrong."

"Are you Ms. Johnson?"

"Yes, Tina Johnson. My friend Linda—Linda Merry—and I had a date to go out for a glass of wine Sunday evening. When she didn't come over, I knocked on her door and called several times. I hardly slept last night for worry. Her car hasn't moved since Saturday after work. She's home because Linda would drive if she only wanted to go to the corner. She didn't answer my knock or call this morning and I tried to get the manager to use his key, but he wasn't in. You might have to break down the door."

"Save your shoulder," Porter said from behind, waving the key.

Ms. Johnson rushed forward, but Zach

stopped her. "Stay here. I'll talk to you later."

Both officers went to apartment 2B. Zach knocked twice, then nodded at his partner and put the key in the lock. They drew their revolvers and entered, Zach in front. His eyes immediately focused on the nude woman lying in a pool of blood in the center of the living room rug. He motioned Porter toward a door he assumed was the bedroom; the two men cleared the apartment, making sure they were alone before holstering their weapons. The body's frozen face made it unnecessary to check for a pulse, but following proper procedure, Zach did; then he called dispatch. "Got a homicide, 2B, Becker Apartments."

~ ~ ~

Ready to go to lunch, Travis Eagle had one arm in his buckskin jacket when the phone rang. "Detective Eagle. Becker Apartments, 2B. Got it. Show me en route." As he left his office, he received another call. "Hi, Zach. Yeah, dispatch just called. I'm on my way."

Zach stood waiting on the street for Travis. "The CSI is here; she was just around the corner when she received the call. It's an ugly scene, Travis." He gazed away a moment. "No. Make that barbaric. The victim is mutilated and duct taped to the floor like a giant UPS box."

"That's a new twist." Travis put on his coveralls, polyethylene gloves and paper shoe covers. At the door, he stopped and added a surgical face mask to protect him from dangerous partials of bacteria and possible decomposing flesh. It would also help ward off the putrid odor already assaulting him.

Zach had already applied a dab of Vicks under his nose and walked over to Travis holding out the open jar. "Want some?"

"No thanks. I don't see that it helps that much." Marion will have a fit, he thought. The first time he'd gone home after investigating a corpse, his wife said he smelled worse than a skunk and insisted he take a shower immediately. It did not help. He'd tried to explain the odor of a decomposing body is permeating and remains in clothes, hair and fingernails even after several showers. His bed became the couch for two days. He himself remembered his first encounter with a body— being stunned when he later broke wind and his fart had the same nauseating stench. Thinking it was his imagination, he asked an old-timer about the incident and was told that he wasn't alone in recognizing the strange phenomenon.

Porter met Zach and Travis at the door, jerking his thumb toward the bedroom. "Hi, Chief. The kike is already here."

Travis's jaw tightened. "Don't call her that. From what I've heard Joella Bar-Lev is damn good at her job and CSU is lucky to have her."

"Okay, Chief."

"Don't call me chief, either."

"Gottcha, Chief."

Travis bit his lip and ducked under the crime scene tape stretched across the door. The small apartment swarmed with police personnel, each doing his or her particular part. He took in the tasteful and neat dwelling at a glance, everything tidy and in its place. No sign of a struggle. "Any evidence of breaking and entering?"

"Naw," Porter said, "which is strange because the lady who called this in claimed the door was locked when she tried it. Still was when we got here. The victim either let him in or he had a key."

When Travis turned around to study the body, his gut revolted in waves of nausea. *Why am I so queasy? I've seen dozens of murder victims worse than this. Must have been that Mexican joint Zach insisted going to for lunch.* Ignoring his unsettled stomach, he peeked at the nude woman again. *Zach's right. A damn psycho's on the loose.* The platinum blonde had been a real beauty, slim, yet well stacked. Her light blue eyes now stared unblinking at the ceiling.

Standing over the body, Travis crossed his hands over his chest, looked heavenward and in a whispered voice, said, "*Naató'si, ko'komíki'somm. Iikimmokinnaan, isspommookinnaan. Usniayi.*"

Porter overheard his whisper. "What the hell kind of mumbo jumbo is that?"

Zach elbowed Porter aside. "Shut up. It's a private thing."

Porter left in a huff, going into the next room.

Zach leaned in closer to Travis. "I've heard you use that prayer many times. What does it mean?"

"*Naató'si* means sun, holy one. Old moon, pity us, help us. That's it. The end. My mother taught me that prayer when I was only a kid.

5

The Blackfeet pray more to the creator today."

"Thanks. Always wondered what it meant."

Travis moved in to study the corpse. "I don't think I've ever seen a victim duct taped to this extent." Her arms taped to the floor over her head, the hands in a puddle of blood. Long strips of tape crossed the chest, waist and hips; the legs splayed, each knee and ankle taped securing the body to the floor. A crumpled strip of tape lay beside the head indicating the woman's neck had once been secured to the floor. Travis gawked. "This victim wouldn't have been able to move a muscle."

Zach flinched. "Shit. Don't tell me she was alive when the killer did this?"

"Looks that way."

While Travis studied the body and made notes, Zach nudged him. "Look at that thatch between her legs. I don't think I've ever seen a natural blonde before. She must be Swedish or something. The only blondes I ever banged were chemical ones with dark roots."

"How can you think about the women you've bedded after seeing the horrifying agony this poor woman suffered? If you spent less time in the weight room pumping iron to impress the bimbos you shack-up with, you might develop a little compassion."

Zach shrugged.

Travis refocused on the body. The thin red wound across the woman's neck stretched ear-to-ear, no longer oozing blood, her face ghostly pale, the carotid and jugular veins severed. Blood matted her long platinum hair and puddled on the floor; duct tape covered her mouth. He observed the right index finger hacked off at the third knuckle and laid into the sliced open vagina; the body's emptied urine pooled underneath. The left breast nipple was cut off and missing. "Sure not robbery," Travis said. "Look at the size of that diamond."

"That's a rock all right, it must be three carats at least." Zach glanced at the victim again. "I have never observed this particular defacement before. But why only one finger and one nipple?"

"You got me," Travis answered. "Seems like the bastard picked a precise and unusual combination of disfigurement all right. Most likely the selection has some special meaning in the killer's twisted mind."

"Okay, but where the hell is the nipple? Don't tell me this sick maniac is a cannibal too."

"Could be or maybe he's a trophy collector. The victim didn't have the opportunity to try fighting the whacko off, there's not a drop of blood anywhere except around the body. No broken nails, cuts or contusions."

Joella Bar-Lev came in from another room. "Detective Eagle, isn't it?"

"Call me Travis."

"Okay, Travis. I'm Joella. I'm not through yet, but our perp is either damn smart or very lucky. The scene is close to clean; I only needed two paper bindles so far. The techs are still dusting for prints. You know the routine."

"Sure do. You're here so I'll go interview the lady who called this in. What say we meet for coffee at Jakes after you finish and we can compare notes?"

"Sounds good. The ME is almost through. We won't know a lot until after the ME and lab completes their work. I shouldn't be longer than an hour or so. I'll stick around to see if the coroner wants help wrapping the body and bagging the hands and feet."

Zach walked by and Travis said, "See you tomorrow. I'm heading out."

"Okay, Chief."

Travis turned to Joella. "Take your time. I'll go by and see if Ms. Johnson can fill me in before I meet you at Jakes."

~ ~ ~

A retired police detective owned and ran Jakes Bar and Grill naming it after himself. Located near the police station, it became a trendy hangout for the cops the day it opened. The rustic wooden building with its pitched roof resembled an old barn without the typical big sliding door. Well experienced in the manner thieves worked, Jake had installed bright lights at every window and door. No fancy trappings decorated the inside. The business boomed because it had the "best damn grub in town" as Jake liked to say.

Travis walked inside Jakes hesitating at the door to let his eyes adjust from the glare of the lights outside. He spied Joella sitting at a wooden table against the far wall. She had removed the jacket of her pantsuit and he couldn't help but notice her well-stacked figure revealed by a form-fitting green sweater. Sliding her glass of wine closer she waved for him to join her. She smiled, flashing incredible green eyes with streaks of blue that seemed to change color like the Northern Lights whenever she turned her head, catching the light at a different angle. A slight twist of the left cuspid prevented an otherwise perfect set of teeth from looking like dental plates. Joella raised her glass. "As you can see, I didn't wait. I'm off the clock." Her light auburn hair shimmered with threads of gold as she swept a strand off her forehead in a graceful gesture. When he'd seen her earlier in the day, she was on duty with the mandatory controlled hair off her face. "Would you like to join me in a glass of wine?"

"No, thanks. I don't drink." Removing his jacket, he laid it on the seat and waved to the waitress. "Hey, June, one coffee, please."

When she brought the brew, Joella waited while he stirred in a sugar packet. After taking a sip of wine, she glanced at him. "What did the woman next door have to say?"

"Too hysterical to make much sense. She couldn't remember the names of the victim's two boyfriends. I'll have to wait until tomorrow to get the full story. How about you? Did you learn anything?"

"At first glance of the breast and vaginal mutilation and the body position, I wondered if we might have a picquerist on our hands, but there weren't enough cuts for that."

"Picquerist? I assume that's a type of serial killer."

"Yes. They get gratification from cutting or stabbing another person multiple times, usually the breasts and groin. Ted Bundy fell into that category. He took pleasure in the victim's pain. One of the worst known is The Butcher of Rostov in Russia. He murdered almost sixty people: men, women and children, in a dozen years."

Travis shifted backward in his chair. "What a bastard. Hard to believe monsters like that exist."

Joella's eyes glanced around the room, as if trying to wipe the horrible images from her mind. "Then I saw the finger, and I'm fairly certain we have a sexual sadist on our hands. They attack the breasts and genitalia too, leaving the face alone. They're hard to catch because they don't have a simple motive—can be about power, profit, anger and a couple of other things. Some strike whenever they have a successful hunt or happen to stumble on an opportunity."

"That description of a picquerist almost makes me glad we have *only* a sexual sadist on our hands," Travis said.

"Afraid I don't have much to add to the case. I did my bit, took the victim's fingerprints and did a visual examination. As expected, found lividity on her back, arms and legs. She died right where the body lay. He's right handed. Her wrists and ankles were mottled red bruises from her struggle with the duct tape."

"Yeah," Travis interrupted. "That's why killers use the tape so much. No way of twisting it loose."

Joella nodded and continued. "No tattoos and doesn't appear she was a junkie, no needle marks. The toxicology report will confirm or deny that." She paused long enough to take another sip of wine. "Her wallet was empty. I don't believe robbery was the motive because of the ring. No thief would leave that behind; but any criminal would certainly grab a few extra bucks from a wallet. Other than pictures, my crime report is pretty blank. Not much to make notes on. I'm hoping forensics might find something. One thing's for sure, this whacko is a hard-core misogynist. I suspect the victim was still alive when the maniac cut her and he got his kicks watching her agony while he jerked-off. If he did, the bastard was careful; we didn't find any semen. The poor victim was most likely near death when he yanked off the neck tape and committed the *coup de grace.*"

Travis cocked his left eyebrow. "He? Do you have evidence the killer is a male?"

"No, but the weird mutilations make me so sure that for the sake of conversation, I'm calling the suspect a he. I've never seen a female do this."

"See your point, but I'll still investigate female possibilities. Did you find her missing breast nipple?"

"That stumped me for a minute or two. When I pulled off the mouth tape, I found the nipple inside her mouth. The killer must have put it there after she died."

"At least we know he isn't a cannibal. What kind of a sick mind prompted such unusual disfigurement?"

"A really warped one," Joella answered.

"Any guess as to the time of death?"

"From the blood drainage, state of rigor mortis and ambient room and liver temps, my best guess would be sometime between noon and midnight Sunday. But you know how unreliable those estimates can be."

"Yes, I know, the science isn't perfect but it gives me a little something to go on. I'll talk to Ms. Johnson again tomorrow and get the names of Ms. Merry's boyfriends. I did find out the victim works as a waitress trying to support her mother who lives in a nursing home. Ms. Merry also volunteered there in her spare time."

"Isn't that typical? Always happens to the good ones," Joella said.

"Yeah, but I'm going to nail this creep. He is one sick bastard."

Joella leaned over, looking at Travis. "You know I'll do everything I can to help."

"Thanks for the update." Travis drained the last of his coffee. "Guess I better get home. The wife will be mad as hell. I was supposed to take her shopping. I'll have to offer a nice dinner out to pacify her."

"I'm sorry," Joella said. "This could have waited until tomorrow."

"Doesn't make any difference. She's always angry about something."

Porter, his big belly preceding him, came in. "Hey, Chief, learn anything?"

"I told you before, do not call me that. You will address me as either Travis or Detective Eagle. Understand?"

Porter rolled his eyes. His mouth twisted into a wide smirk, displaying large yellow teeth in need of cleaning. Winking, he strutted off toward another officer at a nearby table.

Travis picked up his jacket and stood. Joella also rose. "I'm ready to leave too." Once they were outside, she asked, "Why do you get so angry when Porter calls you chief. I noticed Zach called you that and you didn't say anything to him."

"I'm a Piegan Blackfeet Indian, and Zach uses it as a friendly soubriquet. Porter is a damn bigot who calls me Geronimo or any other 'Injun' name he fancies. I'm proud of my heritage, and I don't like his slurs."

Travis hesitated, putting on his jacket. "I can't tell you how many times I've pulverized my tongue to keep from knocking Porter on his ass. But I cannot do it. I'm the only Indian a city police department has ever hired in this state. If I deck him, he'd run to the recruiting officer and tell him I was nothing but an 'Injun' savage—I'd attacked him for no reason at all. The department would never hire another Indian."

"You may be right," Joella said, "but you have more restraint than me. I couldn't turn the other cheek that often."

"It's getting harder and harder—afraid I may lose the battle one of these days."

"Know what you mean. He's called me a few ugly names too, oven dodger being the worst."

Travis's eyes opened wide. That remark was cruel. "If I'd been there, I would have 'lost the battle' right then and knocked him on his ass."

Joella laughed, "I almost did."

His left eyebrow went up. "You mean you

could have taken him? He must have a good hundred pounds on you."

"Yes, but he doesn't have a black belt in karate."

Travis grinned. "Remind me not to cross you." He walked toward his pickup and waved. "See you tomorrow."

The rain began as Travis got into his black Chevy pickup, his stomach still queasy after viewing the murdered woman. No moon or stars peeked through the black, cloud-covered sky, the air heavy. Streetlights reflected in the glistening pavement as the soft flip-flop of windshield wipers kept rhythm with his chaotic thoughts. *Strange...I feel such a nagging impression that I know her.*

CHAPTER 2

Instead of the rain and freezing temperatures the weatherman had forecasted, Travis awoke to a beautiful, sunny day, crisp with the last of winter's chill. He gazed out the window at the row of new Dutch elms replanted along the avenue, the same trees that lined every street in the residential area. Bright new buds indicated an early spring: robins with orange breasts the color of grass fires had arrived, a flock pecking for worms in the front lawn. He opened the window and inhaled deeply. Travis didn't go to the police station; he went directly to re-interview Ms. Johnson. He knocked on her door. When it opened slowly, she appeared unkempt as if she hadn't slept. No longer crying and appearing calmer, she wore an elegant purple velvet robe. She hadn't washed her face for the black mascara smudges around her eyes contrasted the pale, river-like tear streaks that had washed away her makeup.

"Ms. Johnson, I spoke to you yesterday. You were in shock, and I said I'd return today. I need to ask you a few questions."

"Yes, I remember. Please come in. I'm sorry; I've forgotten your name."

"That is quite understandable considering the circumstances. I'm Detective Eagle." He glanced around the room while he waited for her to sit. The inexpensive furniture appeared stylish and in good taste. The room stood out because of the monochromatic beige and ivory color scheme that seemed like the work of a professional decorator. A place for everything and everything in its place. She sat on the couch and indicated the chair beside it for him.

"Thanks. I hope you have remembered the names of the two boyfriends you said Ms. Merry dated."

"Yes, I did. Sorry, I wasn't sure yesterday; I barely knew my own name and I couldn't stop crying. One of the men is Fergus Finnegan, a used car dealer on Tenth Avenue South and the other Timothy O'Toole. He is a doctor at Benefis East."

"Would you happen to know the name of Finnegan's business?"

"It's Finnegan's Car Lot or Used Vehicles, something like that. You can't miss it. The dealership bears his name."

"Thanks," Travis said, jotting the names in his notebook. *An O'Toole and a Finnegan. Ms. Merry had a thing for the Irish lads.* "Yesterday, you said she dated both men. Is that correct?"

"Yes, but she'd fallen in love with the doctor and planned to marry him. He gave her a gorgeous yellow diamond engagement ring." Her eyes opened wider. "Maybe that's why somebody killed her. Was she still wearing her ring?"

"Yes, she had it on which is why we ruled out robbery. Do you know when she broke up with Finnegan?

"Well—she hadn't. At least not completely. Linda tried. He wouldn't take no for an answer. She felt afraid of him and came to expect him to appear every night begging her to take him back. He just wouldn't leave her alone—like he was stalking her."

"Are you sure those were the only men she dated?"

"Positive. She discussed her relationships freely and never mentioned anyone else." Ms. Johnson brushed fresh tears from her cheeks. "A more kind and generous soul doesn't exist, and I can't believe anyone could do this to her. She went out of her way to help everyone. I can't tell you how many down-and-out guys she bought coffee and a sandwich for at the diner where she worked."

"Do you know the name of the diner?"

"Of course. I'd stop often for coffee if Linda was working. The owner is Roy Thumb and he thought it might draw customers if he named the diner Tom Thumb's. It was a cute cliché because it was small, only a few stools. Naturally, everyone called him Tom. He answered more to that name than he did Roy."

Travis noted the information in his notebook

and noticed Ms. Johnson looking at him.

"I just can't believe anyone would kill Linda. She didn't have an enemy in the world."

"Someone wanted her dead. Or the killer merely found her a good opportunity—she may not have even known him."

He observed how Ms. Johnson's facial muscles froze, her eyes wide. "Oh my God, maybe he'll come back. Several single females live in this building. I'm buying a gun."

"Relax. It's not probable he'll come back here, and having a gun most likely wouldn't have helped Linda Merry. Did she have any other girlfriends?"

"She didn't have much time for a social life other than the two guys she dated. We sometimes shared a glass of wine in the evening but rarely went out. Sunday night was special. She wanted to celebrate getting a raise because the extra money would have come in handy with her mom's expenses."

"Can you tell me Mrs. Merry's name and where she lives?"

"Her name is Bridgett Merry. Isn't that a pretty name? She emigrated from Ireland as a child. Linda told me Bridgett means fiery dart and how the name fit her to a T as she bustled about the house at breakneck speed." Ms. Johnson paused, a faraway look in her eyes. "It's so sad. She isn't very 'fiery' anymore and won't be able to help you. She has Alzheimer's and doesn't recognize anyone." She fidgeted, struggling for composure. "Linda visited her every day at the Grandview. She fed her dinner and often took her out for ice cream. Once I asked Linda why she visited so often because her mother didn't recognize her. She told me, 'She may not know who I am, but I know who she is.'"

Ms. Johnson began to weep, wiping the tears away with the back of her hand. While she collected herself, Travis breathed a sigh of relief. *At least I don't have to tell another mother her daughter is dead. No point visiting her, but I will verify her state of mind with the nursing home.*

Notifying family members of a loved one's death was the worst possible task any police official had to do, and typically, most officers had little training for the dreaded chore. They could only use their own core of compassion, and Travis often relived those horrible scenes for years. The more he heard about the victim, the more determined he became to catch the sick whacko.

He stood. "We'll get the guy," he promised handing her his card. "If you think of anything else that might be of interest—anything at all— give me a call. You can reach me anytime day or night." Travis headed for the door. "Thanks for your help."

The diner was within a few blocks of the apartment house. Travis wanted to talk to Roy Thumb and he was lucky, the owner happened to be there discussing menu changes with the short-order cook. He was of little help because he wasn't at the diner often enough to know if Linda ever had problems with any of her customers or not. The cook hailed from China and if any English spoken wasn't on the menu, he didn't understand a word. Only one waitress worked the diner at a time so the entire interview was useless.

~ ~ ~

The Roy Thumb interrogation was a bust. Still, walking to the patrol car, Travis felt confident. Both of Ms. Merry's boyfriends sounded like outstanding prospects—it had to be one of them.

Out of the past, a voice murmured in his mind, clear as a bell. *Good ol' Gus—he never lets me down.* Gus Kalinowski, mentor from Travis's rookie days, still guided him. He heard the voice unmistakably whisper MOM: *Means, Opportunity, and Motive.* Travis grinned. *I have a case.* The soft murmur in his mind no longer mystified him as it had the first time. Back then he'd become unnerved and filled with anxiety believing he was losing his mind. It didn't help matters when he confided in Marion. Instead of reassuring him, his wife usually replied, "You need a shrink. You're always hearing and feeling things that don't exist." He heard her nasty remarks so often he almost began to believe her. Eventually, he came not only to accept Gus's wisdom but also welcomed it, believing his mentor's message was a gift bestowed by *Naató'si.*

~ ~ ~

Travis located Timothy O'Toole's whereabouts and drove to Benefis East hospital just off Tenth Avenue South. When he arrived, O'Toole was still in surgery so he talked to some of the hospital staff. Everyone he spoke to seemed to admire the handsome doctor. One nurse did admit, while he appeared nice, she thought him a bit of a womanizer because he dated another lady while engaged to Linda.

Travis tried to hide his surprise. Both Linda Merry and O'Toole were dating two people. *Wonder if either knew about the other one.* "Do you know the name of the other woman?"

"Sorry, no. It was something like Doreen or Darleen, but I heard recently she'd quit her job."

Travis handed her his card. "If her name comes to mind, please call me."

The nurse left as O'Toole walked over. "Are you the detective asking for me?"

"Yes, I'm Detective Eagle" he said, flashing his badge. "Please sit down. I'm afraid I have bad news." The doctor remained standing so Travis continued. "I'm sorry to inform you your fiancée, Linda Merry, has been murdered. We discovered her body yesterday morning." Travis observed little reaction from O'Toole. *He seems mighty composed after learning his fiancée is dead. Does he already know because he did it?*

"That can't be true. Who would want to kill Linda? She didn't have a dime in the world. Oh, Lord, did they steal her engagement ring?"

Travis cringed. *He's lost his future bride and all he can think of is her engagement ring?* "No, it's in police custody. I need to ask you a few questions."

"I can spare you only a few minutes; I'm due back in surgery."

Those 'few minutes' turned out to be more than enough time—the good doctor had a near-perfect alibi. O'Toole was on call Sunday afternoon and he had spent most of the night operating on victims from a three-car pile-up on I-15. To commit the crime, his window of opportunity was slim. Travis didn't leave his card. Before exiting the building, he verified the doctor's alibi with hospital officials and found it accurate. *But, I won't rule him out.*

~ ~ ~

Locating Fergus Finnegan's Used Car Lot was easy. Travis couldn't miss the size of the letters that covered the top half of the building. He decided to seize the moment and drop in. Hundreds of used cars in every color of an artist's palette lined the lot like shiny bags of candy on a store shelf. From a wood shack in the back of the lot, a pimply-faced salesman who reminded him of a teenager, dashed out.

"Sorry, I'm not in the market for a car." He watched the faux smile disappear when he flashed his police badge and asked to speak to Finnegan.

The salesman raked scraggly, dirty blond hair back before answering. "He ain't here. Took the day off."

"Give me his home address."

"We ain't supposed to divulge personal stuff. I guess it's okay 'cause you're a cop. I'll have to get it in the office," he said, returning to the dapple-gray shack that badly needed a coat of paint. When he came back, he handed Travis a scrap of paper with scribbling so bad it resembled Arabic writing.

"I can't read this," Travis said. "Just tell me the address."

"I couldn't find his address, but I can tell

you where he lives."

"Okay, where is it?"

"It's out near the cemetery. He lives on Fifteenth Avenue South, somewhere around the thirteen or fourteen hundred block. It's next door to a big brick two-story house with a wrap-around porch. Fancy circular driveway in front. Ya can't miss it. The boss lives on the east side."

Preferring the element of surprise, Travis didn't call to see if Finnegan was home. He drove toward Thirteenth Street South, the road to the cemetery. At the stop sign, he spotted a police car approach with blinking blue lights leading a long procession of cars with their lights on. *Must be some bigwig's funeral with that many cars.* When the police car was even with his, a glowering Porter waved. Travis laughed. As glum as he appeared, must be a Jewish funeral. *That's a great job for the bigot. At least he's not antagonizing another cop on a crime scene.*

CHAPTER 3

The redbrick house was easy to spot. *At least the kid gives decent directions.* The huge house was a beauty, but Finnegan's house surprised Travis. The small white cottage had lilac bushes bordering the property line, the air smelling like a flower garden. A long curved concrete walk bordered with pansies led to a bright yellow door. On each side of the door sat a large pot of red geraniums and potted ferns hung from the front porch roof. Even the entrance welcome mat bloomed with painted flowers. He felt like he was in Oz. *I wonder where the Wizard is.* He knocked.

Travis could visualize the occupant already: a small, slight artistic type who would most likely faint if he asked him about a murder. He knocked again. No one answered. Turning to leave, he jumped when the door flew open. Stunned, he gawked at a barrel-chested, mountain of a man who filled the entire doorway. He resembled a sumo wrestler with ballooned biceps. Travis couldn't see around him.

Finnegan, Travis presumed, heaved hard, his curly red hair damp from exertion. His right arm cradled a tiny, yellow tiger kitten that he stroked with the other hand. The kitten purred like a small engine motorboat. "I'm sorry it took me so long to answer the door. I had to get my little Precious out of the tree before she fell." He put the kitten down. "Sorry, Precious. Daddy has company," he said, wiping sweat from his pale, freckled face with the bottom of his T-shirt.

Other than his eyes appearing too small in the round, chubby face, Finnegan was a nice looking man and Travis couldn't picture this gentle giant as the aggressive abuser described by Ms. Johnson. *Mr. Pussycat, a vicious killer? It doesn't make sense, but stranger things have happened.* "Thanks. I'm Detective Eagle," he said, displaying his badge. "May I come in?"

"Sure, as long as it isn't to sell tickets to some cops' benefit," Finnegan said flashing a silly smirk.

"No, I need to ask you a few questions about a police investigation." Walking through the door, Travis glanced around. Flowered curtains hung on the window and the couch had petunia print pillows. He turned to face Finnegan. "I'm afraid I have bad news. Your girlfriend, Linda Merry, was found murdered."

The man's hand clutched his chest. "Mother of God, that can't be right. I just saw her. Who would kill my sweet Linda?"

"That's what we're trying to find out. We believe she was killed on Sunday."

Finnegan's blue eyes stared straight ahead focused on nothing. A few moments later, a low bellow came from the depth of his soul. "No, no, no. Not my sweet Linda. I loved her." The big man's knees gave way and he sank to the floor sobbing.

Travis scratched his head. He couldn't believe the reaction he saw from this great hulk of a man. *If he did it, he is a damn good actor.* He leaned over and gently helped the grief-stricken giant to a Lazy Boy, the man barely fitting between the worn out chair arms.

Finnegan wiped his eyes with a large flower-print kerchief he pulled from his pants pocket. After a moment, he pointed to a chair. "Sit down and tell me what I can do to help find the monster that killed my darling Linda. I loved her, you know. She fell for some other dude and wanted to break it off with me. I couldn't bear to let her go. I figured if she knew how much I worshipped her, she would change her mind, but she didn't."

Travis felt surprised at the guy's rambling. *Doesn't he understand he's a prime suspect?* Following his usual line of questioning, he asked a few trivial questions first to put the huge man at ease. Then he said, "When did you see her last?"

The directness of his query didn't faze Finnegan. "Late Saturday night. I went to her apartment to beg her not to dump me. She wouldn't listen. Said to leave her alone, that she was getting hitched to some doctor. She actually ordered me to leave."

"Were you angry when you left?"

"Damn right. She wouldn't listen to reason."

"You never saw her again?"

"No."

Travis took a deep breath before he asked the all-important question. *Now let's see if he has an alibi.* "Where were you this last Sunday between ten in the morning and midnight, and can anyone verify it?"

"Yeah, uh no. I missed most of it. I felt crappy after Linda kicked me out, and I went to a blowout with some guys from the car lot. Our head salesman wanted to celebrate his divorce and we started partying about noon. Still furious with Linda, I hit the sauce hard. I couldn't tell you how late the bash lasted. I passed out early. My assistant manager took me to his house and I spent the night on the couch. Monday morning he drove me back to the bar to get my car."

"I need his name and number."

"His name is Tucker Williams. Don't know his home phone number off hand, but you can reach him at the car lot."

Travis slapped his notebook shut. *Damn. Looks like his alibi is as solid as O'Toole's is— he has an entire gathering to swear to his whereabouts.* Any hope he had for a quick solution to this grisly case collapsed like the stock market on every 'sure thing' he'd ever invested in.

Before heading back to the station, Travis went to Tom Thumb's diner again. A rail-thin waitress put a glass of water in front of him. "Haven't seen you in a while." Travis thought he'd eaten a sandwich there once but wasn't sure—the food must not have been impressive and he didn't remember ever seeing the waitress before. The interview was brief. She'd never even met Linda Merry.

~ ~ ~

Travis drove back to the station and called Williams, who not only verified Finnegan's alibi but said his wife would gladly vouch for his whereabouts as well. She was not happy about cleaning the mess he left in the bathroom.

Travis was scowling at his disappointment when Zach popped his head in the door. "Hey, you're just the guy I've been looking for. Dexter made detective. Finally, on his third try," he said, winking. "The announcement just came down. He's so excited he can't sit still, running around like a maniac on meth. After we clock out, we're all getting together at BJs to celebrate. Come join us."

"Zach, you know I don't drink."

"I know, but this is a real special occasion, buddy. You can't miss it. Surely you can have one beer or even a Coke."

"Sorry, I won't be there. I've got things to do, but please congratulate Dexter for me."

Disillusionment still fogged Travis's mind and he closed his laptop. He walked down the hall to Joella's office. She smiled when he opened the door, and he plopped in to a chair. "Been that bad a day?" she asked.

"Sure has. When I talked to Ms. Johnson again, she told me Ms. Merry had dated two guys and both wanted to marry her. A doctor and a local used car salesman. She fell for the doctor and accepted that rock on her finger. The other guy wouldn't take no for an answer. Kept popping up at her place unannounced. According to Ms. Johnson, he was abusive and smacked her around. She became afraid of him. I thought I had two perfect suspects."

"What do you mean 'thought?'"

"They both alibied out."

"You're kidding. Both of them?"

"Both of them."

"You might want to take another look."

"Why?"

"When I examined the corpse, the breast wound appeared so neat it almost looked like the work of a surgeon—sure wasn't any hack job. You might want to check on that alibi again. My money would be on the doc."

"Appreciate the tip. The hospital verified his alibi, but I'll double check it."

"Maybe another view of the body might help. I was just about to leave. The autopsy is scheduled now. Come join me in the lab; we can walk over together."

Travis checked the time and agreed but wished he had something urgent enough to keep him from attending. Although necessary, he dreaded post-mortem examinations. Not because he tossed his cookies like some, but because he hated to see the utter destruction and degradation of what was once a warm, loving human being—in this case Linda Merry. Aside from Y incisions made from shoulders to vagina, skull sawed open to remove brains and peel back the face, eyes pierced and internal organs removed leaving a hollow shell, the victim, brutalized and killed by a male, now suffered a final indignity: more men probing and taking swabs of her vagina.

~ ~ ~

After the autopsy, Travis walked out with Joella. With every step, the stench of the cadaver's odor wafted with him, clinging to his clothes and hair. He waved his hand in front of his face as if to swish in clean air, but it did no good. "The autopsy didn't help much other than confirm what we already suspected: the killer was right handed and the ante mortem blood proved she was alive during the sadistic butchery."

Joella shrugged. "You can't expect a lot from some autopsies. We'll have to wait for the lab results. We might get lucky with the nail scrapings and vaginal swab. The ME did say they found hair and fibers after he sticky taped the skin. When the ME said no main arteries were cut with the first mutilations and Linda Merry may have lived as much as an hour or more before her body emptied its five liters of blood, it made me so angry I almost popped a blood vessel myself. The bastard had plenty of time to enjoy himself—more than once."

~ ~ ~

Days went by without hearing from the ME or lab and Travis's impatience grew. He felt it still too early but went to check with Joella anyway. On the way, dispatch routed him to another call and he didn't get back to the station until late. Taking his notebook, he tossed his jacket on the chair and walked toward her office.

Zach met him in the hall. A wide grin spread across his friend's handsome Italian face, displaying even white teeth. The small butterfly-like scar on his chin, exaggerated the cleft the ladies found so charming.

"Make any progress on the Merry case?"

"Not yet," Travis tossed over his shoulder as he went into Joella's office. He sat opposite her desk. "Did you or the ME find anything after the autopsy?"

Joella leaned back in her chair. "Afraid not. I don't think I have ever seen a cleaner crime scene. Ms. Johnson volunteered a hair sample and her fingerprints immediately. The techs also found a bunch of prints. I'm betting most of them will be the victim's or Ms. Johnson's. I would have thought that odd except she told the technician that Linda never took her boyfriends to her apartment."

Travis fumbled for his notebook. "That's sure out of character for most of today's young women."

"You got that right," Joella replied. "Only found a few other smudges and doubt there will be enough prints to register on the database. I suspect the killer wore gloves."

Travis groaned. "What about DNA?"

"I didn't find as much as a single unidentified hair on the scene. The fibers and hair the sticky tape pulled off during the autopsy haven't been identified. In addition to gloves, I'm thinking the killer wore a tight-fitting cap, booties and some kind of coveralls. A lot like what we wear. Most likely grabbed her from behind because I found no indication she fought back."

"That's what I figured too."

"We still might luck out," Joella said, "if the ME finds something under her fingernails or if she was raped. That would be a break for us. I couldn't identify what clothes she was wearing. The hamper held a few items, and there were damp clothes in the washing machine. I have no way of knowing who put them there—the victim or the killer." Joella paused, running her tongue across her lower lip. "The murderer might have washed her clothes to be certain he didn't leave any forensic evidence behind. As I said earlier, it seems as if we're dealing with a very intelligent killer. Hate to think this, but I wonder if he has police experience or has worked in a forensic lab."

"Great. Got any more good news for me?"

"Don't feel bad, Travis. Killers today have the advantage of the Internet and they can see where other murderers made mistakes. Police techniques and retired cops are everywhere online. And movies and TV are full of crime drama. Makes our job a lot harder than it was a few years ago."

"Sure does. Did you find the weapon?"

"No. It was some kind of thin blade."

"Like a doctor's scalpel?"

"Maybe, but didn't seem quite that thin."

He frowned. "Not looking good, is it?"

"No, not yet, but with your experience you know it's way too soon to give in now. How long have you been on the force, Travis?"

"Thirteen years."

"That's a long time. You ever grow tired of it—the frustration of those who got away?"

"No, not really. I get a lot of satisfaction putting as many as I can behind bars. How long have you been with the CSU?"

"Only six years. I trained and worked in Seattle until the pace became brutal. Too big a city for my taste—a lot of crime. When I heard about an opening in Great Falls last month, I applied for it."

"Glad you did; we can use you."

Joella flashed a warm smile. "Hope I can live up to the challenge."

"I'm sure you will. Our lab doesn't have much to analyze on the Merry case right now. Maybe we'll get lucky. When do you think we might get the results?"

"Never know; it usually takes a while. Too long. I did request that they call me before they finished if they discovered anything remarkable or unusual. And, I also asked them to be extra careful. There is way too much compromised evidence coming out of crime labs these days. I don't want to lose this bastard on botched lab work."

"That's for sure. Please call me if you hear anything. I feel like this guy is slipping away from us." Travis closed his notebook and left, a hollow feeling in his gut. He was almost out the front door when Joella came running down the hall.

"Hold on, Travis. The lab hasn't finished yet, but they called a minute ago to tell me something interesting. You may want to take another crack at your potential suspects."

"Why? I planned on checking out the doctor again when you claimed the slash looked professional, despite his ironclad alibi. Why Finnegan?"

"The ME found what I would call a prime, Class A motive for both the suspects. She was pregnant."

CHAPTER 4

Dispatch kept Travis busy all week. It felt like the run on banks during the Great Depression and every small business in town seemed to be on the burglars' honey-do list along with car thefts and home invasions. A group of angry citizens complained about a hooker using their porches to conduct business and he arrested her, a job he hated. By the time he'd finished the paperwork, the prostitute's lawyer had sprung her. He met her orange head of hair and inch-long eyelashes in the hall; she swayed her full hips in a tight miniskirt and suggested he come see her sometime. "I'll give you a freebie, sweetie."

~ ~ ~

By Friday, Travis was thankful to see the end of his shift. He hadn't been sleeping well. Ms. Merry's murder investigation continued to drag out. The lack of clues and progress in the case raised his anxiety level to high. It didn't help that the *Great Falls Tribune* printed daily articles hinting how the police seemed unable to catch the killer they had dubbed the Merry Murderer. Whenever a brutal killing occurred, the newspapers invented fanciful nicknames like The Green River Killer and The Boston Strangler; even the cops used the moniker. For some reason those infamous signature names didn't bother Travis, but he cringed whenever he heard the Merry Murderer. Using the poor victim's name was insensitive and he couldn't bring himself to say it, so he concocted his own soubriquet: MM.

~ ~ ~

On the drive home, Travis turned his wipers to low after the pelting rain had turned to an intermittent drizzle. All he could think about was relaxing, visualizing his butt planted in the black Lazy Boy in front of the television. He hated to admit it, but Marion had done a nice job decorating their apartment. Then again, most people with a modicum of style would do well if they shopped only expensive items. He still shuddered, remembering their shopping sprees for furniture. She asked the cost first. Nothing had ever been suitable unless it had a fancy price tag. Her style favored modern, and two tiger barrel chairs and a caramel sectional couch rested atop an ivory carpet with black coffee and end tables. She had fought the chair he wanted insisting it was tacky until his stubborn persistency finally won at the end of the day. He hadn't known then what a rare victory that would be in the future.

Travis opened the door and proceeded to hang his jacket when he heard Marion call from the kitchen.

"Dinner is ready. Hurry and eat; I'm joining Cora for a special two-hour sale at the mall. She's driving tonight so you don't have to."

A heavy sigh of relief escaped him—going to the mall was the last thing he needed. He wasn't hungry, but rather than face his wife's wrath at being unappreciated, he joined her. "I want to drive to Browning on Saturday. I called Aunt Winona and she said she would arrange for a sweat lodge. This Merry case is getting me down—I need to rejuvenate my spirit and body."

Marion glared at him. "What the hell am I supposed to do while you're sweating your ass off?"

"You could spend time with Aunt Winona; she loves company."

"Yeah? I tried that before. She can't hold an intelligent conversation. All the old hag babbles about is the glorious days of Running White Buffalo. Who the hell was he anyway?"

"Her great grandfather, a legend in his time and a mighty warrior. The entire tribe still honors his grave today."

"Who cares?"

"Okay," Travis said, his voice on edge. "Tell you what, if you go, we will not stay the entire day. We could take the long way home and have a nice dinner in Cut Bank or Shelby."

"Nice dinner. Where? There's nothing except greasy spoons in those bergs. I'm not going. If you weren't so damn cheap and bought me a car, I could do something fun for a change. I'm tired of sitting around here with nothing to do all day."

Travis exhaled a long breath. "If you had agreed to have a baby you wouldn't have to sit around all day with nothing to do. Then you'd have someone to lavish with love." *You're sure not lavishing any on me.*

"I've told you a dozen times, I am not having a damn half-breed papoose ruin my figure. I want a car."

Travis ignored the insult. "You know I can't afford another vehicle. We've talked about it before. If you'd quit spending so much money on fancy clothes you never wear, maybe we could save some money."

"The reason I never wear my 'fancy clothes' is because you're too damn cheap to take me anywhere," Marion yelled. "Besides, we just went to that stupid foot-stomping Sundance Ceremony a couple of months ago; I spent the entire day watching you hop up and down like a jack rabbit on hot coals."

Travis balled his fist, his face reddening. "Marion, the Ookaan is important to me. You knew I was an Indian when you married me."

"Maybe so, but I am not a damn squaw," she screeched, hurling her half-full coffee cup at him.

Travis's jaw tightened, nails cutting into his palms. He snatched the towel on the counter and wiped his face. *I have to get out of here before I choke the bitch.* Grabbing his jacket from the hall tree, he bolted for the door.

"Sure, go get drunk like you always do

instead of having it out with me. Ma will take care of you."

By the time he reached his pickup, Travis still shook with rage. He jammed the vehicle into reverse, backed out and stomped on the gas pedal with no idea where he was going, streetlights flying past in a blur. Trying to get his anger under control, he turned onto Third Avenue North. Driving through the blocks-long, green tunnel of ancient elm branches arching across the street always relaxed him. It reminded him of the forest and mountains he loved—the land where *Naató'si* intended the Indians to live—not on a damn reservation.

~ ~ ~

Travis had been born on the flat open prairie of the Blackfeet Indian Reservation in Glacier County. The detestable reservation bordered Glacier National Park, his beloved mountains; near, but oh, so far away when you were a child. He had hated living there. A lonely boy with no other children nearby, he often asked his mother to bring home a baby brother for him to play with. Later, when he was old enough to attend school the kids teased him about being skinny and tormented him about his weird name. After a particularly painful day of mockery at school, he questioned his mother how she came to name him Travis. "It doesn't sound Indian and the kids always make fun of my name."

When he became of age, he could still recollect every word of his mother's reply. "I know, son, and I'm sorry. After my marriage, I came to the reservation on a travois. I was little more than a child myself. I loved riding the travois. I was so happy, and I got pregnant with you on the trip. I wanted your name to remind me of those joyful days and Travis was the nearest I could come to travois."

He had scowled. "I'd be better off if you just named me Travois. At least it sounds Indian."

Travis loved his mother and he would have had a happy childhood if not for his father, an alcoholic who beat his mother and him every time he got drunk, which was every day after payday until the money ran out. At an early age, Travis recognized not only his father but also many of the men on the reservation were alcoholics. When Travis was five, his father flew into a rage because he ran out of whiskey and his mother wouldn't give him the few dollars she needed to buy us food. He went berserk and beat both wife and son severely, nearly killing them. Right then, Travis swore to his mother he would never drink alcohol. "Not ever," he told her.

A near outcast among his peers, Travis continued to plead for a baby brother. But as he grew older, he understood why his mother prayed to *Naató'si* every night never to become pregnant again.

When his beloved mother died suddenly on his fourteenth birthday, his childhood ended. He ran away and never went back while his father lived. After his father's death, Travis returned often to the only family he had left, Aunt Winona, his mother's sister who had moved into his family home.

~ ~ ~

His face still smarted from the hot coffee
Marion had thrown at him and once Travis left
the calming green tunnel, his mind returned to
Marion's rampage. His fury returned tenfold.
The Third Avenue green arch had not worked
its magic, and he turned around at Gibson
Park and drove back through the street again.
His hands still clutched the steering wheel so
tightly his fingers turned white—First Avenue
South drew him like a magnet.

CHAPTER 5

The sign flashed "Betsy's Bar" in sparkling neon red. Driving past, he resisted the urge to go inside and break the promise he'd made, yet again, to his mother long ago. Travis drove down the street. At the end of the block, he slowed—stopped a few moments—and then made a U-turn. He didn't recognize any cars in the parking lot so he drove around to the alley where there was room for the owner's car and one other behind the building. One spot was empty.

Travis went in through the back door. Inside, his eyes scanned the room taking in a brawny redheaded man at a nearby table, his hand sliding up and down a buxom brunette's leg. He could smell the powerful aroma of her perfume from across the room. Its pungent chemical flower odor nearly gagged him. *She must have bathed in Dollar Store's Eau de parfum.* Two other men sat at the far end of the bar, involved in deep conversation. He detected no one he knew.

Betsy—better known as Ma—stood behind the bar mopping a spill only she seemed to see, a process she repeated often, needed or not. She was so short that patrons across the room saw only her head floating back and forth over the top of the bar. With her tight silver-gray curls atop a round cherub face, she resembled a kewpie doll.

When she spied Travis, her face lit up. "What are you having, Honey, Coke or coffee?"

Travis did not reply. His shoulders slumped and he sat at the bar." Bring me a shot of bourbon, Ma."

"Oh Lord. Don't tell me. You and the Mrs. been at it again?"

"Afraid so."

"You two fight all the time. Why on earth don't you leave her sorry ass?"

"I don't know. I think I'll have to before I do something I'll regret. She's a strict Catholic and believes divorce is a sin. She told me before we were married that she would never agree to a divorce. I can't bring myself to do that to her."

Ma never called him by his name. "Okay, Honey, but you know the Travis Rule."

"Yes, Ma, I know the 'Travis Rule.'" Digging in his pants' pocket, he laid his truck keys on the counter. "Now bring the bourbon."

Ma put the keys in her pocket and pulled a shot glass from under the counter, filling it to the brim. She put the drink on the bar and he threw the shot back in one gulp. "Bring another. On second thought, just leave the bottle."

"Okay, Honey, but I do wish you'd go home instead."

He filled his glass.

~ ~ ~

When Travis awoke the next morning, his head pounded like the beat of a tom-tom. He opened his eyes, squinting from the sunshine pouring through the open drapes. The flickering leaves on the elms outside his window beamed bright flashes of sunlight into his eyes. He squeezed them shut. *Now I know how a suspect feels when we question him under a spotlight. I need aspirin.* He opened his eyes once more and found he was in his own bed, Marion nowhere in sight. He assumed Ma had taken care of him—again. Her friends always drove him home after those rare drunken nights. Still fully clothed, he noticed his jacket on a chair across the room. Rising, he put his hand in a pocket and felt his keys. He couldn't remember anything about last night. Travis closed his eyes. *Damn. Another blackout.*

His blackouts terrified him because he could never remember what he did.

CHAPTER 6

When the weekend came, Marion still refused to go to Browning so Travis went alone to use the sweat lodge, a gift *Naató'si* gave the Blackfeet. After four rounds of singing, he felt purified from the steam of the holy rocks the Indians gathered new for each sweat lodge. Feeling at peace with the world, he spent the night at Aunt Winona's house since Marion wasn't there to insist on staying at a hotel.

Before leaving for Great Falls the next day, he repaired a broken gate and did a few other chores his aunt could no longer handle. When he left for home, he felt renewed, his spirits high. Too early to eat but not eager to face Marion, he decided to take the long way back and enjoy that 'nice dinner' he'd suggested at one of the 'greasy spoons' she'd snubbed.

The drive home gave Travis time to relish the natural high he experienced from the sweat lodge. He rolled down the windows, the brisk rush of spring air filling his lungs, revitalizing him further. Thankful for Montana's generous speed limits and roads with little traffic, he drove fast through miles of rolling, open prairie and slowing only for the river running through the deep, sculptured ravine entering Cut Bank. The town, twenty-five miles from the Canadian border often placed first in the weather report as the coldest spot in the nation. He was glad spring had sprung.

By the time Travis arrived in the small town of Shelby, urgent hunger pains rumbled in his stomach and he stopped at a restaurant near the Interstate ramp. The narrow, shiny aluminum building—made to resemble the old-time-diners of the 1950s—had a long counter and a row of stools. He'd eaten there before. The menu wasn't elaborate, but the food tasted good and the forks and spoons clean.

Entering the vestibule door, he read an announcement taped to the inside glass door: "Specialty of the Day: Sweetgrass Steak." He couldn't believe his luck. Sweetgrass-fed cattle were famous for producing the most tender and rich-flavored meat in the country—impossible to buy privately because all the beefsteaks were shipped to packinghouses in Chicago for conventions. He grinned. *The cook must have a friend in the cattle business.*

Travis sat on a stool near the door, inhaling the delectable aroma that wafted through the entire diner. When the waiter brought the steaming platter, his mouth salivated. He hesitated, and then sniffed the meat like a connoisseur tilting a wineglass. When he cut into the steak, the juices flowed across the platter and he devoured each succulent bite.

After he polished off the steak, he wiped his mouth with a paper napkin and a wicked grin crossed his face. *Marion, you don't know what you are missing in this 'greasy spoon,' but I sure as hell am going to elaborate about it when I tell you.* Steak was her favorite food—it was expensive.

~ ~ ~

Monday morning, Travis left for work feeling an eagerness in his bones to tackle the case again. Dispatch kept him running most of the day and he didn't get back to the office until late. He decided to review his notes and study Finnegan and O'Toole again. *If Ms. Merry was pregnant, I still think I'm on the right track with those two.* Because Finnegan liked to slap women around, Travis assumed he would have a record. He did but had no convictions; his wife—now his ex—refused to press charges. Those cases always left Travis disheartened because he knew it would happen again.

Finnegan's record lacked the necessity to question him further, but that of O'Toole's astonished him. *Well look at this, Mr. Tall, Dark and Handsome has a record. Not one, but two assault cases on women. This is getting interesting.* Faking an alibi would be easy for an important surgeon, a powerful man around the hospital. Spread a little cash around here and there or maybe a few threats to the right people.

Thrilled when he found O'Toole's two assault

cases, his excitement fizzled when Travis learned both women had dropped their charges against the doctor soon after they filed them. *Dammit.* Irritation flashed through his body, making him aware of his exhaustion. He looked at the clock. *That's it. I've had it.*

On his way out, he intended to see if Joella had learned of any new developments but she wasn't in her office. Then, because of a day in court to testify in a dreaded death notification for a family and other assorted assignments, Travis didn't see her in passing until Friday. He found her hunched over some paperwork. Joella raised her eyes when she heard the door open. "Hi. You must be burning the midnight oil too."

"I wanted to bring you up to date. I checked Finnegan for priors. Expected to find assault records and his wife did call the police twice. When the cops got there he'd already calmed down, and she wouldn't press charges when he said, 'It won't happen again.'"

Travis felt great empathy for battered wives because they reminded him of his mother's many beatings. Remembering his involvement in these cases, he scowled—there was *always* a next time.

"Then I checked O'Toole. Didn't expect to find much because everyone at the hospital seems to admire him, but I got a surprise. He also had a couple of priors. A woman called 9-1-1 claiming assault. When the cops arrived, they found her bloody, but she then claimed it was an accident and wouldn't file charges. He was nowhere in sight. Happened again with the same outcome. So I'm going to interview the doctor again—and those two women. Maybe I'll find a different face for O'Toole."

"You never know," Joella said. "Sometimes those nice, handsome guys are the worst abusers. Let me know how it goes."

"Will do, but right now I'm bushed. Been a long day. I'm outta here."

"Me too. Think I'll just relax this weekend, maybe take in a movie. You and Marion have plans?"

"Not really. I wanted to go to the Russell Museum. I hadn't been there in a long time but Marion wants to go shopping."

"Is Russell that self-taught cowboy artist who had one-man shows all around the world?"

"That's him."

"I'm not sure if I've ever seen his work."

"You should check out the museum. His old stone house and next-door studio are open to the public. I like Russell's work because of the detail. One summer he lived with the Blood Indians witnessing their everyday lives and perfecting his painting style. Every detail of clothing and horse tack is authentic—each bead and feather in perfect place." Travis headed for the door. "I think you'd like his work."

"Sounds interesting. I'll check it out one of these days."

Because he and Marion had only one vehicle, his wife's shopping plans for the weekend meant Travis had to play chauffer again. In his disgust, he hadn't realized Joella had already left; he hadn't heard her cheerful "See you Monday, Travis." He stood staring into space, his vision a soft glossy glow as images rambled across his mind like the prairie's homeless tumbleweed—bringing thoughts of an existence he'd felt cheated out of his entire life. In the museum he could relax to lose himself in the paintings of a long-gone world, a world where spindle columns of smoke rose from the lodge holes to blend into sapphire blue skies, the trapping of beaver and the thunderous buffalo hunts requiring prime new feathers for arrow shafts, the smoking of pipes and dancing to the steady, heavy drumbeats that echoed across the plains drowning out the song of the wolf and coyote. War-painted faces and the counting of coup never entered into his daydream. He was a man of peace.

The first chance he had, Travis interviewed everyone on Benefis East's staff connected with O'Toole's alibi and checked hospital records. Everyone admired the doctor and he could not find a chink in his alibi. Travis decided to interview the two women who had claimed assault but later refused to press charges. They might accidentally provide some useful background information. Back in his office, he searched all the available records and files but could not locate the whereabouts of either of the woman. It was as if they never existed. Both had left their jobs without prior notice. Neither left a forwarding address. *I'll bet Mr. Perfect paid them off and they skipped town. Okay, there's still Finnegan. Maybe one of his alibi guys will slip up.*

~ ~ ~

Several days passed before Travis ran into Joella at the station. "Sorry I didn't get back to you as promised, it's been hectic. I interviewed half the people in the hospital, had a couple of robberies to contend with, and some idiot stabbed a guy at one of the local dives on Tenth Avenue just because the lovesick jerk played the same sad song on the jukebox over and over. If the victim dies, I hope he thinks it was worth it."

Joella shook her head. "Hard to believe the silly things that drive some people over the edge, isn't it? What about the two women who filed charges on O'Toole?"

"No sign of them anywhere. Apparently, they left town in a hurry—as if someone paid them off. Think I'll try interviewing some of Finnegan's drunken friends tomorrow."

"*Mazel Tov.*"

Travis's left eyebrow shot up. "What?"

"Sorry. It's Hebrew for good luck."

"Afraid I don't know much about Jewish people."

"That's okay. I don't either. I am Jewish by birth but I'm not a practicing Jew and I forgot most everything crammed down my throat as a child."

Travis's forehead wrinkled. "If that's your heritage, you should be proud of it, learn more about it." Before she could answer, he asked, "Did the ME find any further results?"

"Oh my, yes. Results—but no clues. No surprise on the cause of death, and he found no DNA under her fingernails so it appears as if she didn't fight back. The only blood on the scene belonged to her. The toxicology report came back negative. The duct tape proved to be common hardware store variety, the favorite tool of killers; no amount of twisting and turning ever helps a victim as you said earlier. And he didn't rape her—no semen. Think I was right, the maniac probably jerked-off watching her dying in agony."

"Damn," Travis said.

"Yeah, that's how I feel."

He stood. "Better get going. Catch you tomorrow." Joella stood too, and for the first time his eyes took in her entire figure. *Not bad, and she's nice too.*

~ ~ ~

When Travis arrived home, Marion was gone, but she'd left a post-it note on the refrigerator. "I'll be gone all afternoon. I'm with Cora. Tonight I plan to attend late Mass."

Crap. That means two trips to the church tonight. He had to agree with Marion, they needed a second car, but there was no way he could afford one. *Guess I'm stuck chauffeuring.* In the kitchen, he checked the refrigerator: no leftovers. A glance at the counter rewarded him with a half-full coffee pot. He reheated a cup in the microwave and decided to scramble some eggs until he remembered the Billings Bulls had a hockey game that night. The egg carton went back into the refrigerator, and he flopped in the Lazy Boy ratcheting the leg rest higher. When he turned on the tube, the game was in progress. Finding the score one-sided, he soon dozed off.

~ ~ ~

Travis woke from his sound sleep when Marion returned and kicked the chair, jarring him awake. Her arms loaded with packages and sacks, she wore a new dress in her favorite style—expensive.

She twirled around. "How do you like it?"

He felt too disgusted to comment.

"I'm making a fresh pot of coffee. Want some?"

"Yes," he said following her into the kitchen. Sitting at the table, he rubbed his hand.

"What's the matter with your hand?"

"I moved some heavy boxes and furniture at the office today. Guess I strained it."

Marion rolled her eyes. "Seriously? You are always having imaginary aches and ailments. I told you before that you need a shrink. You're losing it."

"Stop saying that. What are you trying to do, get me committed?"

She didn't answer.

Travis slouched in the chair. "I'm hungry. What's for dinner?"

"I don't have time to cook; I'm going to Mass. You'll have to heat some leftovers."

"There aren't any, and I am *not* driving you to church until I get something to eat."

He observed her lips part in a sweet smile. "You don't have to drive me. I bought a car."

"You did what?" he yelled, feeling his face burning. "I told you before; I cannot afford a second vehicle."

"I am tired of sitting around here with nothing to do while you go to Browning all the time. I saw this cute little baby blue convertible and couldn't resist it. We had enough in the checking account for the down payment so what are you bitching about."

"Did you stop to consider how I can make the monthly payments?"

"If you'd quit making so many trips to Browning, we'd have more money."

The glaring glow of Betsy's neon bar sign flashed across his mind.

~ ~ ~

When he opened the door, Ma looked at him. "This better be a business call, Honey, or you're fast losing this battle."

"I know Ma, but if I didn't get out of there, I would have done something I'd regret. She bought a car knowing damn well I can't afford it."

Ma noticed his shaking hands. "Oh Lord, calm down before you bust a gut. Better here than elsewhere. I'll get the bourbon."

~ ~ ~

Travis awoke the next morning fully clothed, lying in his own bed. *Thanks Ma.* His head pounded like a jackhammer. Slowly, he edged out of bed and checked his jacket for the car keys. They were there.

CHAPTER 7

Monday morning Travis sat hunched over his laptop, his eyes blurry from hours of searching for similar MOs in the FBIs ViCAP. His blackout headache had finally eased but his anger—at himself—still simmered. *I just have to get my drinking under control.* He worked through lunch and discovered a few similar cases but none with the same single breast and finger mutilations. He made notes to check out a couple with a few parallels but they didn't hold much promise.

Travis took his empty coffee mug and walked down the hall for a hot refill, meeting Watson, a new rookie on his way back to his desk, coffee in hand.

"Hey, dude. How did you like the rodeo?"

"Rodeo. What rodeo? What are you talking about?"

"Thought I saw you in Cheyenne last week,

I figured you were there for Frontier Days."

"I wasn't in Cheyenne."

"Really? Thought that was you I saw when I was in the taxi heading to the airport. Sure you weren't sneaking away from the ol' ball and chain? That's sure as hell what I was doing. Gotta get away from the damn nag once in a while."

"It wasn't me." *Wish to hell I could get away once in a while.*

"Well, it was only a quick glance. You ought to go sometime, dude. It's the world's largest outdoor rodeo; I go every year." He laughed. "Those bulls bursting out of the chutes are radical. Like watching that muscled beef on a hoof toss riders in the air like puffy puppets. Those cowboys gotta be airheads."

His mind elsewhere, Travis said, "Yeah, yeah, I'll remember."

Before he swallowed the first sip of coffee, dispatch sent him out and kept him on calls until late afternoon.

When Travis finally returned to the station, he went straight to Joella's office.

"Hi Travis. Making any progress on the Merry case?"

"No, dammit. I'm worried it's fast becoming a cold case."

"I'm beginning to feel like that too. I'm about to clock out. Let's go have a cup of coffee and forget it for a while. Maybe something will pop into our minds when we aren't thinking about it."

"Great idea. Jakes?"

"Yeah. Meet you there."

~ ~ ~

They both arrived at the same time and found a table in the corner where it might be quieter for conversation. "Glad we came," Travis said, lingering over his coffee. *Any place is better than home.*

"Me too. Gives us a chance to become better acquainted. How long have you been married?"

"Seems like forever."

She stirred a packet of Equal into her coffee. "That doesn't sound much like wedded bliss."

"It's not. We fight all the time. Marion is a shopaholic. She bought a used car yesterday knowing full well I can't afford the payments."

"Ouch. Take it you didn't know about that weakness before you popped the question."

"I was too much in love to think about money. I hadn't been off the reservation long when I met Marion. She had long blonde hair, almost to her waist. Not many blondes on the reservation," he said, grinning. "It was love at first sight—'first sight' of that yellow hair. She had a great job when we married and insisted she continue working to put me through college. I couldn't find a job, even a part-time one. Everything I am today—my entire career— I owe to her. I am so grateful I can't bring myself to leave her." His shoulders drooped and he stared at his coffee cup.

Joella broke the silence. "Is money the only problem?"

"Mostly. Everything was fine at first. Once I graduated from the Police Academy, she quit her job. Said it was my turn to take care of her, and she started a new career as a shopaholic. That's when the problems began. If there was cash in her purse, money in our checking account or a credit card not maxed out, she spent."

"We fight constantly about money, and life isn't very pleasant much of the time. I get a little peace and freedom fishing and visiting Aunt Winona in Browning. Two or three times a year she goes to Buford, Wyoming, to visit her second cousin. Gives me a week or more of tranquility before she comes back with a stack of receipts. She loves big city boutiques and always spends time shopping in Billings and Cheyenne during the trip. Those occasional vacations give me a break from our brawling home life, so it's bearable—most of the time. Enough about me. What about you? Ever been married?"

"Yes, once, a lifetime ago. I was only sixteen and it lasted about that many days. My fault. The guy was a control freak, but I married him anyway. Young and stupid, I thought I could change him. Naturally, instead of changing he got worse. I had run away and lied about my age. When I broke with him and went home, my parents showed me the door and said, 'Don't come back.' Claimed that's what I deserved when I married outside the Jewish faith."

"That's really tough," Travis said. "Family shouldn't treat one another that way."

"It was very rough for a while but I lucked out. A friend's father got me a good job and I worked my way through college. Still, my parents disowning me hit like a cannonball to the gut and I spiraled into deep depression. Wound up in therapy. Don't know how I would have turned out otherwise."

Travis had liked Joella when they first met, but sometimes he felt mystified why she gave him the impression of a wandering soul lost in space, never quite grounded. *Now I know why.* "Do you have any brothers or sisters?"

"I have a sister who sided with my parents and quit speaking to me when they refused to let me come home."

"I'm sorry to hear that. Everyone needs family." Travis thought he could see tears welling in her eyes. "Have you tried to make contact after they disowned you?"

"No, they were pretty vehement about it."

"You ought to at least make an attempt. People often change over time."

"Maybe I'll give it a try someday. Do you have any kids or family?"

"After we married, Marion told me she didn't want children." My only kin is my Aunt Winona who lives on the Blackfeet Reservation in Browning. She's a good woman; I visit her often. My parents are dead, and I was an only child."

"At least you have someone," Joella said.

Travis noticed the melancholy expression that clouded her face. He glanced at her with new interest. *I like this woman. She is not only compassionate, but also honest and bright. Easy to look at, with incredible green eyes—or are they blue?* "I'd like to continue our conversation, but I better get home and face the music for being late—again."

"Didn't you call to tell her you'd be late?"

"Wouldn't make any difference. She thinks I should drop everything to accommodate her. She'd be angry either way."

~ ~ ~

When Travis arrived home, Marion sat on the couch. "I got tired of waiting. Your dinner's in the refrigerator. Heat it yourself. I'm watching a program. And, I know why you're late."

"What are you talking about now? I was working."

"Yeah, sure. My friend, Cora, called. She spotted you snuggling with a redheaded bimbo at Jakes, and you damn well better knock it off."

Travis felt his blood pressure surge. "That was Joella Bar-Lev. She's our CSI. We were having coffee and discussing the Merry case."

"Just remember what I said—no divorce."

"I told you we were working."

"I don't care who the hell she is. I won't have you seen alone in public with other women. Makes me look bad—like I can't hold on to my husband."

Betsy's Bar sign beamed bright in his brain, but before he could react, his phone rang. "Detective Eagle," he answered. "What do you mean we've hit the big time, Zach? Why is little ol' Great Falls on the map?"

CHAPTER 8

Dispatch had called Travis right after Zach did. He thanked them and said he had the vital information.

The victim was dead so he didn't put on his emergency flasher. The address lay in the Sun River area. His anxiety to get there made him curse every slow driver in the left lane. *This town is getting too damn big.* Traffic congestion became lighter on the West Side, and he drove into the community of Sun River a few minutes later. Some of the houses had a splendid river view, but all the dwellings were on low land where heavy rain or snowmelt flooded the community every few years. He shook his head. *No Indian would be dumb enough to live on a flood plain.*

Many of the houses displayed the high-water mark from the last overflow, a foul odor still lingering in the air. Owners, who couldn't afford to renovate, had abandoned their homes, rain poured through broken windows, walls turned gray and green with mildew and mold, washing machines rusted in the yard and bare-framed cars went neglected after thieves had procured free auto parts.

When Travis arrived, he spotted Zach waiting on the street.

"Yeah, man," Zach almost shouted, "looks like we've got our first honest-to-God serial killer. We'll make national headlines. The body has the same mutilation—plus, she *is* a blonde although a chemical one with brown roots."

Travis opened the door at the victim's house and eyed Porter.

"Hi Chief." A repulsive smirk spread across Porter's chubby face. "You couldn't solve the first murder; maybe you'll get lucky this time."

Struggling to resist the urge to hit a fellow officer, Travis swallowed the knot in his throat. He walked over to the victim, but before he could chant to *Naató'si*, his gut revolted, bile rising. Knowing he couldn't make it outside, he ran for the nearest door hoping a bathroom lay behind it. Retching twice in the toilet, he flushed and turned on the sink tap, cupping his hands to splash cool water on his face and in his mouth. *What the hell is the matter with me? I feel as though I know this woman too.*

Porter opened the bathroom door and leaned against the wall, thumbs hooked in his pockets. "Great way to go, Geronimo. You just contaminated a crime scene."

Travis's shoulders slumped. *How in the hell could I be so damn stupid?*

Zach joined Porter in the doorway. "You okay, buddy? The blood getting to you again?" He laughed, rolling his eyes. "We didn't eat Mexican today."

"No. Think I'm getting the flu or something."

"Get the hell out of here then, I don't want to catch it. I've got a hot date tonight. Don't worry, Joella is on her way and you can get caught up with everything tomorrow."

"I can't leave, but as long as she's coming, I'll go check with some of the neighbors."

Most of the residents weren't home and after talking to only two, Travis called it a day.

~ ~ ~

Travis felt pure relief when he arrived home and found a note saying Marion had gone shopping with a girlfriend. Thankful for the peace and quiet, he took off his jacket, tossing it on a chair. He stretched out on the couch, his breathing slowing.

A beautiful nude blonde appeared, rising from the floor in a vaporous haze, blood spurting from her slit throat. Holding her hand high, the index finger was missing; she laughed hysterically and lay on the floor in front of him. Her left breast nipple was gone, and he saw her chewing. She lay there a moment, then rose and giggling in a whinny voice, floated out the window. One buxom blood-soaked blonde after another glided in and out with identical mutilations until Travis found himself unable to breathe, his mouth covered with their blood. He awoke gasping for air, soaked with sweat and shaking. The nightmare seemed so real. He looked around but saw no blood.

Is Marion right? Am I losing my mind?

~ ~ ~

He still lay on the couch when Marion opened the door.

"What are you doing home so early?"

"We had another murder. Looks like the city has its first serial killer. Be careful when you're out and don't open the door unless you know who it is. Both of his victims were blondes."

"What is this town coming to?"

"Yeah, and just like the last one, I felt connected to the victim. Her remains made me vomit." His feeling of guilt made him ramble on even though he knew Marion never paid any attention. "Then, to make matters even worse, I contaminated a crime scene. I'm bound to get a reprimand from the lieutenant. Maybe even from Captain Walker. I don't know what's the matter with me lately."

"Here we go again, emotions and pain you can't explain. You have such an overactive imagination I told you to see a shrink," she said, flouncing out of the room.

Travis frowned. He'd heard it all before. Numerous times. *Maybe she really is trying to get me committed.*

CHAPTER 9

Seated at his desk the next day, Travis read over his notes on the Merry murder. He wanted to refresh his mind before talking to Joella and learn what she found out last night while he went to interview the neighbors. He tried to concentrate without success. Memories of his nightmare lingered, circulating through his brain like a revolving door. He flipped through his notebook—nothing rang a bell. A tap on the door startled him. Captain Walker strode in and sat on the hardback chair next to Travis's desk. *Damn, did he hear about my tainting the scene already?*

Warren Walker was a bull of a man with massive arms and chest but unusually small feet. Travis often wondered why the captain didn't topple over. They were close friends, often dining out together with their wives and socializing at parties and dances. Warren was an excellent dancer, a fact that amazed Travis because it didn't seem to coincide with his tiny feet and huge frame. Whenever he watched Warren strut his stuff, Travis felt envy, wishing he had the big man's grace and style.

The two men shared a love of fishing and often went camping in the woods around Augusta. Sometimes they drove to Glacier National Park. On those journeys, they always stopped to visit Travis's Aunt Winona; Warren found the near toothless old woman charming. He listened to her tales of Running White Buffalo with keen interest, and learned a few Blackfeet words like *Oki* so he could say "hello" the next trip. Travis taught Warren how to snare a rabbit and roast it on a stick over a campfire. Their bond was like that of father and son. Only Warren understood Travis's great need to reestablish himself often with Mother Nature, in order to find peace and live harmoniously in the world of the white man. Warren was proud of Travis's enormous accomplishment in that respect knowing how difficult it was to achieve.

When Travis peeked at the captain, guilt coursed through his veins. He had seen the captain during regular briefings but avoided their usual personal chats. He felt sure the captain wondered why he hadn't discussed either of the cases with him as he normally did.

"Hey, Travis," the captain said, "looks like we've got a serial killer on our hands. Believe that's a first for Great Falls. These things are supposed to happen only in the big city. Have you made any progress so far?"

"No, not yet, Captain," Travis said, reserving the use of Warren for their relationship away from the police station. Travis forced a twisted grin. The captain was his best friend and he'd been too ashamed of his lack of success to face him. "For a murderer, he is one smart guy. Ms. Bar-Lev and I wonder if he might be a rogue cop or have forensic training. He is so familiar with police investigation procedures. Appears he might have tossed the victims' clothes in the washing machine to remove possible forensic evidence. This maniac is different from the dumb felons we typically encounter."

"That surprised the hell out of me too. Hang tight. He'll slip up; they all do. I have complete confidence in you." He rose and left with a wink, "A fat rainbow trout sounds mighty tempting about now. Let's make a trip soon; my fishing pole is gathering dust."

~ ~ ~

In the afternoon, dispatch routed Travis to a convenience store robbery. He had tried to talk to Joella all day, but couldn't connect with her. He spent the rest of the day rehashing the notes and records he'd studied a dozen times when she strolled into his office at the end of the day.

"Hey, I saw your pickup in the parking lot. What are you doing here? The guys said you went home sick yesterday. Why aren't you home in bed?"

He studied her with new interest. Her face expressed more concern for him than Marion's ever had. "I wasn't really sick. I felt humiliated and Porter had a field day at my expense. I needed to get out of there before I decked him. I'm sure he told you about it."

"He did. But trust me, vomiting is nothing to be embarrassed about, especially viewing such a horrible, grisly scene."

"You do not understand, Joella. I, um—" Unable to continue, Travis noticed the deep concern in her eyes and knew he could trust this woman. He was about to tell her the whole story when Porter came in.

"Well, Tonto, feeling better, are we? Getting sick was sure a good excuse to let Joella do your job."

Travis felt his face flaming. He leapt toward Porter, fists clenched.

Joella jumped in front of him, grabbing his arm. "No. Don't. He's not worth it." She turned facing Porter. "Shut up and get out of the way. We were just leaving," Out in the hall, she said, "C'mon Travis. Let's check out; I think you need a cup of coffee. I'll meet you at Jakes."

His teeth clenched to the point where he might shatter his tooth enamel. Travis walked toward the door. "Okay, see you there."

CHAPTER 10

The drive over to Jakes had Joella on edge, watching her rearview mirror to be sure Porter wasn't going to Jakes. *I should have suggested BJs; Porter rarely drinks there—not enough desperate women. How does his wife stand such a jackass?*

The tavern wasn't crowded yet, and she selected the corner table against the far wall, ordering two cups of coffee.

When Travis arrived, he hesitated at the door glancing around.

Joella waved, catching his attention and he walked over dropping into the chair, his shoulders slumped. When she first met him, his Indian coloring and jet-black hair struck her foremost, but as he sat seemingly dejected in the chair, her attention riveted on his coal-black eyes, like shimmering pools of coffee. *I could get lost in those eyes and I'd give my anything for those high cheekbones. He's good looking in a craggy way.* She remained silent waiting for him to speak. *It's so refreshing to meet a kind and caring soul. One who doesn't have to toss his macho attitude around. Why are the nice ones always married or gay?*

He tore open a sugar envelope, stirred the contents into his cup, took a swig, frowned and added another packet. After he swallowed two or three gulps of coffee, nearly finishing the cup, the tension in his shoulders appeared to relax.

"I don't know what is wrong with me these days. With both victims, I experienced gut emotions like I have never ever had before. I felt such an intimate connection, yet I never met either one before. It was not the appalling mutilation that made me vomit. I've seen dozens of bloody bodies far worse than those and never had a reaction like that. I feel frazzled these days, drained of any patience. Porter always gets to me, but never like he does these days."

"I don't know what to say. I'm sure it's only a coincidence. You're a compassionate man and those poor, unfortunate women suffered beyond imagination. Go home. Get a good night's sleep. Forget Porter." She hesitated a moment before she spoke again. "You really must learn to ignore him. You know what a blow-hard bigot he is; he gets his kicks out of goading everyone, especially you. Your anger fuels his sick drive and certainly does nothing positive for you. Now go. I'll fill you in on the details of the second victim tomorrow."

Joella watched Travis walk toward the door, his gait slow, head bent. *I don't understand. Why is he so despondent? Several times he seemed on the verge of telling me something and then changed the subject. Does he have some secret gnawing at his gut?*

CHAPTER 11

Travis drove through the park and along the Missouri River as he often did before going to work. The peaceful scene put him in a relaxed frame of mind before meeting the demands of the day. A recent shower had left the world dewy and bright, the sun glistening off the wet grass. Rolling down the window, he breathed in the lingering scent of rain. In the distance, a double rainbow arched the Missouri, behind it a rain curtain of diamonds shimmering in the sun. *What a great omen to start the day.*

At the station, he went straight to Joella's office, once again eager to solve the city's first serial killer case. "Glad you're here early, Joella. I wanted to find out what you learned at the scene before I started questioning the neighbors." Noticing her anew, he paused a moment. "Hey, you changed your hair."

"Yes, I tired of my old style. Now that my

mane has grown out, I am trying a new fashion. So I'll resemble a woman."

"You always looked like a woman to me. It's nice."

Her eyes brightened and she beamed at the compliment.

Travis sat and opened his notebook "Who discovered the body?"

"The victim's employer called us. She worked at the Holiday Village Mall, at that bar in the side wing. He'd talked to her Saturday and knew she planned to work Sunday night. When she didn't show, he got worried and called her home several times, then the police because she lived alone. A party girl, her boss said, she often came in late and hung over. He didn't care because she made up any loss of time by being such a dedicated worker. When he'd hired her, a fleet of loyal male customers followed their favorite bartender to her new job. This made the boss very happy."

"I bet it did. Don't think that bar does a lot of business. What is the victim's name?"

"Cheryl Richmond, according to Zach. Her condo overlooks the Sun River. From what he found out, she lived a very sociable life. You'll have your work cut out for you questioning the neighbors."

"Thanks. Any evidence at the crime scene?"

"As clean as the Merry case. The MO is identical right down to the damp clothes in the washing machine. Now we're fairly certain it was the killer who washed them and not the victim. The body had the same smooth incision by an experienced hand, no ragged edges. It's the same guy all right. Her wallet was empty, but didn't seem like he took much, if anything, and there were some valuable items in the apartment. Still hoping the ME or lab might find something."

Travis raked his hair back with his fingers. "Don't think I've ever run across a killer taking time to wash the victim's clothes to avoid leaving evidence, and whatever protective gear he is wearing must be as high-quality as ours. Now that we know he is a serial killer, I suspect he carries a murder ditty bag—has everything he needs with him all the time."

"A disgusting thought but it happens."

"Any signs of breaking and entering?"

"Not one, according to Zach. But, as I was leaving to come here, I got some updated information about the Merry victim, a profile."

"We don't have a profiler."

"I know. I'm talking about Daniel Higgins, that skinny young instructor from the Great Falls College of Technology who moonlights part-time for the department. The little guy with all the pimples—doesn't look like he's old enough to be a teacher."

"Don't think our paths have crossed."

"Guess the department called Dr. Higgins in when they found we had a serial killer on the prowl. I spoke to him a little while ago. He told me he still doesn't have enough information to compile an individual profile on the killer, but said a sexual predator would be impulsive, self-centered and feel no remorse or guilt. He knows right from wrong, but doesn't care. Most likely a loner and a victim of childhood abuse."

"No kidding. Doesn't take a genius to figure that out. Did he approximate an age?"

"Between twenty-five and fifty."

"That's really pinning it down," Travis said, scowling.

"Aw come on, Travis, give the kid a break. He's ecstatic to be working with us."

"Guess you're right. We all have to start somewhere."

"Once Higgins got started, he gave me the full rundown. He about busted his buttons off enlightening me with everything he learned in school. Said anger expressed through control is what drives serial killers, as if I didn't know." She stopped to brush a lock of hair from her forehead. "He claimed most sexual predators are predisposed to extreme behavior because of an abnormal brain. Can be caused by a brain injury, genetics or womb development even childhood abuse."

"Might be young, but seems to know his stuff."

"Yes, but I had to bite my tongue to keep from laughing. I already knew everything he said and didn't have the heart to stop him. Also found out that Watson, our new rookie, is a real computer nerd and Captain Walker has him working on the case because the city can't afford a computer specialist. Unfortunately, he found nothing useful on the victim's computer or cell phone."

Travis felt his inspirational rainbow omen shatter into crumbled ice. "Did you see the paper this morning, Joella? The damned *Tribune* isn't making life any easier for us with their

Merry Murderer Strikes Again headlines. If they keep on, the mayor is going to be jumping down our throats. He's already hammering the captain. And that line warning all blondes to be wary will have half the women in town scared to death."

"Yes, I saw the article. Typical, they never let up. Headlines sell their product."

"Guess I better get going. I'll talk to the victim's boss and then tackle those neighbors. Catch you later."

~ ~ ~

Travis drove past the two-block-long parking lot on Tenth Avenue South and continued around to the back of the building to enter the wing with the bar. *No need to walk through the entire mall.* Marion spent half her life shopping in the complex—he only went in the line of duty now that she'd bought the damn car—no more chauffeuring.

Opening the bar door, he stopped, the sound of slot machines dinging in his ears. He could see nothing in the darkened room until his eyes adjusted. Little candle lamps casting a yellow glow on each table allowed him to locate the bar, his nostrils inhaling the odor of melting wax, beer and cigarette smoke.

A frizzy-haired blonde, elbows on the bar, flirted with a male customer whose eyes never left her deep cleavage even when she blew smoke in his face. She never stopped talking except to take a drag of her cigarette, popping her gum in between sentences. Entirely engaged with the customer, she appeared not to see Travis.

"Excuse me," he said, flashing his badge. "I need to talk to the manager."

"Yeah? What's going on?"

"I said I want to speak to the manager."

"Keep your britches on," she said, blowing a huge bubble that exploded on her pouty lips. She pulled the gum loose and popped it back in her mouth then patted the customer on the hand. "Don't move, sweetie; I'll be right back." When she came out from behind the bar wearing skintight jeans, her hips sashayed so radically Travis thought she might fracture one. She strutted across the room in five-inch stiletto heels and disappeared through a door at the back of the room.

Moments later, an older, portly man about fifty returned with her. His jet-black hair appeared frosted, so perfect was the blend of black and gray. Sporting a navy suit, white shirt and turquoise tie, he looked more like a banker than a bar manager. "I assume you're here about Cheryl. It's so tragic—a lovely girl. A bit on the wild side but still a nice woman and an excellent bartender. Let's talk in my office."

Through the open door the manager indicated, Travis saw a small desk and two chairs nearly filling the cramped room. When he entered, he stopped, stunned. The wall he hadn't seen was aglow with light, every color of the artist's pallet. Advertisements filled the entire wall: blinking, bubbling and flashing neon beer signs.

The manager grinned. "You've discovered my weakness. When I received the first flashing Pabst Blue Ribbon sign, I was hooked. They were supposed to hang in the bar, but as you can see, they never made it. Please sit and tell me how I can help."

Travis took out his notebook. "Do you know if the victim had any enemies, anyone who might want her dead?"

"No, everyone adored her. I can't think of a soul who would want to harm her." The manager hesitated, cupping his chin in his hand. "Hmm, there was this one strange guy, but he didn't dislike her. Just the opposite. He came in almost every day and pestered her to go out with him, but she didn't like him. Sometimes he became belligerent. One time I had to toss him out."

"Do you know his name?"

"Afraid not. Well-dressed guy, maybe a professional judging by his manner. I say 'professional' because he never came at the same time of day like a laborer would. My bartender, the one you met out front, said he was a 'gorgeous hunk,' if that helps," he said grinning.

After a few more questions, Travis left his card, and the bar owner promised to call if the man came in again. *Okay, "well dressed, gorgeous hunk, maybe a professional." The hospital is only a few blocks from here.*

CHAPTER 12

When Travis arrived at Richmond's condo, he cringed. The two-story U-shape building was huge—a lot of neighbors to interview. He took a deep breath and opened the office door.

Investigating the swinging neighbors in the condo took days, as Joella had predicted. Apparently, the dimpled, curly peroxide blonde with the top-heavy figure blossomed as a lovable woman in more ways than one—she hadn't missed a single male in the condo. They all adored her, saying she was quite the gal about town morning, noon, and night. All the men knew their relationship was not exclusive, but in their eyes, she could do no wrong. Days of interviewing the neighbors had not revealed a single suspect, let alone a motive, but he hadn't expected to learn of a motive. Serial killers didn't need one. By late Friday afternoon, Travis had left his card with several tenants and the landlord before he decided to call it a day.

~ ~ ~

Travis rolled over and glimpsed outside, the claustrophobic gray sky promised a dreary day. Marion had ignored the alarm clock, turned over and gone back to sleep. He dreaded getting up and lay in bed as long as he dared. Finally, acknowledging the time, he rose, dressed and left the house. *I'll grab a bite on the way to work.*

He used to enjoy returning to work after a weekend listening to Marion complain. Now he hated Monday mornings. Not because the day started a new workweek, but because the serial killer seemed to purposely commit his murders on Sundays—at least so far. *It could be a coincidence, or for some reason the killer has a violent reaction to Sundays. Damn it, until we catch him, there will be more victims—serial killers don't stop until they're caught.*

Travis spent the morning filling out reports and trying to find some kind of a link between the victims, anything. But the only similarity he found was they were both blondes. He was on his way to lunch when his scanner crackled with an 11-44 in Black Eagle. *Damn it. Is it MM again?* The Ninth Street Bridge lay only three blocks away. He arrived in minutes.

~ ~ ~

Why anyone wants to live in this old, run down berg is beyond me. The entire town consisted of 1.7 square miles and it averaged a population of two hundred people. Black Eagle had sprung into existence in 1909 to support the workers building the world's tallest smoke stack for the Anaconda Mining Company. The town's only other claim to fame was the production of George Montgomery, the popular 1940s cowboy movie star. Unfortunately, the town remained the same stunted community, never growing beyond several bars and a few restaurants. Other than official duty, Travis went to Black Eagle only when Marion insisted they eat at the 3D Supper Club, one of the more upscale restaurants in the area. The victim's condo was one of the few new buildings in the town.

~ ~ ~

Travis arrived at the scene and Porter greeted him at the door, the usual nasty smirk on his face. "Our serial killer has been at it again, Chief. MM's picking up speed—it's only been a week between the swinging bimbo and this one. Maybe after three victims, you can finally make the Merry Murderer a little *unhappy* by actually catching him."

Travis bit his tongue resisting the urge to hit Porter square in the middle of his girlish, pouty lips. "Who discovered the body?"

"The sister. They shared the house." He winked. "She'd come home from an all-nighter and found the body."

Travis winced at the disgusting juvenile expression on Porter's face whenever he talked about anything hinting of sex. "Where is she now?"

"At the neighbor's next door."

Travis put on his coveralls, gloves and paper shoe covers. He ducked under the crime scene tape, taking out his notebook. He hated working with Porter. "Where is Zach?"

"Had a doctor appointment."

"What about Joella?"

"She's been delayed, be here soon."

"Any sign of breaking and entering?"

"Naw, just like before."

"Did you learn the victim's name?"

"Dorene Burke. Mama was being cute and named the sister, Lorene." Porter snickered. "Who ever heard of spelling like that?"

Travis took out his notebook. *Dorene? Wasn't that the name the Benefis Hospital nurse told me O'Toole dated during his engagement to Linda Merry?* Flipping through the pages he located "Dorene or Darlene" written alongside the nurse's name. *Well, well doctor, you're looking interesting again.*

Porter left to join another officer. Travis waited for his departure and whispered a quick prayer to *Naató'si*. When he began to study the body, he uttered a sigh of relief. *At last, I'm over my vomiting binges.* He took in the room noting the signs of a furious struggle. A small end table lay smashed to smithereens, as if someone had fallen on it. Broken ceramic pieces littered the floor, and a heavy wood-framed painting had fallen from the wall, cracking open. Small pillows matching the couch lay scattered about like sprinkled confetti. The MO did appear to be the same as MM's victims, masses of blood pooling around the body, but...

Not normally a vindictive person, Travis couldn't pass by this golden opportunity. When Porter returned, Travis said, "What makes you think this is the work of our serial killer?"

"Huh? I'd say it's damn obvious. Exact same MO, she's blonde, wet clothes in the washing machine. And it's Sunday."

"All true, but this isn't the work of our serial killer. You're forgetting something."

"And what's that?" the five-foot eight-inch Porter asked gazing up at Travis's six-foot frame.

Porter's attitude often made Travis wonder if he had a Napoleon complex. He watched his beady brown eyes dart about the room to see what he'd missed. "With all your training, you ought to recognize what I'm talking about. The first two victims didn't fight for their lives, and we never released the fact the killer used duct tape to the press. Do you see any duct tape? It is possible the serial killer changed his MO. More likely, this is a copycat crime. Someone wanted to do her in and lay the blame on the serial killer."

Red faced, Porter glared at Travis as though he were the devil incarnate, then turned on his heel and stalked off. Travis couldn't stop the laughter that rolled from the bottom of his belly. *That took the bigot down a peg or two.*

After Joella arrived, Travis went to interview the sister only to learn an ambulance had taken her to the hospital in a state of hysteria. *If she is out-of-control, it might be days before I can get anything from her.* Nearly lunchtime, he decided to check out Dorene's former work place and her old associates. *I can grab a bite at the hospital cafeteria and maybe I'll get lucky and catch a little gossip about O'Toole.*

~ ~ ~

The human resource department at Benefis Hospital confirmed Dorene had quit, stating personal problems as the reason. He corrected the name spelling in his notebook. They referred him to Hannah Kirkland, the head nurse working on the third floor. Locating her at the nurses' station, he flipped open his badge and showed it to her. "Detective Travis Eagle. I'd like to ask you a few questions about Dorene Burke. Did hospital personnel contact you?"

"Yes, they did. Her death shocked us all. She had blonde hair; is she a victim of this serial killer I'm reading about?"

"That's what we're trying to find out. She worked on this floor, didn't she?"

"Yes. She was a CNA and a damn good one."

The gravely deep voice of the woman surprised him. Usually he found a female with a husky voice sexy, but not from this fleshy, unfeminine creature with close-cropped brown hair and skin like sandpaper. Her voice sounded like she was calling hogs to the trough. He recovered quickly saying, "CNA? That's certified nurse's aide, isn't it?"

"Yes. She had worked here for several years before I came onboard. What do you want to know?"

"Did she have many friends?"

"Not that I'm aware of. She was quiet and shy, and everyone on staff seemed to like her."

"Do you know if she dated anyone from the hospital?"

"I wouldn't know. We weren't close."

"How about enemies, anyone who might have wanted her dead?"

"No, as I told you before, everyone liked her, including the patients and that is high praise for a CNA."

"Do you have any idea of why she quit?"

Kirkland closed her eyes a moment. "She only stated she had personal problems."

He asked a few more questions and then pulled a card from his jacket, handing it to her. "If you think of anything else that might help us find her killer, please call me."

"Will do, but I really didn't know her well."

~ ~ ~

Travis found the cafeteria and ordered a BLT. They *can't do much to ruin a BLT.* The place was crowded; his hope of overhearing a little gossip fizzled like a day-old soda when he glanced around the room. No doctors or nurses and he concluded they must have a private dining area. *Guess loose bowel questions from interrupting people wouldn't do much for the digestive system.* He was also wrong about his BLT—it didn't digest any better than his lack of information from Ms. Kirkland. *Why didn't I go somewhere else?* When he left the hospital, the bright lights of a convenience store, shining like beacons, caught his attention and he stopped to buy Tums before returning to the victim's condominium to question neighbors.

~ ~ ~

The complex appeared to be more of a retirement home with most of the tenants either gray, beauty parlor blonde, or bald as a billiard ball.

A white-bearded man using a cane with a fancy silver head laughed, his belly shaking, when he told Travis, "We're a close-knit group. We hold as many social events as we can possibly think of: birthdays, President's Day, April Fool's Day, and Independence Day. Sometimes even Mondays." Laughing again at his joke, he paused looking off in the distance before making eye contact again. "Everyone knows everybody in the condo—and all his or her business too. The young victim and her sister were our adopted pets. They could do no wrong."

The tenants were cooperative, wanting justice for one of their favorite mascots. Travis returned for several days to interview them. A few informed him that Dorene Burke had recently quit her job at the hospital. He already knew but asked each one if they knew why, none did, saying she didn't tell them, and that both sisters never talked about their personal affairs. However, they did know she had a boyfriend but never saw her with him, which they thought strange. Most suspected she might be dating a married man and didn't bring him around because she didn't want them to recognize him.

An elegantly dressed, thin woman with Botox smooth-as-silk-skin told him, "If you want to get the real scoop on anyone who lives here, talk to Agnes. Her window opens onto the parking lot and she spends most of the day watching everyone, a real busybody. She knows who is sleeping with whom and if they are living payday to payday. She lives right across the hall from Dorene's apartment. I don't think Dorene confided in her any more than the rest of us. Believe she thought of her more as a mother figure, but she was Agnes's only friend. People here don't like her for obvious reasons."

CHAPTER 13

Travis knocked on Agnes's door. A frumpy, dyed redhead answered. She wore a pink frayed chenille robe even though it was afternoon. Her wrinkled face looked like a road map with the large brown mole on her chin marking the capital. "It's about time you got around to me. I knew Dorene better than anyone else in the building." Taking a long drag from her cigarette and blowing smoke into his face, she said, "What do you wanna know?"

Travis fanned the air with his hand. "May I come in?"

"Sure, it's cold out here," she said, drawing the robe tighter.

He glanced around waiting for Agnes to sit. If a room could be called frumpy, this one would match its owner. The furniture seemed incompatible, scattered around the room as if the deliverymen had dropped the couch and chairs wherever they found space, the color scheme loud and clashing. The room didn't appear dirty, only jarring to the senses. Travis forced his attention back to Agnes. "I understand you were good friends with Dorene," he lied, not wanting to affront her. "Can you tell me anything about her male friends? Any who were jealous or might want her dead?"

"Don't know about that," Agnes said, lighting another cigarette with the butt of the one in her mouth. She ground out the burnt cigarette in an overflowing, pie-plate of an ashtray sitting on a nail keg next to her chair. A fancy doily laid on top the small barrel attempting to give the illusion of an end table. "Dorene didn't talk about her personal life often. She was the sweet, stay-at-home type."

"Did you see her frequently?"

"Almost every day. She would bring cookies or something she'd concocted for me to taste. I know she had a boyfriend. She'd broke off with the jerk a couple of months ago, but he didn't seem aggravated about it. She only told me because she thought it funny when he began dating her sister, and then Dorene moved on to some guy at the hospital. I suggested she bring him around for a beer. She never did. Don't think anyone here ever saw him. Every time she had a date, her eyes would light up like the Vegas strip." Agnes paused to take another puff of her cigarette. "Dorene was wild about him and felt positive he would propose any day. It never happened." She pulled a large crumpled kerchief from her pocket and wiped away a tear. "I suspect he was married or just

89

using her, and she didn't get the picture, being naïve as a baby."

Travis made a note. "Do you to know the man's name?"

"No. She never mentioned it. Only know how excited she became when she had a date with him—figured he must be some bigwig executive."

Travis's left eyebrow cocked higher. *Bigwig executive—maybe a doctor?* "I understand she recently resigned from her job. Do you happen to know why?"

"That she did tell me because she was so upset. Came home in tears one night. She quit because she couldn't take her boss's butt pats or leering looks down her blouse. She wasn't the type to file a harassment suit, too timid."

That doesn't make sense. I thought her boss was Kirkland. I'll have to check that out again. The blue smoky haze in the room clogged Travis's sinuses and he blew his nose.

"I hear her sister is being released soon. She can give you more details."

Travis gave her his card with the usual speech and left. Thankful to be outside in clean air, he leaned against the building and inhaled deeply. As he walked to his vehicle, he felt a warm glow in his gut. *O'Toole, you're looking better and better all the time. I just need to break that damn alibi.*

~ ~ ~

After days of interviewing condo residents, only Agnes had provided a clue: Dorene dated a mystery man. Even though he thought O'Toole once more seemed interesting, he still felt discouraged. Driving across the Ninth Street Bridge back to Great Falls, he decided he needed a pick-me-up. A healthy dose of Mother Nature would lift his spirits. Turning left, he followed the river to the tiny parking spot adjacent to the road that overlooked Black Eagle Falls, named by Lewis and Clark for the many eagles they saw in the area. He stood mesmerized by the thundering white water that burst from multiple gates releasing the extra flow from Montana's heavy snows that year.

A newly energized Travis returned to the station surprised to see Joella's car still in the parking lot at such a late hour. He located her in the office. "You still here?"

"Didn't have anything else to do so I thought I'd hang around a while to see if you learned anything talking to the neighbors."

He inhaled as he sat, catching a refreshing whiff of green apples. *Must be her shampoo.* "Nothing unusual. All the condo tenants thought Burke a nice, down-to-earth young woman who was in the wrong place at the wrong time. She shared the apartment with her sister. I did establish one possible person of interest, her ex-boss, but haven't checked it out so far."

"What about the sister?"

"She became hysterical a short time after finding the body and is now in the hospital."

He didn't tell her of his suspicions about O'Toole. *I could be wrong again.*

Joella fingered a sheet of paper on her desk. "I hoped you'd come back to the station. I have both good news and bad news. Which do you want to hear first?"

"The way these cases are going, let's get the bad over with."

"This morning I got the lab results on Richmond, the second victim, and learned absolutely nothing. She wasn't raped. All the blood we found belonged to her. There were a couple of blonde hairs in the washing machine and a few fibers on the body, which the victim or the killer could have carried in on his or her clothes. The lab hasn't identified them yet. All the hair found on the scene belonged to the victim except one and CODIS had nothing on the DNA from that strand. The killer's MO is exactly the same as the Merry victim. And as fast as he is operating, he is swamping the ME and the lab."

"Shit." Travis slouched further in his seat.

"Now for the good news. If the Black Eagle killer is our serial killer, he is getting careless. However, that's a big *if*—I don't think it's the same guy. The Burke victim's finger was cut off, the nipple too, but it wasn't a neat a job like the other two victims. Hacked off is more like it. The crime scene team found a few fingerprints that seem promising. She lay naked on the rug. The MO is similar, as you know, except there was no duct tape. If it wasn't the serial killer, he wouldn't have known about the tape, which is why we didn't find any. Remember what a mess we found in the house. This lady fought hard for her life so we'll possibly get some DNA under her nails and if we are lucky, maybe some semen if he raped her or jerked-off."

Travis closed his eyes. "Yeah, I suspect this is a copycat crime—doesn't match MM's MO."

"I came to the same conclusion," Joella said.

"Let me know if they find any DNA. I have to recheck with human resources to see who Dorene's boss was. They gave me the name of Hannah Kirkland which doesn't make much sense because according to the local gossip, who lives next door to the victim, Dorene quit her job because her boss was a letch; wouldn't leave her alone and became furious when she kept refusing a date."

Joella wore a bemused expression.

"What's so funny?"

"Maybe Kirkland is a lesbian."

"Holy shit. I never thought of that. Is she psycho enough to kill because her advances were refused?"

"Hard to say, but I'm sure you'll find out." Joella glanced at her watch and turned her computer off. "Did you ever find those two women from O'Toole's priors?"

"No, I couldn't find hide nor hair of either one. They both disappeared—like they'd been paid off. I'm still looking for them. If O'Toole dated Burke, he's smart enough to try to pin the murder on the serial killer. That is also the main problem. He's too damn smart to have committed so many blunders."

Joella stood, the top of her head level with his shoulders. "Been a long day. Want to join me for coffee. I'll spring for a burger—I'm starved."

"Me too. Jakes?"

~ ~ ~

After ordering, Joella took a sip of coffee. "I took your advice, Travis."

"What advice?"

"Your recommendation to try contacting my family again."

"Good for you. What did your parents say?"

"I didn't call them; thought I'd test the waters first with my sister, Justine."

I knew Joella was one smart lady. "How did it go?"

"Better than I expected. She surprised me. Always the perfect little Jewish girl when we were kids, she wed out of the Jewish faith and our parents abandoned her too. She tried to make contact repeatedly; they always rejected her. After a few years Mom and Dad weakened; they didn't like being alone, without any family. Justine made peace with them at last just a couple of days before I called. She suggested I call them." Joella paused to blow a strand of hair from her temple. "We knew Mother would never admit to being wrong, so I'd have to do the calling. Then Justine changed her mind, hinted I wait a while and let her talk to them first to try and lighten their mood."

"That's a nice start," he said. "Let me know how it goes."

"What are you grinning about, Travis? Every time there's a lull in the conversation, I swear you light up like a Cheshire cat. How about letting me in on what's so funny."

Travis laughed. He told her his conversation about Porter's lapse in memory concerning the duct tape. "I feel like I've gotten a little revenge for all his damn slurs."

"Oh, I'd love to have seen that. How did he take it?"

"Not well. But it sure did jumpstart my heart." He swallowed the last of his sandwich and drained his coffee. "Guess I better get going. Thanks for the burger."

"Yeah, I need to go too." Outside, as they crossed the parking lot, Joella said, "I smell smoke." When she looked, the entire sky was a gray haze, nearly blotting out the sunset. "What is that, a fire?"

"Yeah, there's a huge grass fire near Fort Benton."

"My God, do they get fires that big?"

"Yeah, they burn thousands of acres ever year, most started by lighting. Before becoming a cop, I volunteered and fought several of them. The white man finally learned to use an old Indian trick of lighting an escape fire or backup fire as they call it. Stops the flames from progressing because there's no fuel to burn. My ancestors saved entire villages using that system. Guess no one tried it in Fort Benton and the blaze is roaring out of control."

~ ~ ~

The next day, Friday, was brutal. Travis managed to leave the office at quitting time and planned to retire early. He had reached the point he dreaded going to bed. Every night he tossed in turmoil as bloody blondes floated through the window invading his sleep. The three unsolved murder cases sitting on his desk did not help, and his quick pick-me-up at Black Eagle Falls had disappeared. The moment he walked into the apartment, an urgent need to leave washed across him. *I need to get back to Mother Earth for the inner harmony the forests and rivers bring to my soul.*

Marion walked out of the bedroom. His depression ratcheted up a notch. "I'm going fishing." He didn't ask her to go because he knew from past attempts she wouldn't consider it. Mother Nature was a foreign experience for her.

"Fine, but I need cash to go shopping."

"I don't have any extra money."

"Damn it, that's what you always say."

"Marion, I make a decent paycheck. If you'd just live within our means, we'd be okay. You know I have to be on call. I can't get another job." He hesitated, hating to bring up a subject they had argued about before. "I could cancel that life insurance policy you insisted on taking in case something happened to me. It's very expensive. You really don't need it; you'd have my pension."

Marion rolled her eyes and laughed. "Your pension wouldn't keep me in makeup."

"That's what I mean," he yelled, feeling his face grow hot.

His anger apparent, she softened and turned affectionate, stroking his hair. "I didn't mean to upset you, honey. You know I don't want anything to happen to you, but I'd feel safer if we kept the insurance—just in case."

Travis sighed. *Why argue. It's useless.* "Maybe you could get a part-time job. Then you wouldn't be so bored all the time and you'd have money to buy clothes."

"Don't you dare go there," she screeched. "I didn't put you through college simply to go back to work to support us."

"Okay, okay. I still don't have any money for you to go shopping, and I'm still going fishing." Marion continued ranting as he fled out the door. He didn't bother to ask his friend Captain Walker to go with him because he feared the conversation might turn toward the unsolved cases. *Anyway, I'm unfit company for anyone.* He always stored his camping gear in his pickup; the gun rack behind the seats held not rifles, but fishing poles. The apartment building had a huge storage unit; his canoe was loaded in minutes.

~ ~ ~

The sun, still high in a brilliant blue sky, peeked out between cotton ball clouds as Travis departed the city, his heart warm with the prospect of fine weather. Deep ruts dotted the fifty-nine-mile graveled road, and the rhythmic musical pings of stones striking the undercarriage of his truck soon uncoiled the tension in his shoulders. *If I can just make the drive without a rock from another vehicle dimpling the windshield.* Leaving society and the evils of mankind behind, he felt as if he were returning to the land of *Naató'si.*

Travis felt fishing the Smith River well worth the tailbone-shattering ride. The river, a tributary of the Mighty Mo, actually connected nine miles south of the city, but he sought the majestic jewel of the thousand-foot limestone canyon walls draped in mineral red and studded with evergreens. The river along that stretch was accessible only by boat. There were no rapids and his canoe glided silently along the shorelines flickering shadows. Undercut riverbanks hid radiant rainbow trout and deep, clear pools in the leisurely flowing Smith made it one of the finest fishing rivers in the entire country.

Whenever he visited the Smith, Travis felt anger that the National Forest Service had bowed to public demand and allowed float trips of noisy tourists; however, he was thankful the service limited the number of launch sites leaving one stretch of the magnificent river untouched. Years earlier he had made friends with a landowner and camped on private property on these little getaways, thus avoiding the crowded and raucous public campgrounds he found annoying.

He pitched camp under a grove of cottonwoods along a bend in the river. By nine thirty he set up camp. Deep purple blanketed the lower canyon walls as the sun dipped behind the horizon creating rounded masses of brilliant pink and orange altocumulus clouds. He cast a line in the riffles alongside his encampment, and soon the aroma of roasting trout filled the air as he turned the spit over a crackling fire. Tall pines guarded his secluded campsite like silent sentries. Listening to the river's mysterious melody, Travis breathed deeply. He raised his eyes heavenward and thanked *Naató'si* for the Smith. One more day of peace and meditation followed.

Sunday night he returned to the city.

CHAPTER 14

Travis learned early in life how settlers in 1885 had developed Great Falls in a narrow valley. The deep depression harbored land that was the traditional winter home of the Blackfeet, his forefathers. He had always enjoyed the surprising and sudden view of the city that blossomed out of nowhere at the top of Gore Hill. The city straddled the Sun River and the Missouri River, which drops four hundred feet in ten miles giving the town five nearby waterfalls including the thundering Great Falls that Lewis and Clark heard seven miles away.

The first time he'd flown out of the city, Travis had been astonished at the miles of gold, green and brown strip farming that hug the city limits, a beautiful multicolored mosaic. He loved the Rocky Mountains and considered the Little Belt and Highwood mountains, thirty miles to the east, mere foothills. The city's only scenery other than the waterfalls was Giant Springs three miles northeast. Travis often drove out to stand on the cement path bridging the spring's 156-million gallons of crystal-clear water bubbling up from moss-streaked rocks every day. He always gazed into the sparkling water and wished his life flowed as smoothly.

It was dark when Travis pulled off I-15 at the airport. He parked at the bluff overlooking the city that stretched before him. Where smoke once curled skyward from hundreds of teepees, now twinkling lights danced like fireflies in the wind. Wanting to enjoy the view and to prolong the relaxation and calm that appeased him, he fell asleep.

~ ~ ~

The sun already peeked over the treetops when Travis awoke. He decided to go to work instead of home thus avoiding the usual tirade from Marion. He'd call her from his office.

Travis walked into the police station, his hard-won tranquility evaporated like morning mist over the Missouri River. The very walls seemed to mock him, reminding him of his failure.

He worked a couple of hours reviewing notes and filing reports. When he checked, he learned the techs had completed their work at Dorene's apartment and cleared her sister to return. Travis called the hospital. Lorene Burke had been discharged earlier that morning. After grabbing a quick lunch, he drove to Black Eagle.

When he knocked, a pallid, unkempt raven-haired woman wearing a flannel robe answered the door. Her eyes were puffy and red from crying, her feet in hospital slippers, the kind with wavy rubber-strips on the soles.

"Miss Burke, I'm Detective Eagle," he said, showing her his badge. "I'm sorry for your loss. I hate to bother you at a time like this, but I need to ask you a few questions."

She lowered her eyes, almost whispering, "I understand—it's your job. Please come in and sit," she said, indicating a brown overstuffed chair. "Would you like a cup of coffee, I just made a pot?"

"No, thank you. I'll be brief."

Travis sat and glanced around the room; it was still in the topsy-turvy state from the night of the murder. The bloody carpet where the victim had lain now looked dried and crusty, the couch sprayed with an arc of splatters, the wall freckled with dark red spots. He noticed Miss Burke avoided looking in that direction, keeping her eyes lowered much of the time. He asked the usual questions only to learn nothing new. "The hospital said your sister listed only personal reasons for quitting. Do you know what they were?"

"Dorene didn't talk much about her work. When I asked her why, she only said that she needed to stretch her horizons and seek out different experiences."

"Did she ever mention a doctor named O'Toole?"

"Yes, I recall her mentioning that name. I don't think they were friends."

Travis thanked her and left. *She knew O'Toole. That's good enough for me.* He drove to the Benefis.

~ ~ ~

The pastel green walls and sterile odors of the hospital stripped Travis's weekend escape to nature farther from his mind than returning to work had. He wanted to surprise O'Toole. At the nurses' station, he learned the doctor would be in surgery at least another hour. Travis went to the cafeteria. After his gut-rumbling sandwich earlier, he ordered only coffee. There were few people in the room and he dawdled over the brew, stirring in another sugar. Finally, he checked his watch and drained the cup. *Time to meet the good doctor.*

After notifying hospital personnel he needed to speak to the doctor, Travis went to the waiting room just outside the surgery center. Whomever was 'under the knife' apparently had no kin or loved ones because the room was empty. How sad he thought before realizing he too would have no one to worry about his outcome if he were ever in surgery. Marion wouldn't shed a tear. *Other than Aunt Winona, I am alone in the world too.* Travis reviewed his notes again and then in boredom selected a Newsweek lying on an end table. Flipping through the pages, he read only the picture captions.

The sound of footsteps clicked on the tile floor as O'Toole strode toward him, his face registering irritation. "What is it this time? I've answered all the questions you could possibly need about Linda and me. Yes, we were dating, yes, we were in love and yes, we were going to be married. This is bordering on harassment and better be the last damn time or I'll file a complaint."

"That's your privilege, Dr. O'Toole, but I have a job to do and I intend to do it."

The doctor sat at a nearby group of chairs, his dark eyes glaring at Travis who had seated himself opposite the doctor. "What do you want to know?"

"Did you know your intended bride, Ms. Merry, was seeing another man, Fergus Finnegan?" It seemed to Travis the doctor was struggling not to register a reaction but a new hardness in his eyes gave him away.

"No, I didn't and furthermore, I don't believe you. You're making false accusations hoping I'll incriminate myself. I know how you guys work. Even if she were dating this Finnegan fellow, we weren't married yet and it was none of my business."

Both Travis's eyebrows rose. *That's a curious answer for a man about to wed. Maybe he thinks that answer will make him sound less guilty.* "Fair enough. But wouldn't you say it 'was your business' to let her know you were dating Dorene Burke at the same time you were proposing marriage to Ms. Merry?"

A flush crept over the doctor's deep tan most likely acquired during a Caribbean cruise. O'Toole's eyes narrowed into slits. "That's it, detective. This interview is over." He stood and pushed back his chair.

Travis stood too. "You can answer the question here or at the station. Take your pick."

O'Toole glowered, his dark eyes fixed on Travis as though trying to hypnotize him. He snatched the chair back and sat.

"Like I said, did Ms. Merry know you were dating Burke?"

"We were *not* dating. It was only once. Dorene was a mousy little homebody thrilled to be laid by a doctor. It meant nothing, just sex in a linen closet."

Travis peeked at O'Toole. *Doctor, according to Dorene's neighbors and know-it-all Agnes, I think you're lying.* "Do you know why Dorene quit her job?"

"Have no idea."

"I've been told she couldn't take her boss's butt pats and lascivious leers at her cleavage anymore."

"That's entirely possible. Hannah Kirkland, head nurse on the third floor was her boss. From what I hear, she's friendly with all the women; she can't keep her hands to herself. Frankly, I don't know how the dyke keeps her job. Guess most of the women are afraid she could get them fired."

Travis cringed. *Mr. Fancy Doctor is a bigot too.*

"Dorene never said anything to me," O'Toole continued, "but I was nearby one time when Hannah patted Dorene's butt and I could tell she didn't like it."

Travis fought to get his focus back on O'Toole. "Where were you the Sunday Burke was killed?"

"I don't remember. Unless I'm on call, I spend Sunday resting after a hard week. Have a beer and watch a game."

"Can anyone vouch for that?"

"No, like I said, Sunday is my day to relax. I

do it alone. Now if that's all, I have another surgery waiting."

"Okay for now, but I may be back," he said, stifling a laugh when he noticed O'Toole's jaw clench.

In the elevator, Travis pushed the third floor button. At the nurses' station, he saw Kirkland and walked over. An expression of surprise crossed her face. "I haven't thought of anything helpful yet."

"That's okay, I have another question. You told me before that Dorene never dated anyone on the staff."

"That is correct. At least I never knew of anyone."

As he readied to ask the next question, Travis focused on the woman's eyes. "Did you and Dorene date?"

She paled, her eyes glaring at him. "What do you mean asking a question like that?"

Oops, not out of the closet yet, are we? "Sorry," Travis said. "Would you like to continue this conversation somewhere more private."

"No. We did not date. Why would you ever ask that?" Her higher pitched voice startled him.

"I learned the reason Dorene quit her job was because she couldn't take her boss's butt pats, lascivious looks and constant requests for dates. You were her boss, weren't you?"

Kirkland's face turned crimson, her eyes looking over his shoulder. He waited a moment to give her a chance to collect her composure. Finally, she made eye contact again. "For the record, we did not date. If you don't have any more questions, I must get back to work. Excuse me please."

Travis suppressed a grin as she left. *You could be telling the truth. You pitched; she didn't receive.* Opening his notebook, he jotted down the time and date, as well as several notes on their brief conversation. He couldn't help but feel sorry for her. *Lady, you just need to come out and be honest with the world—would be less embarrassing for you.*

~ ~ ~

Travis returned to the station where he met Zach and Joella leaving the building.

"Hey, Chief," Zach said, "we're off duty, heading to Jakes for a burger and a little firewater. Why don't you join us?"

"Sure, I could use a cup of coffee."

Walking out to their vehicles, Joella said, "Are you limping, Travis?"

"I twisted my leg establishing my camp site last night. Just a strain."

"Setting up camp? Where were you?"

"I spent the weekend fishing on the Smith River. It's a beautiful place, peaceful and quiet. Helps me to regain my sanity."

~ ~ ~

Waiting for their order, Zach asked, "Did you have any luck in Black Eagle?"

"Not really. The sister confirmed Ms. Burke knew O'Toole, but insisted they weren't friends. In addition, none of her co-workers knew about any budding relationship between them, but I interviewed him again anyway."

"And?" Zach said.

"He still has that near-perfect alibi but I did learn O'Toole and Dorene had sex at least once, according to the fancy doctor. Apparently, the sister didn't know. Many of Burke's neighbors said she dated a mystery guy. Nobody knew his name. I suspect it was O'Toole. I did find another person of interest, though I don't really think she did it."

"She? That kind of knife mutilation is almost never done by a female."

Travis winked at Joella. "How about that penis amputating lady a few years ago?"

Zach grimaced. "At least not to another female," he said, subconsciously crossing his legs.

"My gut tells me she didn't do it even though Dorene's neighbor, Agnes, said Dorene quit her job because of her boss's advances," Travis said. "I was surprised to learn Dorene's boss was a lesbian. She didn't strike me as violent, but I'll check her out more."

"That adds another piece to the puzzle," Zach said. "I know you were leaning towards O'Toole, and it's too early to stop scrutinizing him. He still seems like a fine possibility to me, especially since Joella said the cutting was done by an experienced hand." He checked his watch, and drained his beer. "Gotta run guys, I got a hottie waiting for my eager butt." He laughed, emphasizing his dimples, as he made for the door.

After he left, Joella said, "You seem to be losing weight. Do you feel okay?"

"I'm not getting much sleep, that's all."

"Why? What's the problem?"

Travis never had any luck discussing his problems with Marion. She was not interested. He hesitated, raking back his jet-black hair. *I need to talk to someone.* Taking a swig of coffee, he began slowly. "I—I'm not sleeping because the minute I close my eyes I see bloody blondes all night." Once he started, the entire nightmare spilled out. "It's the same one every night. I can't banish the horror from my brain." Even telling the story, his stomach turned sour.

"That doesn't sound strange to me. After all, you're investigating three gruesome murders, all blondes. Bound to make anyone relive such atrocities."

"Maybe, but my gut tells me it's something more."

"I can't think of anything it could be. If there is anything I can do to help, let me know."

"Nothing anyone can do. I want to know why I was emotional enough to vomit viewing the first two victims. I didn't with the Black Eagle case, so maybe I'm over whatever it was. It still worries me though." Travis glanced at his watch and stood. "I have to go too. Sorry to leave you alone, I've another important stop to make before I head home." Once behind the wheel of his pickup, his roiling stomach felt better. *It was good talking to Joella. I'm sure I can trust her.*

~ ~ ~

Travis parked his car, went in the front door and sat at the bar. "Hello, Ma."

She stopped polishing an invisible spill at

the other end and walked over. "Oh Lord, please tell me you're on duty this time."

"Yes, 'this time' I am." Seeing the relief on her face, he grinned. "Bring me a Coke."

Her face beamed. "Coming right up."

"Thanks, Ma. And double thanks for the other night. My keys were in my pocket, like always."

"You're welcome, Honey. Please try not to let it happen again. That's twice in the last few weeks. I'm afraid you are fast losing this battle."

"I do my best, but sometimes I have to get away from Marion before I do something I'll regret."

"If you don't want to divorce her, why don't you just pack and leave? The church couldn't call that a sin or blame her."

"It may come to that. I can't take much more, but the guilt would eat me alive. You know I owe her for putting me through college."

"Well that doesn't mean you have to suffer a life sentence." She put a napkin on the bar and placed a tall Coke on top. "On the house, Honey. You said you were on duty. What can I do for you?"

"Do you remember when I had my last blackout? I don't mean the recent one—the one time before." He observed her look at the ceiling, her brow wrinkled.

"Gee, I remember the night, but couldn't tell you the date."

"Do you happen to recall the day?"

"The day? Afraid I don't. Is it important?"

"No. It's not important." *No sense worrying*

her. He finished his Coke, said goodnight and walked toward the front door. On his way to see Ma, he had prayed she might be blessed with an exceptional memory and could tell him his previous blackout was on a Monday or Tuesday—any day but Sunday.

~ ~ ~

Driving home, his brain spurted a cluster of suspicious thoughts in all directions. He'd fallen in love with Marion's yellow hair but over the years of their ugly marriage, he'd come to loath blondes of all shades. His blackouts, coupled with his queasiness at seeing the bodies of the two serial killings, terrified him. Both he and Joella thought the killer might be a cop or forensic worker because he knew police policies and procedures. The whirlwind of dark thoughts slammed his secret fear into full focus. *Did I kill those women during a blackout and not remember?*

CHAPTER 15

Travis's legs were still shaking when he arrived home, his stomach churning. From the bedroom, Marion's soft snores echoed into the living room. He stretched out on the couch. Afraid to close his eyes, he glared at the ceiling. His tortured mind exploded with possibilities. 'Possibilities' that accessed the darkest corner of his soul. *Am I capable of such horror? Why not? It's in my genes. My forefathers did a lot worse after the white man taught them how to scalp.*

His gut roiling and knees shaking, he called in sick the next day and the next. It was useless to talk to Marion. She already thought he needed a shrink for his overactive imagination. He finally returned to work on the third day. *I must talk to someone before I lose my mind. Joella. I'll see if she can go for coffee after work.* He planned to wait until quitting time to ask her, but she opened the door a few moments later.

"I heard you were back. I'm worried—you're not yourself lately. I wanted to call to see how you were, but thought better of it when I remembered how jealous you said Marion was." She paused, glancing at his face. "You still look awful. Have you been to the doctor?"

"No, I haven't. If you are free after work, I'd like to talk to you. I'll buy you a drink."

"Sure, I don't have any plans. Jakes?"

"Too many of the guys go there. How about you ride with me?" He saw her eyebrows arch.

"Okay. If dispatch doesn't send us out, I'll meet you in the parking lot."

"Good." Travis shifted in his chair, his eyes locked with hers, hands shaking. *I need to change the subject.* "Anything new on the Black Eagle case?"

A broad smile spread across her face. "Actually, that is what I came in to tell you. The ME just lightened your heavy caseload by one. I've never seen two such different results from crimes supposedly committed by the same person. Our serial killer is so smart I wondered if we would ever catch him. The lab solved the Burke case in mere days. Zach and Porter arrested Manny Ryker yesterday. Scared shitless, he confessed after a few minutes of interrogation."

"Are you serious?"

"Sure am. He doesn't appear too bright, and he has watched too many TV mysteries. Made a clumsy effort to clean blood off the walls with Clorox. Couldn't do much about the carpet and couch. He left fingerprints everywhere, and he raped Burke so the ME had DNA, both semen and his skin under her fingernails. She fought hard. He looked like he'd lost a battle with a barbed wire fence; scratches still covered the guy's face and arms."

Travis gazed out the window, his eyes unfocused. *That's why I didn't get sick looking at the victim. The serial killer didn't do it.* There wasn't a cloud in the sky and he felt as if the sun pierced his brain. He crossed the room to close the blinds. The Burke case was a clumsy crime from the start. If he hadn't been so weak-minded, the collar would have been his, with forensics furnishing the proof, of course. His failure at solving the three recent murders wouldn't go unnoticed by the captain. He looked back at Joella prolonging eye contact for several seconds before his curiosity got the best of him. "So who the hell is Manny Ryker?"

"He's a hospital maintenance employee. A couple of previous felonies supplied the ME with prints and DNA already on file that matched the murder's immediately. The other detectives were busy so Zach questioned hospital staff and several of the nurses told him how the guy had pestered Burke for weeks, wanting a date."

"None of the staff mentioned him when I interviewed them," Travis said.

"You questioned them about any rejected suitors or stalkers; Ryker didn't register with the nurses because he had a thing for her. And they didn't consider him violent, only lovesick. But he can't be Dorene's mystery man if this was their first date. That is, if it was a date. Maybe he appeared at her place uninvited."

Travis needed to lighten the conversation, away from his feeling of failure. "Bet turning Zach loose on a floor with a bunch of young women made his day. He most likely has them all neatly categorized by bust size in his little black book."

She rolled her eyes and laughed. "You're probably right. But back to Burke's murder. When they questioned Ryker, he broke down. Admitted he became enraged when she fought off his advances. Claimed he didn't mean to kill her, only wanted to scare her. When she fell to the floor and wasn't breathing, he panicked. Then he remembered reading about the serial killer and decided to stage it to look like another of MM's victims. He didn't know that the police never released all the facts, nor was he aware that the serial killer used duct tape and his victims didn't put up a fight. You were right—a copycat crime."

~ ~ ~

Travis tried to center his thoughts on the two unsolved murders after Joella left, but his mind still swirled with failed effort. His forehead tensed. *Focus, dammit.*

Investigating the lesbian for priors had simmered on the back burner for days. He booted his laptop only to discover nothing anywhere to indicate a raging psycho. In fact, Hannah Kirkland had no criminal record at all, not as much as a speeding ticket. Apparently, none of her butt-pat victims filed a complaint. Afraid of losing their jobs, as O'Toole had suggested. His gut told him she didn't do it. She didn't seem the type. He put Kirkland on the 'back burner' again.

He looked up when Zach sauntered in, flopping into the chair next to his desk. He'd changed out of his uniform and wore what Travis assumed were his date-hunting duds to attract the women at BJs: skintight jeans and an even tighter Billings Bulls T-shirt that emphasized his triangular torso and small waist. Bulging biceps and abs rippled the T-shirt that clung like wet Kleenex. He wore black gaucho boots with large iron side rings and a gray gambler's hat with a feathered hatband that sat on the back of his head completing his hunting garb.

"Wasn't that something—solving the Black Eagle case so fast?" Zach said.

"Yes, it was great work."

"No work involved—the ME solved it. All we had to do was bring him in. And man-oh-man, Chief, I enjoyed that. That wigwam is one great happy-hunting ground. Most of the nurses and aids are young single chicks. I got a hot date tonight. A tiny little brunette that almost comes to my armpits. Hey, glad you're feeling better, but gotta run. Don't want to keep the little lady waiting—I'm dying to see if those humongous boobs are real."

After hearing news of the solved case, Travis's thoughts shifted gear to a new problem: Joella. *I'm sure I can trust her. But how much do I dare tell her. She is a cop.*

CHAPTER 16

At quitting time, Joella strolled out to her minivan; a stiff wind whipped at her, hair blowing across her face. She tried to hold her tresses in place, but it was useless. No sign of Travis. She checked her watch. *I know dispatch didn't send him out. He's running late.* She opened the passenger door and tossed in her briefcase, the wind slamming the door closed almost catching her hand. Familiar voices grabbed her attention. She waved to Zach and Porter exiting the building and heading to their respective vehicles.

Zach called out, "The wind about to blow you away?"

"Sure is." Joella leaned against the rear of the minivan. *What's keeping him?*

After Porter drove out of the parking lot, she spotted Travis. *Guess he wanted to wait until the bigot left.* His furrowed brow and arms clasped around his chest raised her concern. *What is bothering him?*

Travis seemed to be scanning the parking lot for her, and she noticed his shoulders relax when he spotted her.

Joella walked toward his pickup, the wind almost knocking her off her feet. "Doesn't this damn wind ever ease off?" she asked.

"Not really. It seems to funnel at full gallop through the depression the town nestles in."

He unlocked the passenger door and opened it. She quit trying to hold her hair in place and stepped inside.

Travis walked around the pickup and slid in behind the wheel. "Ready?"

"Yes." *Now let's see why he couldn't talk at Jakes.*

CHAPTER 17

Travis parked behind Betsy's Bar and guided Joella through the back door. He looked around, troubled to see so many patrons, but thankful there were none he knew. He guided her to his favorite corner table. "This was a mistake. We can't talk here, but I promised you a drink. I'll go order. What would you like?"

"White wine if they have it, otherwise a beer is fine."

Ma greeted Travis with her usual, "Hi, Honey. Why don't you bring the missus over and introduce her?"

"The lady isn't my wife, Ma. She's a fellow officer, and I need to talk to someone. I gave in trying to converse with Marion a long time ago." He leaned in, lowering his voice. "I have problems far worse than my blackouts and she is someone I can trust."

Ma raised her eyebrows, a worried look in

her eye. "What are you drinking?"

"Don't worry. Give me a Coke. My friend will have white wine."

Ma inhaled audibly. "Thank God for small favors. I'll bring your drinks to the table."

"Thanks, Ma."

As Travis walked away from the bar, a pang of guilt hit him. *Damn.* He stopped abruptly in the middle of the floor. *What was I thinking? I shouldn't have said that to Ma. She'll think I don't trust her. I'd trust her with my life, but I didn't want to burden her.* He continued toward his table. *I'll explain to her later.*

At the table, he watched Joella's eyes scanning the room. "How did you ever find this cozy old bar? I love it. I've been admiring the beautiful oak floor, and those great wooden rafters, not to mention the beautiful carved bar with a mirrored backdrop. This building must be very old."

"It probably was old when Ma bought it years ago."

"Ma?"

"Sorry. Her name is Betsy, but everyone knows her as Ma. If you called her Betsy, she most likely wouldn't answer. I'll introduce you to her when she brings our order. We can drink up and then go somewhere quieter." When Ma brought the drinks, he made the introductions and Joella seemed to like Ma right away. He knew Ma would withhold judgment until she knew Joella better.

~ ~ ~

The bar door opened. Ma turned to see a tall, gaunt man with an elegant salt and pepper goatee enter wearing an expensive navy suit. His crimson necktie matched his lady's dress and five-inch stiletto heels. When he observed the laborers wearing jeans seated at the bar and neighborhood folk, he stopped, appearing to be uncomfortable. He hesitated, and then headed for the table nearest Travis and Joella, away from the crowd. Ma, ever protective of her Honey, stepped over to block the way. "Sorry, that table is reserved. Please sit at one of the others."

When Travis and Joella had almost finished their drinks, Ma brought another round. "On the house, Honey." Ma knew him so well she recognized his furtive glances around the room and knew he wanted privacy. "I figure by the time you drink those, it will be quiet enough for private conversation—see, half of the one-for-the-road crowd has left."

"You're right, Ma, as always."

"Besides," Joella said, "anywhere else we went would be as crowded and I'm enjoying this place being free of television sets and pool tables."

"Wouldn't have those damn ball knockers in my place," Ma said, knowing her words might offend the prim and proper looking Joella.

Joella laughed.

"You're all right, Miss. You can bring her back any time, Travis."

~ ~ ~

Travis relaxed, happy that two of his favorite people had hit it off so well.

When Ma left, Joella took a sip of wine, smiled in approval and put the glass back on the coaster. "What did you want to talk to me about, Travis?"

Other than the staid couple, two men at the bar were engaged in conversation while four others sat at a table across the room, none close enough to hear. Now that he was free to talk, he fought for words. *How do I tell her such horror? She could go to the captain with my story.* Finally, after a long hesitation, he decided. *No, I can trust her.* "Joella..." His voice cracked as he said her name. "The other day when I didn't come to work, I wasn't really sick. I was shaking so bad after the realization hit me that I couldn't stand. I couldn't sleep. I couldn't breathe."

"What 'realization?'"

Hesitating, he drew a deep breath and then as if afraid he might lose his courage, he blurted, "I'm scared shitless I might have committed those first two murders, Merry and Richmond, and not remember it."

Joella recoiled, confusion glazing her eyes. "What on earth do you mean?"

"Do you remember how queasy and sick I got viewing the first two victims? I felt such a strong personal connection—like I knew them. Never felt anything like it before when inspecting a brutalized body. I can't begin to describe the depth of my emotion. I'm always feeling pains and emotions I can't explain and Marion gets so disgusted with my imagination that she threatens to commit me to an institution. She once made an appointment for me with a shrink but I wouldn't go."

"Travis, that's crazy talk. You are far too

compassionate a man to ever commit such heinous crimes."

"Then why do I feel such a strong emotional connection?"

"I don't know, but it is not because you killed them. Maybe it has something to do with Marion being a blonde. Anyway, I'm sure it's just plain coincidence."

"Both times?" Travis wet his parched throat with a gulp of Coke. "There's more. I told you I fell in love with Marion's blonde hair; but after our farce of a marriage, I've come to detest flaxen hair of all shades. And now I have that recurring nightmare of golden-haired women floating in and out my window, all with the same mutilation the killer used. The blood keeps flowing until I am covered and I wake gasping for air. It's the same dream every night, and I relive their pain every night."

"That's horrible but hardly evidence you are a murderer."

"Unfortunately, there's more."

Joella shifted in her seat, downing half of her wine.

"No one knows what I'm about to tell you except Marion and Ma." He watched Joella's eyes dart around the room as she twisted her napkin to shreds, saying nothing.

He leaned closer, lowering his voice. "I tell everyone I don't drink, and I don't—normally. My father, a raging alcoholic, beat my mother and me whenever he drank. I swore I would never drink." He paused and wet his lips. "And I never did until after I married. The early years were fine until Marion quit work. Our money problems mounted and so did our arguments. Hell, our lives have become a nightmare."

He gazed around the room, took a deep breath and continued. "When our fights were especially vicious, I'd leave the apartment in a rage to keep from choking the life out of her. I always ended here intending to have one drink to calm down. But one never was enough" He stopped and breathing briskly peeked at Joella, whose face appeared frozen, her eyes glassy. She didn't utter a word. He began talking faster to get the story out before he lost his courage. "When I got roaring drunk, Ma always took care of me, making sure I got home safely. The next day I could never recall what happened. I had total blackouts and had no idea what I might have done after I got home. I knew only what Ma and Marion told me." He swallowed, feeling as if the wind had been knocked out of him. "My last blackout was the Sunday of the Richmond murder."

Travis swore he could see the blood draining from Joella's face. "Remember last night when I said I had another important stop to make? I came here and asked Ma if she could remember the date of my blackout before the Richmond case. She couldn't. It could have been the Sunday of the first victim—I don't know, the odds are against me—most of my blackouts are on a Sunday, after a weekend of terrible arguing with Marion. Both of MM's murders occurred on a Sunday."

He watched her face tense, eyes staring into his. Joella remained silent for several moments. Finally, her face relaxed and she said, "It's all circumstantial. I don't believe you are capable of murder."

"Have you forgotten, you said yourself the murderer might be a cop because of the clean crime scenes."

"My God, Travis, that was only a comment. The killer may be well-read or just plain lucky."

They both sat not speaking, as if afraid to say anything more. Finally, Joella broke the strained silence. "There is no way in hell I'll believe you committed those two murders. There's one thing I know for sure—if you can't bring yourself to leave Marion, you *must* get your temper under control. You can't allow her tirades and shopping splurges make you so angry that you start to drink. You *cannot* change her. You must change the way it affects you. Walk away. Cool down. Your anger is hurting no one but you. It won't stop Marion's outbursts or shopping addiction." She stopped, gasping for air. "Sorry for the long-winded soap-box speech. Tell me you aren't angry."

Travis noticed her solemn expression. "I'm not angry." He paused digesting what she said. "And you are absolutely right."

"Thank goodness. I didn't mean to get so carried away, but it needed to be said. I only shared what I learned in therapy." Joella hesitated, as if trying to find the right words. Then she looked into his eyes. "I hate to say this, but perhaps Marion's idea makes sense. Maybe you should see a shrink. I don't know if it is even possible to commit a crime during a blackout and not remember. A doctor would know. If it isn't possible, you would solve your concern right there. Have you done any research on the Internet?"

He shifted in his chair. "To be honest, I am afraid to check. 'Afraid' of what I might find. And I don't have a lot of faith in the Internet. Anyone can put anything on there."

"Yes, you do have to be careful of what site you trust. It would be better to talk to a doctor. You could be tearing yourself to pieces for no reason. Maybe it's not possible." She drained the rest of her wine, looking deep into his eyes. "Are you going to make an appointment?"

"I don't know. If the department found out, I might lose my job."

CHAPTER 18

Travis spent another horrifying night with his procession of blonde beauties. He awoke lying in sweat-soaked sheets with a headache and knotted muscles. *Shit. I can't go on like this; I've got to find out—one way or the other.*

"Travis," Marion called from the kitchen. "Breakfast is on the table. I made pancakes and bacon; if you want them hot, you'd better get out here."

Pancakes? Bacon? What has she bought now? Too mentally exhausted to care or even ask, he rolled out of bed. He wasn't hungry but dressed and went to join her. "Thanks, I like pancakes. We don't have them often enough." He ate several cakes and two pieces of bacon, then pushed his plate forward. He hadn't been hungry until he started eating.

Marion glared at him and threw the spatula down. "See," she yelled, "that is exactly why we don't have pancakes more often."

"What are you talking about?"

"They take too much damn time to make and by the time I finish flipping the stupid cakes, you're through and I wind up eating alone."

She's got me there. "Sorry. I'll have another cup of coffee with you. I want to tell you something. I've decided to take your suggestion and see a shrink."

"Hallelujah. It's about time. I swear you're losing your mind. You should have gone when I made that appointment for you ages ago. The girls at Tish's beauty parlor tell me Dr. Jackson is a miracle worker, and Blake is fantastic too. Which one are you going to see?"

"Neither one. I'm driving to Helena to see Dr. Paul."

"What?" She threw her hands in the air. "You're always complaining about me spending money and now you're driving ninety miles and then ninety back when we have perfectly good doctors in Great Falls."

"Maybe so, but if someone saw me going into the shrink's office or thought I was seeing one on my own, it would not be good for my career. I'd most likely lose my job."

"If you can afford to spend that much for gas, I can buy that cute little black cocktail dress I saw in the window at the mall."

Travis bit on his lower lip. He started to say something but stopped. *What difference does it make? I'll never pay off her credit cards in my lifetime anyway.*

~ ~ ~

Finally having made the dreadful decision, the world seemed brighter, the trees greener, the air sweeter. On his way to the station, Travis checked his watch and drove to Gibson Park, only a few blocks out of the way. He was surprised to detect the aroma of flowers. The garden had only bare soil yesterday, but now blossomed in a Technicolor assortment of newly matured plants, required because of the short growing season.

He parked in front of the lake. When he spied the Canada Goose goslings swimming in a tight cluster behind mama, he scanned the water for cygnets, his favorite. Not finding any, he tossed the geese a handful of corn he kept in the jockey box for such occasions. A little boy in short pants, holding his mother's hand, stood at the edge of the pond tossing stale bread to the ducks and huge golden carp. Every time a duck tilted its tail in the air to grab a sinking tidbit, the little boy shrieked with laughter. Travis laughed too. *It is a beautiful world—sometimes.*

Arriving at the station, Travis wanted to tell Joella of his decision, but she wasn't in. A drug store robbery investigation kept him busy the rest of the morning. The thief, a young punk without his fix, had destroyed half the store searching for drugs when the clerk refused to fill his obviously fake prescription. Bottles and boxes lay scattered across the floor. Travis jotted down the outstanding description the pharmacist gave: a short, bony guy with blue eyes and a thin red Mohawk to draw attention from his blotchy face and arm tracks. Travis's lips stretched to a smirk. *I know the guy—he got out of jail last week.*

~ ~ ~

Back in the office, Travis was filing his report, when Joella opened the door a few minutes before quitting time. "I looked for you earlier," Travis said. "Wanted to tell you I thought about what you said, and I made an appointment with a shrink. Can't live like this—not knowing if I committed these horrible crimes or not."

Joella sat in the chair by his desk. "I'm glad. The doctor will be able to clear your mind of all those ridiculous suspicions. Who are you going to see?"

"Dr. Frances Paul in Helena. Didn't want to take a chance someone might see me go into a psychiatrist's office here in town or word leak out that I made an appointment. It's one thing if the department sends me because I killed someone in the line of duty, but it would not read well on my record if I went on my own. I called Dr. Jackson with a phony story and asked for a recommendation in Helena. Made an appointment with him for tomorrow."

Joella rolled her eyes. "Thank heaven. I think you'll find out it isn't even possible to not remember something so heinous as committing mutilation and murder. You'll be glad you went."

~ ~ ~

After a night of parading blondes, Travis rose early battling a queasy stomach. He passed on breakfast. *I need to calm myself. Can't arrive a nervous wreck—I'd act guilty. Whatever I tell the doctor is privileged information unless he believes I'm about to commit a crime. I only want to know if I could commit an offense during a blackout and not remember it.* That thought jolted him back to reality. *What the hell will I do if he says it is possible?*

~ ~ ~

As terrified as he was, Travis looked forward to driving to Helena because it took him through one of his favorite places: Wolf Creek Canyon. The interstate followed the canyon rim and the old road wound through the floor alongside the Missouri River, the water flowing gently with no rapids. Both views were stunning, but he preferred the old road.

At Ulm, Travis exited the Interstate for Cascade where the canyon opened slowly. The gorge always worked more magic for his soul than the green tunnel of Third Avenue. Today, driving through the colorful canyon did little to relieve Travis's mind. Anxiety surged through his body. His heart beat like a tom-tom, every nerve twitched. He felt a desperate need to be in touch with the Great Spirit. Stopping at a favorite spot, he hiked part way up a steep mountain that overlooked the bend of the river. Off to the side, he could see Little Prickly Pear Creek's crystal-clear flow. The canyon walls winked in orange, green and gold, studded with evergreens glinting in the morning sunshine.

Standing on a rock face and gazing at the sheer beauty, he could sense the creator's presence surround him. He raised his arms to the sky and gazed heavenward. "Hear me now, *Naató'si.* If I am guilty of these horrendous crimes and my time comes to join you, whiteman laws forbid our traditional burial rights so I will have my ashes scattered here on this spot to nourish Mother Earth's trees and grasses. The rabbit will eat the grasses and the coyote will eat the rabbit, my ashes replenishing the cycle of life."

His heart rate slowed and Travis felt his spirit lifted. He grabbed a quick burger at the Wolf Creek bar to satisfy the rumbling in his stomach and reentered the Interstate to ensure he would arrive in time for his appointment.

When he located the address, he parked and walked slowly toward the entrance of the doctor's office, once a private home. A large white sign with black, old English print read: *Dr. Frances Paul, MD.* A white picket fence bordered the property, and its gate squeaked when he opened it. It wasn't loud but to Travis it sounded like a death toll. At the door, he stopped. *Get a grip. I must know one way or the other.* He took a deep breath and then another. He went in.

The receptionist, a chunky brunette with tight curly hair, quickly slipped a magazine into a drawer. She flashed him a warm smile. "Good morning. Do you have an appointment?"

"Yes, I'm Mr. Eagle." Never having thought he would be in such an office, he knew his cheeks were flushed. He filled out the required paperwork and showed his driver's license. The receptionist led him into the doctor's office, trailing an overpowering scent of perfume in her wake. "Make yourself comfortable. The doctor will be with you in a moment."

When Travis's feet sank into the plush navy

blue carpet, he couldn't help but admire the ultra-handsome décor. There were no windows; indirect lighting near the ceiling provided a quiet, soothing mood for the room. A gilded cartouche graced one wall with a heavy bronze Greek mythological figure; he couldn't recollect which one. Two mint-green mohair chairs sat in front of a heavy oak desk. A third matching chair sat off to the side next to a small table that held a tape recorder and notepad. He took one of the chairs facing the desk. Glancing around the room, he recognized a painting by Jean-Baptiste Corot above the cartouche. His college years had acquainted him with the French impressionist and he admired his work. *I wonder if the painting is an original. With the prices these doctors charge, it might be.* He started to go inspect the painting when he realized something in the office was missing— the ubiquitous couch. *Thank you Naató'si, I sure as hell don't want to talk to a guy with me flat on my back.*

The door opened and he fought off his surprise when a woman with long, flaming red hair walked in. The dark green business suit she wore failed to disguise the voluptuous figure beneath. He marveled at her freckle-free pale skin and beautiful facial features.

A sweet woodsy aroma floated his way, and Travis inhaled deeply wiping out the stench of the receptionist's intense cheap scent. "I'm wa—waiting for Dr. Paul."

"That's me. Frances Paul."

Travis shifted in his seat. "I guess the name threw me. I thought my appointment was with a man." *How can I concentrate on my problems eyeballing her?*

She sat down, crossing her legs, exposing a tawny thigh from a side-slit skirt. It wasn't a lot of thigh—just enough to be distracting. "Easy mistake. It's Frances with an E. Happens a lot, but my receptionist should have made that clear when you made the appointment. I'll speak to her. If you aren't comfortable talking with a woman, I can easily refer you to another doctor."

"No. Doesn't matter," he lied. *I can't wait that long.*

"Fine," she said, sitting in the lone chair next to the small table. "Shall we begin?"

"Yes." *Now I find out if I am the monster.*

CHAPTER 19

Joella didn't see Travis before he left for Helena on Friday. He'd told her he was leaving at the crack of dawn to be sure of arriving in time for his appointment. Dispatch didn't send her out and she worked in the office all day. Whatever she did, thoughts of what distress Travis might be experiencing distracted her. *Maybe I shouldn't have suggested he take Marion's advice. I could have gone with him for moral support. No, that wouldn't have worked. If his wife discovered we'd gone out of town together...* She flipped through papers on her desk and shuffled them about, not absorbing much.

~ ~ ~

By late afternoon, Joella was gazing out the window every few minutes to search for Travis's pickup in the parking lot. *He should be back by now.* Quitting time rolled around and

THE GREEN TUNNEL

he still had not appeared. Worried, she wanted to call his apartment, but could think of no believable excuse to do so. She drove home unable to get Travis off her mind.

Joella rummaged around her house all weekend, accomplishing nothing. *Surely, he'd call if something delayed him.* He didn't call. *Something must have happened. Shit. I hope the news wasn't so bad he got drunk. If he had a blackout in a strange city with no Ma to take care of him...*

~ ~ ~

Monday morning Joella arrived at the station early, going straight to Travis's office. She saw him staring out the window, his back toward her.

"How did it go?" When he didn't answer, she called again, louder. "Travis."

He swiveled around. "Huh?"

"I said how did it go? I expected you back Friday. Why didn't you call?"

"I'm sorry. I was in no condition to talk to anyone. I didn't get back until late Sunday night."

Her lips trembled.

"Oh my God. Did the doctor think it was possible that you could have committed those crimes and not remember?"

"I didn't tell her what I was suspicious of, only asked the doctor if committing a crime and not remembering it were possible during a blackout."

"Her? I thought the doctor was a male."

"So did I. The name fooled me. She noted my surprise and said if I felt uncomfortable

135

talking to a woman, she would refer me to a male doctor. Rescheduling would have meant another trip and more time to worry. I turned the offer down."

"What did she say?"

"Wasn't good news. Turns out the subject is highly controversial. Some doctors swear it is impossible, while others consider it feasible. Of course, every lawyer in the country says it is not only possible but also very credible. In fact, several have won cases using that defense. Dr. Paul believes it is very possible. That news sent me into orbit—I'm sure she caught my shocked reaction."

Joella's brow furrowed, her eyes darting around the room. "No wonder you appear so drawn. What else did the doctor say?"

"I didn't mention my blackouts but did state I had a problem with alcohol because of Marion and me constantly fighting over money. We spent most of the session talking about our appalling arguments. Seems that is the main problem with most of her clients, and she didn't seem surprised. Recommended I look into Alcoholics Anonymous." Travis turned and looked out the window before continuing. "I described my depression over not solving the serial killings. I didn't mention the murderer seemed to be as smart as a cop. Because my life is at stake, I watched what I said. Doctor visits are confidential, but only to a point. I mentioned my floating blonde visitors, and Dr. Paul was certainly interested in that—wants to talk more about that next week. This visit was devastating. I'm not sure I will go back."

"You have time to consider it," Joella said. She felt the frown creasing her forehead, afraid to ask the question spinning in her mind. Finally, she could wait no longer. "If you didn't come back to town, where did you spend Saturday night and Sunday?"

"I spent the weekend in Wolf Creek. The bar has decent chow and I had my sleeping bag in the truck—camped out in the mountains, trying to think, to reap a little peace of mind. Regenerate my soul. You know, Indian stuff," he said, trying to lighten the conversation.

Joella felt her heart pounding. *Bar?* Her mouth dried. "Did it help?"

"Always does. After a day and a half in the mountains, I returned home emotionally calm. Actually, had some new ideas about our serial killer. When I went to bed, my social-gathering guests returned. They even added a couple more ladies to the lineup. My stomach is still in knots. I'm beginning to wonder if they will cease their nightly floats when this case is solved. Pardon me—I mean if it is solved."

"We'll get him, Travis. There are too many unsolved crimes already. We won't let this become another one."

Neither said a word for a long time, then, a loud gurgling sound shattered the silence. She peeked at Travis and burst into laughter. "Was that you?"

"Yeah. I didn't eat breakfast. Want to go to Betsy's later for an early lunch?"

"Sure, around eleven?" When he nodded, she said, "See you then if dispatch doesn't grab us first."

As she started out the door, Joella hesitated when Travis's phone rang.

"Detective Eagle. What's up, Porter? Shit. She's right here. We're on our way."

Her brow rose. "What was that about?"

"Our nipple and finger maniac has struck again."

Joella felt shivers race up her spine, her blood turning cold. *Oh my God! Did it happen yesterday, Sunday?* She swallowed the lump in her throat. *Am I misreading him?* Her thoughts began to doubt her past reasoning as they walked toward the parking lot. *I hate to do this, but I must know.* She put out her hand to stop him. "You said you stayed the weekend in Wolf Creek spending some time in the bar. Were you drinking?"

He didn't hesitate answering. "No, the bar is the only place that serves food."

Joella closed her eyes and bit her lip until it was numb. *If this murder happened Sunday, can I believe him?*

CHAPTER 20

Travis followed Joella to the victim's house, which wasn't far from the station. Arriving at the address, he noticed a small stone building with a front porch of the same stone. Bowing to modernization, the city long ago demolished the impressive Grand Theater, the library and the other stone structures, leaving only the courthouse and a few small houses in the oldest part of the city to represent the styles at the turn of the century when the town was born. Most of the houses were dilapidated eyesores, but the victim's home seemed well kept with a low wood-rail fence and pansies planted along the sidewalk He was glad to see someone appreciated historic buildings.

Porter met them at the front door. "The ME and techs will be here shortly."

Inside, Travis asked, "Who discovered the body?"

"The brother, Luke Randenberg. His work requires traveling, and they share the house when he's in town. He returned from a lengthy trip around Montana late this morning, drove in from Missoula. Apparently, they were close. The wimp is crying like a baby."

Travis shook his head. *Why can't this clown show a little respect?* It was useless to comment; advice sailed over Porter's head like a flying Frisbee. "Where's the brother now?"

"He's across the street with a neighbor."

"Any sign of breaking and entering?"

"Naw, just like the others."

"Damn strange," Travis said, looking at Joella but speaking to no one in particular. "Appears this is MM's third murder and no sign of breaking and entering at any of them. Unless he dated them, either they all let him in or left their doors unlocked. Hard to believe anyone would leave their doors unlocked with a serial killer on the prowl and the *Tribune* reminds readers of it every day."

"Maybe he poses as a delivery man like a florist," Joella said. "What woman wouldn't open the door for flowers?"

Travis turned to Porter. "What's the victim's name?"

"Emma Randenberg. Same last name as the brother. Wasn't married and you can see why— she's frumpy. Wasn't a looker like the other victims, but she is a blonde with an inch of brown roots."

Travis clenched his teeth to keep his lips from trembling as he glanced at the body. His stomach began to rumble. He didn't regurgitate after the last victim and thought his strange sieges were over. Now it made sense—the Burke case was simply a copycat crime. The phenomenon was back. *I'm only getting sick in the gut with MM's victims.* He didn't want to lose it in front of Porter. "I'll leave the body to you, Joella, and I'll go question the brother and some of the other neighbors. Let's have that lunch when we get done and you can fill me in."

"What's the matter, Chief—afraid you might puke again?" Porter said, rolling his little piggy eyes.

"Shut up, Porter," Joella said. "Come back here when you finish, Travis, and we'll get that lunch."

~ ~ ~

After Travis left, Porter edged in close to Joella as if confiding a secret. "This is no copycat killing this time, La-dy. Same MO and mutilation, blonde victim and duct tape," he said, emphasizing the words duct tape.

Joella frowned. "Seeing as you've done my job, I guess I can leave too."

"Aw, don't get all huffy. I was just making conversation because our hot-shot detective flew the coup."

"If that's your idea of conversation, you can 'fly the coup' too. Travis is doing his job—I suggest you do the same."

Porter stalked off in characteristic fashion whenever the conversation took a turn against his sarcastic remarks. Joella had come to dislike working with him as much as Travis did, often catching a whiff of offensive body odor in his presence. Either Porter didn't use antiperspirant or maybe he was one of those unfortunate people for whom no amount of the product worked. *He's right about one thing; this looks like the work of our serial killer.*

Like the others, this victim appeared to be in her mid-twenties. The killer not only seemed to hate blondes, he picked them young. The body, taped to the floor, face up like the other victims. The longer Joella worked, the more disturbed she became. *How can this maniac commit so many crimes without leaving clues?*

Continuing her inspection, Joella made a few quick notes before aiming her camera at the reddish-purple splotches on the victim's arms and legs. She had already removed the duct tape from the body's limbs and focused on the discoloration where the blood had drained from gravity. *This body wasn't moved either. Why always in the living room?* Discovering that full rigor mortis had set in and had recently begun to release the body back to its limp state, Joella's face froze. *Oh God, this woman lost her life Sunday. Travis said he didn't get home until Sunday night.* She gazed at the body a long time, her mind discharging despicable thoughts. Finally, she pulled herself together and continued the examination. *The fact he returned home Sunday doesn't prove anything—does it?*

The ringing phone on her hip startled her. "Hi, Travis. Yes, I have almost finished; I'm waiting for the coroner to come for the body. Why don't I meet you at Betsy's. I shouldn't be long." She put the phone back in its holster and again turned her attention to the corpse.

Mike, one of the technicians, came in from the bathroom. "Found damp clothes in the washing machine again and a couple of prints."

"I suspected we would. We'll have to get the brother's prints to rule him out, but seems encouraging. Let's keep our fingers crossed and pray the killer slipped up this time. Every blonde in town is hysterical, afraid to leave the house. Some natural blondes are dying their hair dark. We've got to get this whacko." She gave the room another quick scrutiny. "If you guys are done, go ahead and take off. I'll wait for the coroner."

"You sure, he might be awhile?"

"That's okay." *I need time to think.*

Joella stood over the body, deep in thought. When her eyes refocused on the inert form, a glint of black under the blonde's thick hair caught her eye. She hadn't seen it earlier, against the navy blue rug. Joella brushed a few hairs aside with her pen. A black matchbook lay on the floor. *Damn. No advertising.* She pulled a plastic bag from her kit and turned it inside out to pick up the matchbook. *I didn't see an ashtray. Did our killer get careless?* When she turned the bag over to see the other side of the matchbook, her breath caught in her throat. Electric red letters read "Betsy's Bar."

CHAPTER 21

Driving east to the bar, Joella's mind exploded with possibilities splintering in all directions at once. Bumper-to-bumper traffic crawled from one traffic light to the next, typical for Tenth Avenue South, it having the heaviest vehicle congestion in the state. Her anxiety matched the congestion, but she was in no hurry to see Travis. She had always considered all those so-called clues Travis mentioned as coincidental. *Is this matchbook another coincidence? Or...*

At the bar's parking lot, she recognized only a few vehicles, one of them Travis's black pickup. He had used the front parking lot this time since he was on police business. Arriving before the lunch crowd, Joella had her choice of empty spots. When she pulled in next to his vehicle, her body began to shake involuntarily. *Am I eating with a serial killer?* Unable to face him, Joella sat in her car a long time staring into space. In her heart, she still felt him innocent, but she couldn't ignore the hard-core logic, which had raised its ugly head. *I don't think he has it in him to murder anyone.* Still, her body seemed incapable of movement. She lowered her head, debating both sides of her ugly dilemma a long time, looking up only when she heard voices coming from the opening bar door.

Travis stepped outside and walked over. "I was about to leave. Thought you got hung up somewhere."

"Sorry. I'll be right in. Have you eaten yet?"

"No. I intended to drive back to see if you were still working. Glad you made it. Let's have that sandwich."

The bar's cozy atmosphere did little to relax her tense shoulders. Rubbing her neck, she walked to their usual corner table, away from anyone who might overhear their conversation. Two laborers, with paint-speckled coveralls, sat at the bar; at the other end of the room, a fat, bald man plied a frowzy, bleached blonde with drinks. His gaping eyes never left her perfectly round silicone boobs, the size of extra-large grapefruit.

Betsy waved. "Glad to see you again, Joella. Are you keeping my Honey out of trouble?" she said, grinning at Travis.

"I'm trying," Joella joked back. *The only way he will keep out of trouble is to leave Marion.*

"Ma," Travis said, "I've been bragging to Joella about your Reuben sandwiches. How about making a believer out of her."

"Will do, Honey. What are you drinking?"

"Coffee for me. Joella?"

"Make mine coffee too."

"Coming right up," Ma said over her shoulder as she walked back to the bar.

Joella squirmed in her chair. *I need more time to think.* "Let's enjoy our sandwiches first, and then I'll tell you what I learned."

"Good. No sense ruining a great Reuben with shop talk."

Joella heaved a sigh of relief. She wasn't really listening to Travis ramble on about the tasty sandwich, only nodding once in a while as though she were.

A few minutes later, Ma rejoined them, carrying two large plates.

"That tangy aroma smells heavenly," Joella said, as Ma returned to the bar. While they ate, she studied his face, the craggy features, the furrow between his brow and the deep-set black eyes. She remembered his consideration and sympathy for the victims and their loved ones, his determination to catch MM. *No way can this compassionate and gentle man be a murderer. I don't care what the evidence suggests.* The uncertainty that had revolved in her mind after finding the matchbook, the mental debate flipping back and forth, ended. *He did not do it.*

When they finished eating, she asked what he learned talking to the victim's brother.

"Not much. Luke Randenberg was so distraught he couldn't stop crying. The two hadn't lived in the house long. He's a traveling salesman, not home a lot. They moved here from Havre last month and don't know any of their neighbors so none of them were of much help." He leaned back from the table. "Did you have better luck or is our killer still as clever as before?"

Joella braced herself for what was coming. *I'm sure he's not guilty, but how do I convince him?* She toyed with her coffee cup, wiped her mouth with a napkin and pulled out a lipstick to freshen her makeup.

Travis drummed his fingers on the tabletop. "Well?"

She took a deep breath, exhaling slowly. "His MO is exactly the same. The victim is another young blonde. Wet clothes in the washing machine, duct tape, everything the same as the prior crimes."

His lips tightened into a thin line. "Damn."

She hesitated a moment. "Everything was the same, only this time he made a mistake. He left a clue."

Travis let out an audible gasp. "At last, something to work with. What is it?"

She hesitated, then leaned over and took a matchbook resting in the slot of the ashtray. "He left one of these."

Travis's gaze was riveted on the matchbook. His complexion turned niveous, his black orbs resembling the coal eyes of a snowman.

Joella saw his body shaking.

"Naató'si, the monster *is* me."

CHAPTER 22

Travis sat stunned from his sudden realization, unable to speak, unable to stop the trembling. His veins felt frozen and his eyes stared, lost in time and space.

"Stop it right now," Joella yelled, shaking his shoulders.

His body jerked back from limbo.

"It might seem bad with all that 'contrived evidence' you think points to you, but it is all circumstantial. You are incapable of such horrendous crimes."

"Why not? The mutilations are like the work of my ancestors. It's in my genes."

"I don't buy that heredity crap. Does anyone on the force know you go to Betsy's Bar?"

"I always check the place out first, and I've never seen any of the guys come in while I was there. But still..."

"Okay. I'm not turning the matchbook in, at

least for now."

He felt his breath stop. "You'll get fired when the captain finds out you withheld evidence."

"I'll take the risk. He might give me another chance after you catch this maniac. You seem to have some kind of emotional attachment, and you need more time to find out why."

"All right. Don't turn it in, but when the time comes, I'll tell the captain I found the matchbook and didn't turn it in. That way you'll be in the clear."

CHAPTER 23

Ma kept glancing across the room at Travis and Joella, while she polished the same spot on the bar top again and again. *Something is wrong. He's looked troubled for weeks, ever since he brought Joella here the first time and told me he had more problems than blackouts. Good God, if something is worse than that, it must really be bad. Maybe I should go see if I can help.* She took a few more swipes at the counter. *No, if they need my help, they'll ask.* Her thoughts sounded convincing, but she couldn't help herself; laying the bar towel down she walked toward their table.

"Hi, guys. Can I get you another drink?" *Please, tell me what is wrong.*

Travis glanced at Joella. "Do you want another coffee?"

"No, I need to get back to the office."

Travis shook his head and looked at Ma. "I

hate to tell you this while you're working, but you need to know. Our serial killer has been in your bar—he could be a regular patron. He could be here now."

A noticeable gasp escaped Ma's lips. "He's been in here? How do you know?"

"He left one of your matchbooks at the last murder scene. It's possible he got it from someone else. More likely, he has been here—at least once. Joella and I are trying to work out our next move. I can't go into detail now, so one of us will get back to you later. Don't tell anyone what I just said, and be very careful and alert."

"Okay. I'll keep my eyes open. Get back to me as soon as you can." She went back to the bar and turned over in her mind every possible creepy character she had seen in the place for weeks. She concentrated so hard she barely heard one of the patrons yell, "For God's sake, Ma, get me a brew. How many times do I have to ask?" She snapped to attention. "Sorry sir," she said and rushed to fill his order, her mind refusing to stay focused on business. *Guess not all killers are creepy. I must consider everyone.* She shuddered. *Hope it isn't one of my nice customers.* Then a memory pierced her mind. Travis said that he had more problems than just blackouts. *My God, is he involved? Is he trying to shield someone?*

CHAPTER 24

Travis watched Ma walk away feeling pride in her composure. "Ma's a tough ol' gal. I knew she could take it. When we decide what to do, we'll bring her onboard. Her eyes can be damn useful."

Joella didn't reply and sat quietly. Unable to stop the bombardment of questions flooding his brain, Travis closed his eyes, sitting in a trance-like state. When he finally opened his eyelids, he stared at his coffee, now cold as an arctic wind. He took a sip and muttered, "Dammit, Gus, where is the path?"

Joella's mouth dropped open. "Path? What path? Who the hell is Gus?"

Travis jerked back to reality. "Sorry. I was thinking about what my mentor always told me when I was a rookie. You know, I never intended to be a detective when I joined the force. Never wanted to be anything but a cop so

I could put those damn wife-beating bastards in jail." He stared into his cup as though it held the answers. Getting none, he drained the last of the cold coffee. "I can't imagine why, but somehow Gus saw potential in me. He took me in hand, and considering he was the best damn detective in this state or any other, I learned a lot. Every time he worked a case, he tutored me on the clues that would solve it. Educated me about what to look for, what to be suspicious of and where to find it. And, taught me everything he had learned the hard way." Travis paused remembering his friend's words as if it were yesterday. "Whenever I was stuck on a case, he'd say, 'A smart detective analyzes all the paths to find the right one leading to the culprit.' After a few years, he encouraged me to take the detective exam, and no father could be happier than he was when I passed."

Joella smiled. "Sounds like a great guy. I'd like to meet him. Is he retired?"

Travis gazed off into the distance before refocusing on Joella. "No, he died a week after I got the results. Before the promotion became official."

"I'm sorry. At least he knew you passed."

"If he died from natural causes it wouldn't have bothered me as much, but he'd been after a particularly violent drug dealer for a long time. So long, in fact, that he got desperate and used an informer he'd never used before—a double-crossing informer—to get the dealer's name and location. The drug lord set up an ambush. Shot Gus execution style. He didn't have a chance."

"What a terrible way to lose your comrade."

"Yeah, the best friend I ever had. If he were still here, he would have found this bastard long ago."

Joella shook her head. "Maybe yes—maybe no. This perp is one of the most intelligent criminals I've ever run across. Still can't help but think he might be a cop." She clamped her jaw shut as soon as the words were out of her mouth. "Another cop—not you."

His attempt at forcing a smile failed. He glared at his empty cup. "Well I know one thing for sure, we better find him soon because I can't go on like this. I'm shaking so bad I can't do my job. I might as well confess and be done with it."

"Look," she said, "you're unable to do your job because you're convinced you did these horrible crimes. You're much too close to this situation. Do you have any vacation time?"

Travis cocked his left eyebrow. "Yes, but I can't leave now."

"No time better. Take Marion on a trip and let me investigate the case while you're gone. If our killer left the matchbook behind and didn't get it from someone else, we can assume he has visited Ma's place. He might be a regular customer and I can spend my spare time here. I might find something. If money is a problem, I can loan you some."

"Thanks, but no need. I managed to squirrel away a few nuts for the winter that Marion doesn't know about. She's been begging me to take her to Vegas for years. Wants to see those elaborate stage shows. Guess I could take her

154

for a few days."

"That's a great idea. Make it a week to give me more time to probe the situation. I'll clue Ma in about our plan. She'll be a great asset since the matchbook is from her place. And there is something even better that might work in your favor if you take a trip now."

Both Travis's eyebrows shot up. "What?"

"As fast as the killer has upped his pace, he could very well strike while you are out of town. Then you would *know* you are innocent."

Travis didn't say anything for a moment. "Didn't think of that. Maybe you're right. I'll call in and pretend I have an emergency. Guess 'pretend' is the wrong word. If I stay here, I'll either confess or Marion will have me put in a straightjacket—and oh, how she'd love that. Okay, I'll leave this weekend. That will give me a couple of days to connect loose ends. You be careful. This guy isn't human. If you need help or run into trouble, get Zach. You can trust him."

"Perfect. Two heads are better than one. If it's okay with you, I'll go ahead and tell him the entire story tomorrow. Now go home. Give Marion the happy news and get some sleep."

Travis nodded. *I'll give Joella a week, but if she doesn't find something...*

CHAPTER 25

Joella sprang out of bed when her alarm clock went off. She dressed in the clothes she'd laid out the night before. Anxious to get Zach onboard, she didn't bother with breakfast. *I'll grab a bite later.* She drove straight to the station but dispatch had Zach and Porter on a call as well as Travis. She checked and learned Travis had put in for emergency leave. Finally, at ten o'clock, she collared Zach and Porter filling out their report. "May I talk to you a moment, Zach? In private."

"Sure, Joella. Porter's just leaving, aren't you?"

"Okay, okay, I don't need a brick shit house to fall on me." As he walked out the door, he eyeballed Joella over his shoulder, snickering. "Hear Tonto took a few days off. Pressure must be getting to him because he can't catch our Merry Murderer."

Joella cringed. It was getting harder every day to ignore his insults. *Confronting him does no good—the jerk doesn't learn.*

After Porter left, Zach reacted to her question. "What's up?"

"Travis and I need your help, but I don't want to go into it here. Too many ears and don't want to get interrupted. I know it's early, but let's grab some lunch."

"Damn, Joella, sounds serious."

"It is."

"Travis is my best friend. If he's in trouble, I'm your man. Let's go. Where do you want to eat?"

"Anywhere close. I'm driving out to Ma's tonight. We're bringing her in on this too. You'll understand why once you've heard the entire story. We can eat at the tea and sandwich shop around the corner. Let's walk. They never have much business until noon."

When they arrived, there were only two customers sitting near the door. Joella picked a far corner table by the window, no one within listening distance. The cozy room had pastel peach walls, tiny round tables and stackable teardrop back banquet chairs upholstered with burgundy fabric. Each table held a plastic lace doily and tea cozy.

Zach gawked at the menu. "They don't have burgers."

"No, but I've never had anything bad here."

"What are you having?"

"I usually get the shrimp and pico de gallo wrap." She peered over the menu at Zach and saw his expression change from puzzlement to consternation.

When the waitress came Joella ordered the wrap and a pear luna white tea. "What do you want, Zach?"

He looked at the waitress. "Um, bring me that wrap thing she's having."

She nodded. "Excellent choice. What kind of tea would you like?"

"Just tea—Lipton's fine."

Joella caught the tiresome expression on the waitress's face before she turned to leave. Zach was oblivious—he was too busy admiring her saucy hip action as she walked away. Joella couldn't help but laugh, and rolled her eyes. She liked the always-grinning Zach; his self-assured cockiness came across as humor and charisma, blending with the old-world charm he had inherited from his father. Joella had met his Italian butt-pinching father once, a traditional chauvinist and she was thankful Zach hadn't inherited *all* his charm.

After ordering, Zach looked at Joella. "Okay, fill me in."

"Zach, you have to swear what I am about to tell you will go no further. It has to be a secret; no one except the three of us can know, well four, counting Ma. Travis told me I could tell you because he trusts you."

"Of course, he can trust me. He's my friend. I acted as best man for his wedding, tuxedo and the whole enchilada. I do not plan to be stupid anytime soon so he won't get to return the favor. We've been fast friends ever since he joined the force. There's nothing I wouldn't do for him."

"Before you decide to help, you need to know Travis and I have withheld evidence from the captain. We'll certainly be fired if he finds out."

Zach's Adams apple twitched. He sat in silence for several seconds before He refocused on her. "Shit, now you're really scaring me. This is sounding more than serious."

"It is. Travis's life might depend on us."

"You're kidding." Zach appeared stunned. "Good God, you're serious, girl. Why are you both keeping evidence quiet that might help catch the killer?"

"Because he feels somehow connected to the homicides and wants to keep it a secret until he figures out why he feels so emotionally involved with the victims."

Zach didn't hesitate. "I can always get another job, but a friend like Travis is once in a lifetime. How can I help?"

As the waitress returned, Joella put a finger to her lips to warn Zach. The server asked if they wanted anything else and Joella said, "No, thank you."

Zach turned to watch the lady sashay away and then, grinning, looked back at Joella.

She inhaled a deep breath. "Travis thinks he killed those women."

Zach reared back in his seat, his face paling. She gave him a moment and then filled him in on the details that had Travis convinced he was a murderer: his hatred of blondes, his vomiting at the murder scene, his floating ladies of the night and their gut feeling the killer might have police experience.

When she finished, Zach rolled his eyes. "Is that all? That pussycat couldn't kill a fly. I've seen him stop the car to take a turtle across the street so it wouldn't get run over."

"I know. That's how I feel too, but I cannot convince him otherwise." She picked up her wrap and looked him in the eye. "There's more. Remember how I mentioned we had withheld evidence from the captain? At the Randenberg homicide, I found a clue, the first slipup the serial killer has made. No one else saw it, and I didn't turn it in or note it on my report."

"What did you find?"

Joella didn't hesitate. "A used matchbook from Betsy's Bar. There were no ashtrays in Randenberg's home so our victim didn't smoke. Travis goes to that bar all the time. It's his second home."

"Never been there but that's not proof. Anyone can take a matchbook from a bar, or acquire one along the way."

"I know, but it gets worse. Did you know Travis has occasional blackouts?"

Zach's forehead furrowed, his deep-set blue eyes popping open. "Blackouts? You mean he's sick?"

"No, blackouts from excessive drinking."

"Now I know you're kidding. Travis doesn't drink. Not at all. I couldn't even get him to have a beer with the gang when Dexter got promoted."

"I know. He tells everyone he doesn't drink and he doesn't—normally. You're aware that he and Marion don't get along, aren't you?"

"That's putting it mildly. I've met her a

couple of times. She is a real piece of work."

"I've never met her, but from what I hear, you're right. Whenever he and Marion get into a knockdown, drag-out fight, his rage gets the better of him and he goes to Betsy's to cool off and have a drink. His anger fuels another drink and another. He blacks out. Ma, the proprietor, always sees that he gets home safely. Apparently few cops go there and none have ever seen him at her establishment."

"My God, we've been friends for years and I never suspected he was an alcoholic."

"According to AA, if someone can't stop after the first drink, they are alcoholics—and Travis can't. He only drinks after fights with Marion. I think an anger management course would go a long way toward curing him of blackouts. That and a divorce."

The flippant grin that usually graced Zach's face was now a serious scowl. "I can see where he certainly would be worried, but all that is circumstantial."

"I realize that, but Travis is devastated and nothing I say will convince him he isn't guilty. Are you ready for more?"

"Shit. There's more?"

"Yes. He went to a psychiatrist in Helena to find out if a person could commit a crime during a blackout and not remember. The doctor confirmed the possibility. Finding the matchbook put the final nail in the coffin as far as Travis is concerned. He is convinced he committed those murders during one of his blackouts. And he has no alibi for any of them."

"That doesn't help."

Joella leaned back in her chair. "Now you know the full story, are you still in?"

"Damn right. If it weren't for Travis, I wouldn't be here today. The man saved my life. There's nothing I wouldn't do for him."

"What do you mean?"

"It happened years ago; when we were rookies. We were on a drug bust on the outskirts of town, almost to Ulm. The raid sprung a leak somewhere because the suspects knew we were coming. We never got anywhere near the building. Bullets flew. They had more weapons and ammo than the Big Timber Armory. The captain finally got someone in the house on the telephone and tried to talk them out without much luck."

Zach stopped to take a swallow of tea. "We were about to fire a teargas canister when we learned they held a hostage. Guess they realized that would be our next move and they threatened to kill their captive if we used gas. We had no idea who or even if they had a hostage, couldn't risk it. While there was a lull in the firing, I volunteered to sneak around the building to search for weak spots. I used the woods and brush for cover. The captain was still talking to them when I attempted to get back. Someone spotted me. I got shot with what had to be a 44 magnum because it knocked me on my ass. I spouted blood like a busted water main.

"Figured I'd had it because the bullet obviously nicked an artery. Next thing I knew a blur zigzagged across the opening like a rabbit dodging a coyote. Never saw anyone move that fast—must be that Indian B negative blood. Travis dragged me to safety with bullets flying everywhere. I can't imagine why he didn't get hit. But damn right, I *am* in on this caper—if it weren't for him, I'd be on the wrong side of the grass in Highland Cemetery."

"My God, Zach, I didn't know. He's never mentioned it."

"No. He wouldn't. Where is he now?"

"I persuaded him to take Marion to Vegas for a week and let me do some further digging. I'm going to Betsy's Bar to talk to the owner tonight. Travis found a few possibilities in the ViCAP that he wanted to check again but didn't have the chance yet. You might recheck for him."

"Will do. Get back to you later. We gotta find this guy before Travis goes off the deep end."

"I think it's too late."

CHAPTER 26

Joella clocked out and walked outside feeling a slight lift of mood after bringing Zach up to date. The dry, stifling hot day made her skin feel ready to crack. While backing out of her parking space, she glanced at the low-slung clouds over the Highwood Mountains. *Sure hope those clouds mean rain. If it gets any drier, my weeds will die.*

Twenty minutes later, she walked into Betsy's Bar. The ever-present swamping towel in hand, Ma stood joking with a couple of men dressed in grimy jeans, the only two in the bar. "Glad to see you, Joella," she called out. Joella waved and even though she was alone proceeded to the table at the far end of the room where she and Travis usually sat. Ma walked over. "Where's my Honey? Is he okay? I'm worried about him."

"That's why I'm here. Can we talk?"

"Oh Lordy yes. Can you fill me in on the details now?"

"Yes, as much as we know so far."

"Let me get you a glass of wine, and we'll talk."

"Make it coffee. I'm still on the clock."

"You got it. I'll get Jaxson to watch the bar so we won't be interrupted." When he came from the kitchen, she took two cups of coffee to the table. "Now tell me all about it and what I can do to help?"

As she had told Zach, Joella filled Ma in on the same 'contrived evidence' Travis claimed made him a killer. She omitted telling Ma about the matchbook found at the Randenberg scene because Ma already knew.

"None of that is evidence," Ma said.

"I know, but I can't convince him of that."

"Where is he now?"

"I suggested he take Marion on a vacation and let me do some investigating. That means I'll be spending a lot of off-duty time here."

"Is there anything I can do?"

"Not as yet, but when I come in don't let on that you know me or that I'm a cop. If our killer didn't get the matchbook from someone else, he has patronized this bar. You and Travis might even know him. Just keep your eyes and ears open. Particularly if you hear someone bad mouthing blondes, talking about cops or serial killers, even as a joke."

"You got it."

Joella thanked her and drove back to the police station. She had a report to file and wanted to tell Zach that Ma was onboard.

~ ~ ~

Dispatch didn't send Joella out the rest of the day. The hours dragged until her shift ended and she headed home to change for her next visit to Betsy's Bar. After a quick shower, she pulled several things from the closet and inspected them in front of the full-length mirror. *Don't want to look like I'm on the prowl.* She quickly discarded those that made her stand out: too tight, too frilly or too revealing. Finally, in exasperation she pulled on a pair of jeans and a green plaid western shirt with pearl snap buttons. *Might as well go full tilt and wear the boots too.* Looking in the mirror, she giggled. *Now all I need is a Stetson and a pack of Marlboros.*

Joella walked out to the hall closet and began searching through boxes. *Where the hell is she? Haven't used her in a long time, but know I didn't throw Rita away.* At last, she opened a box and carried it to the hall mirror. Extracting a mop of kinky red curls, she positioned the wig in place. Then she pulled a pair of wire-framed, granny glasses from the same box; she plopped them on her nose and gazed in the mirror. *Not good enough.* To complete her disguise she returned to the bedroom and applied fire-engine-red lipstick, long thick false eyelashes and a heavy coat of bright blue eye shadow. Admiring herself in the mirror, she grinned. *Well, hello there—whoever you are.*

Joella drove to Ma's taking one of the last parking spaces. *Great, a full house will work to my advantage.* Dressing casual didn't stop two men seated at the bar from ogling her as she sat a few stools away.

Ma walked over and laid a coaster on the bar. "Welcome to Betsy's Bar, Miss. What's your pleasure?"

"What kind of white wine do you have?"

"We have Chardonnay, Rhine or Riesling."

"Riesling, please."

"I have domestic and also a nice German Schmitt Sohne if you prefer."

"Oh, I love the Schmitt Sohne. I'll have that."

Ma reached in the cooler under the bar pulling out a bottle. She took a stemmed glass from behind the counter and while pouring the wine, leaned in and whispered, "I didn't recognize you at first. Didn't know you were coming in disguise." Then, in a louder voice she asked, "You from around here, Miss?"

"Not really. Only arrived in town a couple of weeks ago and I'm looking for a watering hole near home. You know, a local 'Cheers.'"

"I don't know about 'everybody knowing your name' but we get a lot of friendly folks from the neighborhood."

Another customer came in and Ma left to wait on him, leaving the way clear. The nearest man at the bar, a fat, bald guy with pimples made his move. "How about I buy you a drink, sweetie?"

"Thanks, I have one, and that's my limit. I'm driving."

He shrugged and returned to his barstool. The other man made a pass a few minutes later; neither was obnoxious and both took her "no thank you" well. Joella listened to the conversations around the bar, but didn't hear anything interesting or suspicious. The patrons did seem like neighborhood folks. When Ma came back to ask if she wanted a refill, she said, "No thanks," in a louder than normal voice, "I like this place. I'll be back. And, just so you'll know, my name is Rita."

"Glad to have you any time, Rita."

Joella returned the next night, and Ma welcomed her. "Nice to see you again, Rita. Having the Riesling?"

"Yes, thanks. You really have an amazing memory."

Ma poured the wine and then went to the other end of the bar.

Joella fended off the usual number of letches and tried to listen in on as many conversations as possible. *Damn. Wish there was some way I could move around the bar and be inconspicuous. I can't learn much sitting in the same chair all night.*

The evening proved uneventful, and she took her purse to leave when she noticed the swarthy, stocky man two stools away glaring at a lovely longhaired blonde and her redheaded friend at a nearby table. His dark eyes glared at the blonde so long and so intently that she squirmed in her seat, looking down at her glass. He continued staring and finally she and her friend downed their drinks and stood. When he watched them leave, he muttered something inaudible in what sounded like Italian to Joella. *If he can't say it in English, he's cursing.*

When the ladies left, an expression of pure disgust crossed his face; he stubbed and then ground his cigarette into the ashtray, muttering to himself. He pulled another weed from the pack on the bar and lit it with one of Betsy's matchbooks. Joella couldn't help but notice he didn't use a lighter. When he bent over, the neck of his shirt opened slightly and she noticed a large gold crucifix nestled in a gorilla thatch of chest hair.

Joella slid her wine glass toward the next stool. "Sorry, I didn't hear you. What did you say?"

"Huh?"

"Oh excuse me; I thought you were talking to me." *He obviously didn't like that blonde— could it be blondes in general he hates?* Her heart beat faster. *Could he be MM?* She swished her hair off her forehead and flashed him a warm smile. "You didn't seem to like that blonde woman."

"Don't know the damn slut. If God wanted women to be bleached blondes, he would have made them that way. It's a sin to go against His creation. If I had my way, I'd shave every one of them bald and knock some sense into them."

This guy sounds like a religious nut. Maybe psycho too? "Know what you mean. Women shouldn't go against God's creation. I'd never do that." *I need to keep this guy talking.* "You come here often?"

"Every night. My boss is a son-of-a-bitch. I need to relax after work; otherwise, I'd knock him on his ass."

"Been there myself. Having a lousy boss is tough. Where do you work?"

"I'm a short-order cook. Sling hash at Bandit's Hole down the road and there's no pleasing the pea-brain I work for. Say, you look familiar. Haven't I seen you here before?"

Joella winced. "Maybe. I've been here a couple of times. My name is Rita. I'm new in the area and seeking a friendly watering hole on this end of town. What's your name?"

He abruptly leaned back in his seat, eyes narrowed and his stoic face expressing deep suspicion.

CHAPTER 27

Joella shifted in her seat. *Maybe he's seen me in here with Travis, but neither of us was in uniform. Hope he hasn't pegged me for a cop.* She flashed him a brighter smile. "Well, I can't very well say, 'Hey, you.'"

His shoulders relaxed yet his face remained somber. "My name is Tony."

"Tony what?"

"Uh, Tony Gambino. No connection."

"No connection to what?"

"To the Mafia Gambinos."

Wow, he's Italian all right, if that is his real name.

They talked for more than an hour. Joella couldn't get anything incriminating from him other than his hatred of bleached blondes and his deep conviction those women were sinning against God. She could find no diplomatic way to ask what he'd been doing on the Sunday of the last homicide. Joella took a slow sip of wine and gazed over the rim of her glass into his eyes. "Are you coming by tomorrow afternoon?"

"Yeah. I always stop after work."

"Perfect. Then I'll come too. Look forward to getting to know you better, Tony." She took her purse from the bar and left. *Not really a lead, but it is something. He doesn't seem sharp enough to be MM, but he smokes. Doesn't use a lighter, and he hate blondes. At least bleached ones.*

The next morning Joella went to work early to check Tony Gambino for priors. She assumed he didn't use an alias, because he took such pains to establish he wasn't one of the Mafia Gambinos. The results were what she expected: several bar altercations and a couple of speeding tickets. His wife called the cops a few times when he'd used her for a punching bag. Apparently, she lacked the courage to press charges. Tony was a scrapper and a wife abuser, yet nothing indicated the deviant mind of a serial killer. *Could his excessive hatred of bleached hair turn him into a raving maniac? Doesn't seem likely, but...*

~ ~ ~

The next day after lunch, Joella's looked up when Zach popped into her office.

"Have you learned anything at Ma's place the last couple of nights?"

"Nothing concrete. I found a possible person of interest, though it seems far-fetched to think he might be MM. His name is Tony Gambino." After seeing Zach's eyebrows rose, Joella added, "He claims he isn't one of the Mafia

Gambinos." She filled him in on the details.

"Not much to go on. You're right; we can add him as a person of interest. We're running out of suspects with O'Toole and Finnegan's alibis. That leaves us with Kirkland, the lesbian nurse, and this Tony Gambino."

Joella closed the file she'd been working on. "And neither one seems promising. I took one of Tony's cigarette butts for future evidence, just in case. Might come in handy if the ME finds any DNA on the next victim." She felt her brow tense. *And there will be another.* "I'm meeting Tony at Ma's after work. He said he always pops in for a quick one, but he had far more than that when I met him. Maybe I can encourage him to add another couple of drinks tonight to loosen his tongue."

Rita arrived at Betsy's early the next evening. Tony never showed. *My God, did he peg me for a cop after all? Am I slipping?* Still, she spent every night at Betsy's Bar for a week, receiving numerous passes each time because there were always more single male customers than female. The good ol' one-for-the-road type definitely favored Ma's place after work. There were always a few soldiers from Malmstrom Air Force Base, construction workers from a road crew repaving Tenth Avenue South, plus the regular locals. Every night Joella hoped Tony would return, but he never did. *Damn, that lead fizzled like a damp firecracker.*

Joella even attracted the attention of a lesbian one night, which required a diplomatic refusal to be sure the woman wouldn't be offended and start a ruckus. *I don't need that kind of attention.* Still, of the many patrons every night, the most interesting conversation she heard other than Tony's was whether to put in a sprinkler system now or wait until summer ended, hoping for a nice sale price.

~ ~ ~

Monday morning, Joella could hardly wait to get to the office. Travis would be back. She had convinced herself earlier that she looked forward to their coffee breaks and catching-up conversations. *Hell girl, admit it. You miss him.* She missed getting lost in those jet-black eyes and Travis's cute, charismatic habit of cocking his left eyebrow when he was surprised—both, when shocked.

Dressing with extra care, she selected a pink tailored blouse he once said looked nice on her. She arrived at the station early and saw his pickup in the parking lot. Rushing inside, she walked straight to his office. Travis sat at his desk, a coffee cup in his hands. He seemed rested, his eyes clear and the dark circles under them gone. *The trip must have gone well.*

Before he could speak, she did. "You look relaxed. How was Vegas? Did you have a nice time?"

"Hardly. It became a nightmare before we got on the road. Marion was thrilled when I told her we were going to Vegas. So 'thrilled' she actually made me a nice big breakfast the next day. Then I ate lousy TV dinners until we left because she was too busy to cook. She hauled everything she owned out of the closets and tried it on so she could decide what to pack. Then, she rushed to the mall for items she claimed she needed and didn't have. I clenched my teeth so hard I nearly shattered my tooth enamel. Her closet is filled to capacity—and mine."

"Oh my God, I forgot what a clothes freak she is. Did you at least enjoy the drive south?"

"The first part was great. Instead of the Interstate, I took US Route 93 and enjoyed the mountains and scenery through Montana and Idaho. Marion kept hounding me to get on the Interstate so we could make better time. Once we got to Nevada, I obliged her. I couldn't get out of that sand furnace fast enough."

"I bet Marion enjoyed those high-rent boutiques in every casino."

"You got that right. She wanted to buy everything in town. She'd never gambled before and *almost* quit shopping to gamble. Tried everything in the casino and fell in love with roulette. I put my foot down at that. It's the worst odds in the house. If she had won occasionally, I wouldn't complain, but whatever she tried, she lost. However, losing didn't faze her. I finally refused to give her any more money. She got mad as hell and we had another fight."

"Wasn't there anything you enjoyed?"

"The food mostly. We took in a couple of shows that weren't bad, but far too pricey."

"Oh, Travis, I'm so sorry I recommended Vegas. I forgot about those casino boutiques. I know their prices are outrageous for stuff they probably bought from China. When I saw you just now, I was sure you had a good time because you appeared so relaxed."

Travis smiled and stood. He walked toward her with a spring to his step, grabbing her hands and squeezing them. "I *am* relaxed *and* calm. I did not need to go to Vegas. And I definitely will not be going back to the shrink."

"What happened?"

"I did not kill those women."

CHAPTER 28

When Travis let go of her hands, he was happy to see her eyes brighten in relief in case she had the slightest doubt in the back of her mind.

She grabbed his hands again. "I've been telling for weeks you weren't guilty, but you wouldn't listen. What on earth happened to change your mind?"

"The trip was miserable, but when Marion and I returned from Vegas, I found a note slid under our door. Apparently, it was after the Randenberg killing. I'd already left town."

"A note? From who? What did it say?"

"I know I can trust you, but you need to promise me you won't tell anyone about what I am going to show you, and that goes for co-workers too, except Zach." His lips drew into a thin line when he noticed her confused expression change to distress.

"My God Travis, you're scaring me. Of course, I won't say anything to anyone if that's what you want."

"Thanks. You'll see why when you read this. The psycho is after *me*. He's trying to frame me as the serial killer."

"What? How the hell can he do that? Let me see that note."

Travis watched her face turn ashen as she read the crumpled scrap of paper now enclosed in a plastic-sleeved sheet.

Hey flatfoot, I thought you were supposed to solve crimes. You fucking pigs are so stupid you ain't ever gonna catch this guy! Took me so long to find you that the last state I hung my hat in still has three cold case files, and G.F. will have more than that before the cops finally pin the killings on YOU! But I want YOU to suffer a long time first. Make up for the years of hell YOU caused me. This time I left the first clue pointing to you—look familiar, buddy boy? And there'll be another clue next time.

By the way, it's a fucking good thing you caught that copycat guy because I'd have blasted him for stealing my style and grabbing the headlines in the paper.

Hey, I kinda like the Trib's dubbing me the Merry Murderer. That's me—a laugh a minute, Ha! Ha!

P.S. The first time I see any mention in the newspaper about a letter to you from the killer, there will be NO more fucking correspondence. And I know how you pigs always think a killer's note is going to trip him up. Not this guy!! And I'll save your lab guys some work. No need to check the envelope for DNA. For a couple of bucks the dumb kid on the street obliged me with plenty of spit.

Joella handed the note back to Travis. "Good Lord, this does sound like he's after you."

Travis nodded. "Sure seems that way."

"Do you have any idea who it might be? Why would anyone want to frame you?"

"Not a clue. I don't have any enemies—at least none I know of, but a cop always has jailbirds seeking payback for the injustice they think they received. And he's been watching me a long spell if he knows I spend a lot of time at Ma's place."

"Damn," Joella said. "We'll have to search the records for all the names of those you put away and then check to see if any of them are out of jail now. In thirteen years, I'm sure there were a lot of them. That's going to take weeks if not longer. Glad we brought Zach in on this; we'll need all the help we can get. Let's meet at Jakes after work and put our heads together to find a strategy."

"Fine. Confiding in Zach and getting his help was a great idea, but it may not take that long. We need to check only those guys who were recently released."

Joella shook her head. "You're forgetting something. He said in the note that it took him 'so long to find you.' How long is 'so long?' Two weeks? Two months? Two years?"

"You got a point, Travis said. I'm still thinking this guy might be a cop or forensic worker. He's clever enough to know we can get DNA from the stamp although I guess most crooks know that these days with the Internet. Knew about the imbedded code in computer-printing paper and didn't use it either. His crude printing on that cheap paper is untraceable."

Travis gazed into his coffee cup as if it were a crystal ball. Then he raised his head. "I just remembered something. I busted a cop years ago for swiping drugs from the evidence room. I walked in on him and caught him in the act. It was the hard stuff, not weed, as I recall. It happened so long ago, I'd forgotten about it. I was a rookie at the time. He'd been replacing the thefts with look-alike packages for a long time. Since no one checked the product before they burned the drugs in the incinerator, he got away with it. Had a good thing going and offered to cut me in on his sweet deal when I caught him."

Joella's eyes widened. "Hate to believe a cop would do such a contemptible thing. Still, it happens. Sure gives the rest of us a black eye. I hope they threw the book at him." As soon as the words left her lips, she covered her mouth with her hand. "Here we are both withholding evidence," she said, automatically lowering her voice. "But it's only until you can find the killer. We're doing it for a good reason—isn't like stealing drugs." She straightened, but still wore a guilty expression on her face.

"They threw the book at him, which is why he threatened to get me when he got out. He shouldn't be out yet. I'll check to see if he received an early release. They're doing a lot of that on non-violent offenders these days because of the overcrowded prisons."

"Sounds like a probable prospect."

Travis drained his coffee cup. "If you're free tonight, let's meet at Ma's. Bring her up to date. She will be a tremendous help if the killer frequents her place."

"I'll be there and we need to let Zach know too. This deserves the full team's attention."

Joella walked toward the door. Travis called after her, "Hey, did you learn anything at Ma's while I goofed off?"

She turned around. "Oh Lord, I was so excited when you said you knew you didn't commit those murders that I forgot to tell you. Didn't find anything positive until I came across a person of interest. Tony Gambino, no connection to the Mafia, has a few priors. He's some kind of religious nut. Most important is his unwarranted hatred of bleached blondes. Natural blondes may not bother him, I don't know, but he sure detests bleached hair."

"That doesn't sound like him then because Linda Merry, the first victim, was a natural blonde."

"Yes, I know, her hair was so light he might have thought it was bleached. He smokes and doesn't use a lighter—but used one of Ma's matchbooks which all fits. We were to meet the next evening, but he never showed and I went every night. Don't know why he didn't come back. Maybe something spooked him."

"What could have?"

"Have no idea, unless he pegged me for a cop. Glad we have Ma in on this. She said she'd call if he came in again. Admit it's not much, but it is something—more than we've got now. Haven't had a chance to check further and not even sure where he lives. Does he sound like someone you might have seen or talked to?"

"Not that I know of. I saw a swarthy-looking guy cussing out a female one night. I don't remember what color hair she had."

CHAPTER 29

While driving to Betsy's that evening, Joella wondered what Ma would be wearing on this third of July. Travis had told Joella of Ma's joy celebrating two holidays of the year in a big way: Saint Patrick's Day and the Fourth of July. He described Ma's emerald green outfit and bar theme from last Saint Patrick's Day. Along with green slacks and shirt, her gray curls popped like corkscrews from beneath a brown bucket hat with a shamrock pinned to the side. The tables held green napkins and shamrock coasters. Two bar fonts produced green beer for the faux leprechauns who probably hailed from Siberia and elsewhere. Ma loved her Irish heritage and took every opportunity to display it. She was equally proud to be an American.

Joella arrived at the bar before the others. She didn't see Ma anywhere, but it wasn't much of a stretch to guess what she'd be wearing following Travis's description. Minutes later, Zach and Travis arrived at the same time and joined Joella seated at their usual corner table. Ma exited the backroom resplendent in red, white and blue and wearing an Uncle Sam top hat.

Her always-happy smile faded when her gaze caught sight of the trio's expressions. "Hey, Jaxson," she called, pouring a Riesling, a Coke and two Coors. "Come tend bar; I'm joining friends." After serving the drinks she took a seat. "Okay, guys. Fill me in. What's going on?"

Joella grinned. "Ma, you must be psychic."

"Humph," she snorted, "any quack would know something is wrong. You all look like death warmed over."

"Don't let her fool you, Joella. I've sworn she is psychic many a time," Travis said. "And yes, something is wrong. We're here to hash out a strategy."

"Count me in."

Travis reached into his jacket pocket and pulled out the plastic-enclosed note. Before he had a chance to show it to Ma, Joella clutched his arm. "Oh my God, he's here."

"Who's here," Travis asked, barely audible.

"That guy walking in is Tony Gambino. He's the one...oh no, he spied me. He's leaving. We were supposed to meet the next night and he never showed. Don't know why unless he later remembered me being in here sometime with you, Travis. He might have figured I was a cop that way, but we weren't in uniform so doesn't seem likely. Quick, Zach, follow him and see what you can find out."

The minute Tony disappeared from sight, Zach shot toward the door. "I'll catch you tomorrow," he said, tossing the words over his shoulder.

Joella turned to Travis. "I know he isn't much of a lead, but why did he run out of here when he spotted me? Did you recognize him?"

"I only got a quick glance, but he looked familiar. I might have seen him here before."

"Yeah," Ma said. "He's been fairly regular for a year or two."

During the burst of excitement, Travis had put the serial killer's note back in his pocket. Now he retrieved it and laid it in front of Ma. "You know, Marion and I were out of town for a week. When we got back, I found this note inside the apartment, slid under the door"

Ma read the note. "Good God, someone is out to get you."

"Travis and I interpreted it like that too," Joella said. "We're trying to figure out who it might be. Travis has put away many jailbirds who would like to get revenge. Whoever it is, we have to find him. He's threatening to provide evidence that will convict Travis of murder."

CHAPTER 30

Travis and Zach arrived in the station parking lot at the same time. "Hi, Zach. Looks like we're all early—there's Joella's car. Let's go to her office and you can clue us both in on what you found out about Gambino."

After they greeted Joella, Zach said, "I followed Tony home last night like you wanted. Got his address and license number." He tossed a folded paper on her desk. She copied the information and gave the paper to Travis. "Didn't find out much else." Zach continued. "He drives a new Buick yet lives in a neglected house out near the base. Might be he's single or just plain lazy. Didn't see any other cars in front of the house so don't know if he lives alone or not."

"Thanks," Travis said. "I haven't finished investigating him yet, so any information is helpful."

~ ~ ~

Travis didn't get a chance for a serious talk with Joella for several days, only mere waves as they passed in the hall or a quick hello when they opened the door passing each other's office. Dispatch kept him running like a greyhound behind the elusive rabbit. Finally, late in the afternoon she found him at his desk. "I like your new décor," she said, pointing to the city map on his wall. It had three yellow pins and one red.

"Thanks."

"What's the matter, Travis? Your computer down?"

"No, I use it too. I like the map better because it is always in front of me. One time a few years back, when I walked in the office, the sun shone on the map and a light bulb idea popped into my mind out of nowhere. It helped solve the case."

She grinned. "Has it helped?"

"No, hasn't done a damn thing for me this time. As you know, most serial killers work in a familiar place, a zone they feel comfortable in. MM is all over the place."

Joella sat in the chair opposite Travis's desk and studied the map. "It might not depict a cluster of his killings, but it fits the pattern of his knowing how the police work. He might be doing that on purpose to throw us off. Have you had a chance to check on recent prison releases—guys you put behind bars who might want revenge?"

Travis turned his laptop on. "I did. There were more than I remembered, but the drug-stealing cop was a bust. He's still in the slammer. Haven't had time to check them all yet, but did find a possible suspect: Sam Lone Wolf, a half-breed from the reservation—only thirteen the first time he got into trouble with the law. He's spent more than half of his life behind bars. This is his mug shot," he said pointing to the computer screen.

"How sad," Joella said, "and it happens so often. Some people never learn."

"That's Sam. He's a violent man when drunk, which is most of the time. If he doesn't have money to buy booze, he resorts to robbery, usually liquor stores where he can get cash and whiskey at the same time. His wife called the cops a couple of times after he almost killed her, and then she refused to press charges. She feared he'd finish the job next time. Sliced a few other women bad too— he's never without his knife. He usually carries a bigger weapon, not the thin blade you described used on the victims."

"He sounds like bad news all right and a damned good suspect. He might have a whole arsenal of knives. When did he get released?"

"Two weeks before the Merry murder."

"Geez, that's perfect timing." She leaned forward, elbows on the edge of his desk. "Tell me more."

"I have arrested him a couple of times for robbery. He always became enraged. Thought I should let him go because, in his words, we were blood brothers. He pleaded not guilty and like all cons, swore his innocence. Claimed it was someone else, which didn't sway the judge because I caught him red-handed coming out of the store—he was too drunk to remember." He paused to catch his breath. "One time he cussed me out for not marrying an Indian—said I was a traitor to the tribe, especially marrying a damn blonde. Being a habitual offender, the judge gave him a lengthy sentence last time. They dragged him out of the courtroom screaming he'd get even with me no matter how long it took. I'd heard that before so didn't pay much attention until I saw his release date. He is violent. Hates women in general; I wouldn't put murder past him."

Joella stood to leave. "Do you know where he is now?

"My money's on the reservation. He never strays far away for any length of time. I'm going to drive to Browning tomorrow to track him down. See if he's working or still a thieving drunk. Find out if he has an alibi for the Randenberg murder. No point asking about the others—he'd only claim he couldn't remember that far back."

"Good luck. A knife wielding, drunken woman hater sounds like a prime suspect."

~ ~ ~

Travis drove to Browning early the next morning and returned later in the day. He forced a smile when Joella strolled into his office. Over their many conversations, he recognized she had learned to read his moods and facial expressions almost as well as Ma did.

"Doesn't look like the news from Browning is good. Didn't you find Sam Lone Wolf?"

"No, and none of his drunken friends knew where he was, said he'd been gone a long time. I finally located his wife. She told me he'd gone to Canada to visit a Blackfoot cousin to borrow money."

"Blackfoot? I thought you said the tribe was Blackfeet."

Travis grinned. "That's right. It is a little confusing. The Blackfeet and Blackfoot are technically the same tribe. An Anglicization occurred back in the early history of the white man. Montana is the only place they are called Blackfeet.

"Oh, sorry for the interruption, you threw me there for a minute. What were you saying about the suspect being in Canada?"

"The cousin Sam visited to borrow money from happens to be a woman. Sam's wife told me the story. He was roaring drunk when he asked for the supposed loan—he never paid any advances back. When she refused, he became furious. Used his knife and nearly killed her. Unfortunately for us, he has an ironclad alibi for the Randenberg murder."

"Oh, no. What is it?"

"He's rotting in a Canadian jail. I checked it out with the local authorities."

"Damn. He doesn't sound smart enough to be MM, but he was the best lead we've had in a long time. I simply cannot understand how so many leads pop into focus out of nowhere, and develop a perfect alibi just as fast. I've never had a case like this. It isn't logical."

"I know. I feel the same way. Talked to Zach a few minutes ago and we're meeting at Betsy's tonight. Can you join us?"

"Wouldn't miss it."

Travis, Zach and Joella spent so much time together that Porter began calling them the Unholy Alliance. When he passed Travis and Joella in the hall as they were leaving, he snorted, "Hey, buddy boy, you're sure keeping Joella and forensics hopping. How many bodies do you need to find this freak?"

Travis stiffened, but felt Joella nudging him forward by the elbow.

She opened the door pulling him outside. "Never mind him; he's jealous. Zach is Porter's only friend and he's been spending so much time helping us that he doesn't join Porter for a beer at Jakes after work as often. It's no secret Porter dislikes you. Ignore him. Don't let him make you angry and lose control."

"I try not to, but his relentless insults make me want to slug him whenever I see his flaccid face."

"Consider the source; it delights him to see you angry. And, getting angry only hurts you. It won't faze Porter. I'd better get back to work. Want to ask Zach if he found anything on Gambino. He's been investigating him in his spare time. I hope he's found something by now. Gambino is the only decent suspect we have left."

When Travis returned to his desk, the phone rang. "Detective Eagle. Yes, mayor, I know there have been four. No sir, one of them was a copycat murder." Listening, he felt his face flush. "Yes, mayor. I'll be sure to do that." *Damn, he was breathing fire this time. He calls me or Captain Walker nearly every day. He's almost as bad as the Tribune's daily taunts about the unsolved cases.*

Travis arrived at Betsy's first and Ma came over with a Coke. "Is Coke okay or would you rather have coffee?"

"Coke is fine, Ma."

"How you doing, Honey?"

"Not good."

"Nothing new?"

"I found a new suspect, but he didn't pan out. The only thing we have now is the guy who Joella met here the week I was gone, and an unlikely nurse. We're still investigating both but it doesn't appear promising."

"Well, it isn't from lack of trying on Joella's part," Ma said. "While you were gone, she spent every night here listening and watching. She tolerated a bunch of guys hitting on her but never gave them any encouragement. Of course, that didn't stop them—she's a mighty good looking woman."

Travis grinned and hefted his Coke in salute. "I've noticed, Ma."

The front door opened and Zach walked in, spotted Travis and went to join him. A few minutes later Joella entered and joined the pair. She looked at Zach. "You louse. You grabbed the last parking spot and I had to go to the next block because I knew Travis would park in back."

"I'm sorry about the lack of parking, Joella," Ma said. "I can't do anything about it, no vacant land nearby. One Riesling on the way. Your usual, Zach?"

"Yeah, a Coors would hit the spot."

Travis pushed his half-full glass away. "I'm tired of Cokes, Ma." He noted the questioning expression in her eyes. "I don't mean alcohol. Bring me a cup of coffee, please." He could not miss the look of relief breaking through Ma's face.

When Ma brought the drinks, she asked, "Okay if I sit in to hear the latest?"

"Of course, you're part of the team," Travis said.

Joella turned toward Zach. "You've been checking on MM's note. Have you had any luck?"

"No. Travis tore off a small piece on the bottom of the note for me. The guy in a private lab did me a favor. Just as we suspected, it's cheap note paper available at any Walmart or convenience store."

Travis stirred sugar into his coffee. "Even though MM's note said it was useless, I took it to a private firm to check for fingerprints. MM said he had a kid lick the envelope and the only fingerprints were small like that of a child so I'm sure he was truthful about there not being DNA on the envelope and stamp."

Joella sipped her wine. "I can't get over how smart this guy is about police procedures. If he isn't a cop, he's damn sure done a bunch of research. As much as the computer makes our work easier, it sure as hell educates the criminals. Every crook in the country knows better than to lick a stamp today. Do you have the note with you, Travis?"

"Of course. I never let it out of my sight."

Joella rose abruptly. "Excuse me guys. Gotta powder my nose. When I come back, I want to read that note again. I can't put my finger on it, but there's something about it..."

CHAPTER 31

Travis had dark circles under his eyes and Ma couldn't help but notice.

"Travis, are you getting any sleep? You look awful."

"Thanks for the compliment, Ma," he said winking. When Joella returned, Travis stood and reached inside his jacket for the plastic-enclosed message. "You said you wanted to see this again?"

"Yes." She scanned it, frowned and reread it again before handing it to Travis.

As he reached for the paper, she snatched it back as though pulling her hand from a flame. Her voice rose to a higher pitch. "Let me see that again." The sudden burst of enthusiasm caught everyone by surprise.

Ma's eyebrows rose higher. "What is it?" she said, in unison with the men.

"My God, this never registered before."

Joella laid the note in the center of the table and pointed. "Look at the fifth line. Who else calls you buddy boy?"

Ma narrowed her eyes and read the line. Nothing jumped out at her, but Travis and Zach appeared stunned. Joella repeated her question. "Who calls you buddy boy?"

"Porter," Zach and Travis said at the same time.

Travis seemed to regain his composure first. "Surely you don't think it's Porter. I dislike the guy, but his being a serial killer seems a bit of a stretch."

Zach's mouth still gaped.

"I admit it's a way-out idea and he doesn't seem that smart," Joella said. "Being a cop, he knows all the ins and outs. He could leave a clean crime scene behind and he's made no secret of his hatred for Travis. Don't know if he detests blondes or not. I had begun to think he might be gay. I've never seen him with a date or heard him mention one in conversation. Does he even like women, Zach?"

"Damned if I know. He's married but that doesn't stop him from trying to pick up chicks every night at Jakes. I usually leave before him, so don't know how successful he is. Not a lot of women go for a fat, bald bigot."

Joella swished her hair back with a flick of her wrist. "It may be far-fetched, but what else do we have? We ought to at least check it out."

Zach took a swig of beer. "Wouldn't his background check have spotted something?"

"Maybe," Joella answered, "but he hasn't been in Great Falls long. If Porter is the killer and left those cold case files in another state, he might have changed his name. I say we investigate it. Things are looking better. After four duds, we now have two persons of interest: Porter and Tony Gambino."

Ma had remained quiet throughout the discussion, but she wasn't silent any longer. "You're damn right you need to investigate this guy, Porter, whoever he is."

"He is a cop, Ma. Guess it wouldn't hurt to do some quiet sleuthing," Travis said, breaking his stunned silence. "Just the three of us though. Let's not question anyone on the force, at least for now."

Joella nodded. "I agree. Travis, why don't you back check duty rosters and see if his time off matches any of the murder dates. I'll check his background. Track down where he came from and see if I can find any record of a name change." She paused to wet her lips. "Zach, you're his friend. You'd be the best one to investigate his relationship with women. Watch to see if he picks on blondes for his intended conquests. I know he's married, but that doesn't mean much. Numerous gay guys have taken a wife as a cover up if he didn't want to come out—and suspect that would be doubly true for guys on the force."

"Thanks a heap, Joella. You want me to investigate my drinking buddy?"

"I'm sorry, Zach, you're the only one for that job. If you don't want to do it, I understand."

"I'm kidding, Joella. If he is the killer, he needs to be caught and if he's not, no harm done as long as we don't let anyone else on the force know about our suspicions."

With the matter settled, Ma clasped her hands. "Hold on, I'll get us one for the road." She went back to the bar, poured the drinks and spoke to a couple seated at the bar. She was returning to the table with a tray when the door opened. Ma turned toward the door, the streetlight spotlighting the new customer—a stranger.

The new arrival's beady eyes glanced around the room and locked on the trio. He put his hand to his mouth as if to magnify his voice. "What the hell are you guys doing on this end of town, slumming? Couldn't you find a better joint than this dump?"

Taken aback, Ma stopped in her tracks, eyes glaring. *Who is this creep?* "I'll have you know this is a respectable bar, and if you think anyone here is slumming, I suggest you go elsewhere."

The portly bald man ignored her, laughing.

Zach put his beer down. "Hello to you too, Porter."

So this is Porter. The jerk even smells like trouble. Ma placed the drinks on the table and said, "Can I get you folks anything else?"

Travis winked at her, as though thanking her for not letting Porter know she was part of their team. "No thanks, we're good."

Porter flipped open his wallet. "To hell with that; bring me a Bud."

Ma went for the beer, put it on the table and went to mop off a nearby table so she could eavesdrop. She couldn't help but see Travis's balled fists and clenched jaw. Then

Joella reached over to take his hand, and he slowly unclenched his fingers.

Zach downed his beer. "How did you know we were here, Porter?"

"I didn't, buddy boy. I was returning from Belt and I missed the gas station so I drove around the block to go back. I spotted that zombie of a yellow convertible you drive."

Travis's lip tightened. Swallowing the last of his coffee, he slammed the cup on the table. "I'm leaving." Zach and Joella stood too.

Porter lifted his glass. "Hey guys, I just got here. Don't be such party poopers."

The trio ignored him and left. Ma knew why they didn't say goodbye. When Porter called Zach 'buddy boy' and not Travis, Ma saw the glint in Travis's eye. He'd caught the remark too. She wondered whether that would blow their theory of Porter being a suspect.

~ ~ ~

Travis drove home, a black cloud of gloom hovering over his head. *I know I'm not the killer, but we can't find any evidence against O'Toole, Finnegan, Kirkland, Gambino, Sam Lone Wolf and now Porter might be out.*

Parking, Travis automatically checked his mailbox when he entered his building. Marion never bothered because bills didn't interest her. Withdrawing two envelopes from credit card companies, his brow puckered. When he unlocked his door and stepped inside, he spied an envelope on the floor. *It's from him.* He tossed the bills on a table and put on his polyethylene gloves. He slit open the envelope and pulled out the note. Stomach churning, he read:

> *How about that Betsy's Bar matchbook, flatfoot? I bet it got your heart bouncing like a ping-pong ball. I can just see your mind spinning...'have I seen him, do I know him, have I talked to him?' You're too stupid, copper, you'll never know. Been exciting, but I'm getting restless—time for another bitch to go down and guess what? A little more evidence that will really make your heart race. Now don't you go having a heart attack on me, there's more to come. Another clue this time. Then Bingo, clue three will flip you into orbit and the fucking cops will finally nab you. Can hardly wait, buddy boy.*
> *MM*

Travis barely slept, his parading blondes sharing equal time with a new worry: *What evidence?*

CHAPTER 32

When Travis arrived at work, Zach was on call and Joella sat at her computer. He laid the plastic-sleeved note on her desk. "Got a new one."

"Oh my God, let me see." She read the note and said, "What evidence could MM possibly concoct?"

"I don't know but he must have something. He doesn't sound like he's bluffing."

~ ~ ~

That night at Betsy's the team talked about the Porter incident. Now they knew Porter called Zach buddy boy as well as Travis, he might call many people that. He didn't seem as likely a suspect. They had no one else to scrutinize so they decided to explore the situation anyway even though his hatred of Travis seemed to be the only reason for suspicion. Dispatch kept Travis and Zach running for the next several days and they had little time to devote to checking Porter's background.

~ ~ ~

Entering the police station a few days later, Joella wore a mint-green blouse paired with forest green slacks. She had a spring to her step and a bright beam on her face when she met Zach in the hallway.

"Hey there lady, you're looking mighty sprite today. You win the Lotto or something."

"Better than that," she answered, and kept walking. She called over her shoulder, "Have you seen Travis?"

"He just came in with a cup of coffee. He's at his desk."

Entering Travis's office, Joella saw him at his laptop. He raised his head and grinned. "You look nice this morning."

"I'm so happy I took your advice about contacting my family. My sister, Justine, tested the waters for me. She called last night and said she spoke to my father. They want to talk to me. Really more than talk, they want to see me," she said all this in one breath. Gasping for air, she continued. "They are flying in from Seattle today." Her eyes opened wider as if she'd just realized what he'd said. "Oh, thanks for the compliment. I bought this outfit to meet them at the airport later this morning. Daddy loves me in green."

Travis laughed. "I wondered when you were going to come up for air. I'm happy you have an opportunity to bond with your family again."

"I owe it all to you. I wouldn't have called if

you hadn't encouraged me. Daddy loves Mongolian Bar-B-Q so I'm taking them to the 3D Club tomorrow night, but tonight I'm cooking dinner and I'd like you to come meet them. They are only going to be here a couple of days."

"That's not necessary, Joella. You should spend all your time with them."

"No. I want you to come, please. Actually, I'm a little afraid to be alone with them. Don't want the old argument about religion to surface again. If you keep us company, the subject may not arise."

"Okay, if you put it that way. What time?"

"Is six all right? I mean, can you find an excuse to be away from home at dinner time?"

"Hell, I don't need an excuse. Marion will be so happy not to cook and she won't care why."

~ ~ ~

When Joella left, Travis called Marion. The phone rang several times and he was about to close the phone when she finally said, "Hello."

"I won't make it home for dinner tonight. I'm going to…"

"Great," she interrupted. "Doris Walker called a little while ago to invite us to their twenty-fifth wedding anniversary party in two months. It's going to be a huge bash at the Country Club. She and Warren are going to tie the knot again at the party and they want us to stand up for them. Isn't that fantastic? They're having a Champagne fountain and everything, the works. Didn't Warren say anything to you?" Without pausing long enough for him to answer, she rushed on. "I'm glad they gave us plenty of notice. I need to get a permanent and go shopping for the perfect dress. I don't have a thing to wear."

"What do you mean, you 'don't have a thing to wear?' Your closet is full of clothes and you've taken over most of my space too."

"Yes, but the Walkers have seen them all before."

Travis groaned. *Why bother arguing, she'll go shopping anyway.*

~ ~ ~

On his lunch hour, Travis drove to the nearest liquor store. He asked the clerk what kind of wine Jewish people drank.

"No idea," the overweight clerk snarled, "I'm not Jewish."

"Sorry, thought you might know your being in the business and all."

The clerk gave him a dirty grimace.

"Give me a bottle of Riesling then."

"What brand?"

"I don't know. Just make it one of your better wines."

~ ~ ~

Dispatch didn't send Travis out that afternoon giving him a chance to finish some paperwork. Before leaving for dinner, he showered and changed his clothes. A massive Dutch elm in Joella's front yard shaded the small white frame house with a charcoal roof and bright red door. Sparrows and jays flew in and out of the tree that was decades older than the house; Travis felt thankful at least one construction company hadn't followed the current trend of mowing down every living thing in sight before building. Hanging from the porch roof, wind chimes tinkled in the breeze as two wooden rocking chairs with plump purple pillows moved to and fro as if enjoyed by silent ghosts.

Travis knocked on the door and it swung open. *She must have been watching for me.* Joella still wore the green outfit he'd seen that morning. He handed her the bottle. "Hope this is a good year."

"You didn't need to do that, but thanks. It will go fine with dinner. Come in and meet my parents." She led him into the living room. A man and a woman stood when he walked in.

"Mom, Dad, this is Travis Eagle, my friend and fellow officer." A wonderful aroma drifted from the kitchen. Joella lifted her head and sniffed the air. "If you'll excuse me, I have to check on the roast. Go in to the living room; I'll only be a moment."

Mrs. Bar-Lev, wearing a light blue, form-fitting dress, put out her hand first. "How do you do? Eagle is certainly an odd name, where does it come from?"

Travis didn't appreciate her rudeness. He wanted to say, "From my mother and father," but didn't want to sound flippant and start off on the wrong foot with Joella's parents. "Eagle is a common Blackfeet name, Mrs. Bar-Lev."

A slight flush colored her face. "Blackfeet? You're an Indian?"

"Yes, ma'am. I was born on the Blackfeet Indian Reservation."

Before she could open her mouth again, Mr. Bar-Lev shouldered her aside. "Hello, I'm Joella's father, Jacob. The lady with the foot in her mouth is my wife, Judith. It's nice to meet you, Mr. Eagle. Let's sit and get acquainted."

Travis already knew Mrs. Bar-Lev was as 'acquainted' as she wanted to be. He could see where Joella got her looks and figure. Her mother had the same auburn hair and those incredible green-blue eyes. *Glad Joella didn't inherit her mother's personality.*

Travis shifted in his seat glancing around the room as if afraid to make eye contact for fear of inviting conversation. Feeling relief when Joella returned moments later, he said, "That aroma coming from your kitchen smells wonderful." *Maybe I can guide the conversation in a different direction.* He looked at Judith's face and knew she was not about to be guided.

Judith glared at Travis. "Mr. Eagle, are you and my daughter romantically involved?"

Joella's eyes widened. "Moth-er, I told you we are friends. Good friends."

"You've made one mistake marrying out of your faith," Judith said clipping off her words, "and I want to caution you about doing it again."

Jacob's lips tightened into a thin line and he leaned toward his wife. "Shut up, Judith. It's none of your business. You cannot control our daughters. They are grown women. Let them make their own mistakes. Then, support them when they do."

Shrinking back on the couch, Judith's eyes filled with unshed tears. "Jacob, you've never spoken to me like that before."

"Well, I should have."

Judith's complexion paled only to recover

quickly. "I want Joella to marry a nice Jewish boy and give us grandchildren. Apparently, Justine either can't, or won't, and I want grandchildren, someone to carry on the family name."

Jacob scowled. "Family name be damned. I only want our daughters to be happy."

With great effort, Travis suppressed a grin. *Atta boy, Jacob. Even if you are twenty years too late.* Then his concern turned to Joella who listened to her parents arguing without saying a word. As though she could stand it no longer, she jumped out of her chair. "I think the roast beef is done. Please, let's go in and eat. Travis brought us a nice bottle of wine to go with dinner."

Judith grimaced. "Apparently, our daughter has forgotten that we drink only for Jewish celebrations. Do you drink, Mr. Eagle?"

Travis felt his face redden, but before he could say anything he heard Jacob say, "Mind your own business, Judith."

Joella took Travis's arm and ushered everyone into the dining room. The table looked as though she had used her best silver and dishes; fresh flowers embellished the center. Judith appeared not to be aware of anything, sulking throughout dinner. Travis tried once again to get the conversation flowing in a different direction. "I just now realized, Mr. Bar-Lev, that everyone in your family's name begins with a 'J.' Is there a special religious reason for this?"

"Please call me Jacob," he said with a warm smile. "No, no religious reason. After we married and our baby girl blessed us with her birth, we named her Joella because we loved the name. Didn't realize until later there were now three J. Bar-Levs in the family. So when our next daughter arrived, we deliberately picked a name starting with "J" to make the shared initials a tradition. Always hoped for a Jedediah, but it wasn't meant to be."

Travis smiled. *Lucky kid. Who'd want to be saddled with that moniker? It's as bad as Travis.*

The minute everyone finished eating dinner, Joella brought out a triple-layer, chocolate cake, as if eager to have the disastrous evening over.

Travis excused himself after dessert saying he had an early call the next day. He turned to Joella's parents and said, "It was nice to meet you."

Jacob put out his hand. "It was very nice to meet such a good friend of our daughter's."

Mrs. Bar-Lev said nothing.

Joella walked him to the door. "I'm sorry you had to witness Mother's tirade," she whispered. "She's always been a control freak. I don't recall her being such a bigot."

"Don't apologize. It's not your fault. You can't pick your parents."

"Thanks for understanding."

He grinned. "Your mother doesn't hold a candle to Porter." Travis opened the door. "Goodnight, Joella, and I hope the rest of their visit is more pleasant." He winked. "What is that phrase? Oh yeah, *Mazel Tov.*"

CHAPTER 33

The next morning, Travis awoke early. The sun filtered through the elm leaves creating patterns on the bedroom wall. He opened the window and inhaling the fresh sweet air, he smiled. *What a great morning.* He dressed and went to the kitchen for coffee. His mood soured during breakfast when Marion confronted him for money. After another argument of the century, he stormed out of the apartment. Backing out of his parking space, his temples throbbed, knuckles white on the steering wheel, yet at the same time, he felt a flush of pride. He hadn't considered going to Betsy's Bar—just getting away from Marion. He drove his customary green tunnel route and then to Gibson Park to toss some corn to the ducks, waiting for his blood pressure to drop. Dispatch reached him at the park and routed him to a domestic dispute case.

Travis detested these cases. Not because they were one of a cop's most dangerous assignments, but because on each drive to his destination the horrors imprinted on his mind begin to flow: His mother's blackened eyes, bleeding mouth and a nose broken so many times he couldn't remember its original shape. When his father finished pounding her face, he turned to pummel the breast, stomach and legs to mottled red splotches. Young Travis always charged his father trying to pull him away from his mother but it only resulted in him flying to the corner of the room after his father backhanded him. There he would lie, softly whimpering—he was next. When his father finally fell to the floor panting and exhausted, Travis could only pray he might pass out before remembering his son. He never did.

~ ~ ~

Checking the address dispatch had given him, Travis parked in front of the south side of the house. His spirits lifted when Zach pulled in from the opposite direction. The department always sent a backup on these cases, and he was glad to see Zach, not Porter. An ancient, rusted Ford sat on the weeds replacing grass, one door hanging open, half off its hinges. Beer cans and trash littered the front yard and two shattered house windows had plastic taped across them.

They knocked. By this time, the screaming and loud noises the neighbors called in had turned to a low simmer. When the woman answered the door and eyed Zach's uniform, she backed inside, her face pallid. Travis noticed one eye turning to a dappled purple. Splotchy bruises on her arms indicated earlier attacks. He questioned the women fully—her husband said nothing. Travis wrote their names and other pertinent information in his notebook. When he again glanced at the women, she was shaking.

He shook his head guessing the outcome of the case. "I'll write the paperwork and you can file charges."

"No, no," she sobbed. "It was an accident. I ran into the door."

Zach rolled his eyes. "Lady, it will just happen again if you don't file charges."

She looked at her silent spouse who leaned against the kitchen door, smiling, his fists clenched at his side where his wife could see.

Travis sighed. Not enough physical evidence or testimony from neighbors for a prosecutor to file charges. The prosecutor could file as a misdemeanor rather than a felony but it was rare to file charges of any kind without the cooperation from the victim unless the crime had documented facts by corroborating witnesses. There were no witnesses.

When Travis and Zach shut the door, Travis's eyebrows drew together. "Another bastard walks."

~ ~ ~

Arriving at the station, Travis dreaded to write a report where another wife beater got away with his crime. He gawked at the open laptop as if wishing the facts would change by waiting. They didn't and he had just opened his laptop when he heard a rap on the door.

Joella came in. "Got a minute?"

"Sure. Need a break."

She wet her lips. "I want to apologize again for the wretched dinner last night. I'm never able to stand up to Mother. Everything always has to be her way. My father obviously has had enough. He told me that he straightened her out last night. There would be no more discussions about my being Jewish, and I should consider their house my home. It must have been brutal because Mom's eyes were still red-rimmed and puffy. They decided to leave today instead of tomorrow. And my mom actually apologized and wants to see me again, soon."

"I'm glad it worked out for you, Joella; you have your family again. And the dinner was not 'wretched,' it was damn good." Travis glanced at his watch. "Better get my butt in gear and file my report. Another damn wife-beating case where the guy walks. Why don't they realize it will happen again and again until she does something about it?"

Joella sighed. "I hate those cases too."

She had no sooner left than Zach came in throwing his hands in the air and shaking them. "What the hell is going on today?"

"What are you talking about?"

"The whole town has gone nuts—stark raving mad. Every officer on duty is out on call and dispatch is routing them to another one before they even finish their investigation."

"Yeah, they nabbed me on my way to work for our domestic violence case."

Zach took a deep breath. "You name it, and it's happening. Some idiot robbed the First National Bank using the back of his deposit slip to write the robbery note. Talk about stupid. Dexter is picking the dummy up now. A hot head threw his girlfriend through a department store's plate glass window, a couple of thugs got into a knife wrestling exhibition at Jakes and some guy drove out of a gas station on Tenth Avenue South without paying. He left in such a hurry he tore the hose off the pump. That's just to start with. Is it a full moon or April Fools' Day? We've had everything happen that could except for our serial killer to strike again."

Travis grimaced. "Bite your tongue."

CHAPTER 34

The day continued in the same farcical manner and when Travis finally caught Zach and Joella at the end of the day, Zach merely shrugged, "Ma's place?"

Joella nodded.

"Not really sure that's a good idea now that Porter has discovered it," Travis said.

Zach grinned. "Don't worry; I took care of that little problem. I told Porter we had gone to help Joella move some furniture and accidently ran across the bar when we headed for BJs. Said we decided to stop there for a nightcap because it was late."

"He bought that?"

"Sure, Porter's not too bright. I told him he'd been right all along; 'slumming' was the right word for the place. I hinted we wouldn't be caught dead in that fleabag again."

"Good. Ma and I have been close friends for

years, but it wouldn't be the same if Porter started coming. As much as I love Ma, I'd have to go somewhere else."

~ ~ ~

The team had all missed lunch during the frenzied day and was hearing hunger rumbles. When Ma greeted them, Travis looked at the other two. "Reubens all around?"

Joella and Zach nodded and Ma called, "Hey, Jaxson. Three Reubens, please. Make 'em extra special." A few minutes later Ma brought the sandwiches. "Sorry, I can't join you tonight. My granddaughter is in town, and I want to spend the evening with her. She lives in Billings and is so busy with college and work, she hardly ever gets a chance to come see me."

Joella smiled. "That's why you look so nice tonight—all dressed up. Had your hair done too. Go. We're only going to compare notes on Porter."

"Thank you. Wanted to look my best, I see her so seldom. Let me know everything next time. Keep me in the loop."

Joella saluted her. "Sure will. You're an important part of this lineup."

Travis watched Ma take her purse and go out the back. At the same time, the front entrance opened. A streetlight outside haloed the new customer. Whenever the door opened, it was like a magnetic draw, every patron checked to see who had arrived. This time they saw a flaming redhead strutting across the room wearing five-inch stiletto heels, her long hair flipping with every stride. Her shimmering iridescent purple dress clung to her like snakeskin, exposing drop-dead curves and a plunging neckline. She seated herself at a table and pulled out a cigarette. Every male in the bar stared bug-eyed and hyperventilated.

Zach launched from his chair, lighter in hand, and said over his shoulder, "Excuse me guys, this is one hot tomato."

Travis laughed when Joella rolled her eyes as she watched Zach, like Sir Lancelot, dash to the redhead's assistance.

Joella took a sip of wine before returning her eyes to Travis and their conversation. "I didn't know Ma had a granddaughter. Didn't know she'd even been married. Does she have any other family?"

"Afraid not. Ma's had an appalling and painful life. You'd never know it from her attitude today."

"What happened to her?"

"It wasn't so much 'to her' but to those she loved. She told me about it one night when I came in for a sandwich. Her face looked strained, depression seeping from every pore. I told her to forget the sandwich and took her out to dinner instead. Once away from the bar, she relaxed over a couple of beers and told me the whole story. We've been great friends ever since."

Joella's eyes fastened on Travis. "Well?"

"Sorry. Didn't know you wanted to hear the whole wretched story."

"If it concerns Ma, of course, I do. I think she's great."

"It's a despairing story," Travis said. "Ma

had dropped into the dumps that night because it was her daughter's birthday. She married late in life—never managed to find Mr. Right and finally accepted being a spinster. Then she met and wed the love of her life. She became pregnant on her honeymoon. It wasn't actually a 'honeymoon,' more like the hotel they stayed at—the fanciest place in town called the Rainbow Hotel. Ma felt the name an omen promising them a blessed life. When she learned of her pregnancy, she was overjoyed."

Travis took a bite of his sandwich before continuing. "Her joy was short lived. The baby girl was born blind and the doctor told Ma she couldn't have any more children. In those days there wasn't a lot of help for the blind. Ma doted on the child and took care of her every need. Later she sent her to the Deaf, Dumb and Blind School, as it was called in those days, for an education."

Dumb? My God, what a disgusting name for a children's school."

"Yeah, they changed it quite a few years ago."

Jaxson came to the table with a tray holding a Coors, glass of Riesling and a cup of coffee. "Here, Ma bought these for you before leaving."

"Thanks, Jaxson." Travis closed his wallet. "That's Ma, always buying drinks for me and my friends."

Joella remained quiet until Jaxson left. "Yes, she is a wonderful, caring and generous person. Tell me the rest of the story."

"Ma's husband worked in the coal mines so

they didn't have a lot of money but they were happy. Then a cave-in buried him and his men. The crew managed to dig him out, although he never was the same. Crippled and with lung problems, he couldn't work so Ma needed to become the breadwinner. She didn't have much education and slinging drinks was the only job she could find. Times were tough, and yet she managed to support her family."

Joella's eyes were moist. "That's awful."

"It gets worse. I don't recall the little girl's name. Some bastard raped her at twelve. She became pregnant and died giving birth. The shock was too much for Ma's husband and he had a heart attack. Died the next day. Ma completely lost it then and spent a year in a mental institution. Warm Springs, I think."

Joella's eyes were no longer moist—tears streamed down her cheeks. She opened her purse, retrieved a Kleenex and then another. "It isn't fair. No one person should have to suffer that much pain in a lifetime. It's hard to believe anyone could bounce back from that kind of trauma to have the positive personality she presents today. Is that the granddaughter visiting now? The one working her way through college?"

"Yes. Ma would never tell you. Aside from raising her granddaughter, she's paying for the tuition, fees and most of the school expenses."

Joella wiped her cheeks again though they were now dry. "You know, Ma thinks the world of you too—like a son."

"Yeah, Ma adopted me after that dinner. She's like a real mother to me. I'd do anything for her."

A jubilant Zach swaggered back to the table, as if he'd conquered Mt. Everest. He pocketed his little black book, a broad grin on his handsome face, a twinkle in his deep-set blue eyes. He pulled out his chair. "Did either one of you find out anything about Porter? Hope so, because I sure didn't."

"Sorry," Joella said, "we haven't even discussed Porter. Now that you're back, did anyone learn anything at all?"

Travis stifled a yawn. "All the crimes were committed on Sunday, Porter's normal day off. So, I wasn't surprised to find him off each of the crime dates.

"That doesn't prove anything. How about you, Zach—anything?"

"No. But with Porter, it would take more than a few nights to learn if he had any success with women."

Joella brushed her hair back. "I did better than you guys, but not much. I couldn't find any evidence of a name change, but I did learn he came from Cheyenne prior to coming here."

After divulging what little information they had discovered, their faces looked blank. They had nothing stronger than bigotry to pin on the portly Porter.

Zach frowned. "Shit. That's a whole lot of nothing."

Travis drained his coffee. "I know, let's call it a night."

~ ~ ~

Walking out to the parking lot, Joella glanced skyward. "Look. The Northern Lights. I never get tired of seeing that awesome display."

Travis glanced at the sky. "That's a really rare sight this late in the year. The sun obviously had one hell of an explosion. Hope it doesn't disrupt satellite communications— there's a game on TV tonight."

Enormous swirls of frothy green light streaked the heavens. The rays ebbed and flowed creating a lacy kaleidoscope, a colossal display that flooded the entire northern sky. "It's like angels waltzing in heaven," Joella said. "Someday I'm going to Fairbanks. They tell me these displays can go on for hours."

Travis grinned. "That's bound to be a good omen."

Joella laughed. "Is that what the Blackfeet believe?"

"Damned if I know, but I've always felt it a good sign. Maybe our luck will change tomorrow."

Zach groaned. "Fat chance. We don't know anything more than we did yesterday."

"True," Travis said, "The situation doesn't seem good, but there is one thing I think we could check out again. Now that we know Porter came from Cheyenne, we might look at ViCAP once more. I found a few similar crimes there earlier."

"I looked into those a few days ago," Zach said, "but then I had no idea Porter hailed from there. I'll take another gander."

~ ~ ~

For two weeks, in their spare time, the trio investigated but found nothing to confirm Porter might be their serial killer. Gambino still had not surfaced. Confused and depressed, Travis hoped tomorrow would bring better news for a change.

The next day, Travis received news, but not the kind he wanted. He was in the weight room when Zach walked in. "Hey, I've been looking for you."

"What's up, partner? You seem mighty cheerful; find a hot new girlfriend? Maybe that flaming redhead in the purple eye buster?"

A sheepish grin spread across Zach's face. "Yeah, Cynthia and I have been seeing a lot of each other. I never felt like this about any other broad—it's scaring the hell out of me."

"I guess it would, a confirmed bachelor like you. Why were you looking for me?"

"Oh yeah, your talking about Cynthia, sent my mind spinning in a different direction."

"I can see that," Travis laughed noting Zach's crotch.

"Almost forgot what I came to tell you. You're not going to believe this."

"Try me. Nothing surprises me these days."

"You know how the three of us have investigated Porter for days and didn't find anything except that he came here from Cheyenne?"

"Did you find a lead?"

"Could be. I ran into Lillian, Porter's wife. To say she was upset, would be putting it mildly. Started asking me questions about Porter's activities right off the bat."

"What kind of activities?"

"The usual. Did I ever see Porter with another woman, what did he do when he left

221

work, did he report for duty when scheduled? Even asked if he was two-timing her. She started to cry so I invited her for coffee both to calm her and to see what I could learn. Lillian is a nice lady. She deserves better than Porter. Turns out she's been suspicious for a long time. Thinks he's cheating on her."

Travis shrugged. "That's not unusual for a cop's wife. With our crazy hours, half of the department's wives feel that way."

"I know, but one night Porter didn't come home. He claimed he had worked an all-nighter. They had a hell of a row because she knew he lied."

"How could she know?"

"Family emergency. His brother died in a car accident and she called the station to find him. Dispatch told her he wasn't on duty."

"Ouch," Travis said. "But why is this of interest to us?"

Zach grinned. "That's the best part. She knew the exact date because of the brother-in-law's death. His all-nighter was the Sunday of MM's first murder—that Merry gal."

Travis's eyes opened wide. "Damn, did we finally hit pay dirt? Did you question her about any of the other murder dates?"

"Of course, but she'd had no reason to remember those specific dates. Didn't you investigate Porter's duty roster to see if any coincided with the murders?"

"Yes, and he was off those Sundays during the hours of the murders, but I had no way of checking into it more without questioning some of the department personnel. We agreed not to do that."

"Shit. How can we investigate a person of interest if we can't talk about it? I could try talking to Lillian again. Doubt it would be worthwhile. If we don't find something else, it's another dead end."

"Have you told Joella?"

"No, but I will when I leave here. She'll be disappointed. I think she was leaning as much toward Porter as you were toward the doctor."

"Don't remind me."

CHAPTER 35

Travis had looked forward to the weekend. He planned to unwind and watch the Bull's hockey game, but Marion had other ideas. He'd no sooner turned on the TV when Marion's voice rose above that of the broadcaster.

"What are we going to do this weekend? Let's go to Spokane. They have some great stores and we could have a nice dinner at that new restaurant they've been advertising on TV. We might catch a nice show. It would be wonderful to spend a weekend in a *real city* where there's something to do."

Travis groaned. "I have no intention of driving that far just for you to spend more money on clothes. I've had a hard week. I want to relax and watch the game."

"You never take me anywhere, you cheap bastard."

Damn, she could give lessons to a screech

owl. Travis felt his jaw tightening. *I am not letting my anger drive me to Betsy's.* But unable to bear another weekend of fighting, he stood and went to the closet. "You do whatever you want. I'm going fishing."

Marion dashed across the room and grabbed him by the arm, lobbing him around to face her. "Don't you dare run out on me again, Tonto."

His eyes blazing, he slapped her across the cheek. Observing the bright red handprint on her face, Travis crumbled, sick at heart. *I have become my father.*

"I'm sorry, Marion. I don't know what came over me. I've just had more Indian slurs tossed at me lately than I can take. It won't happen again."

"It sure as hell better not happen again, or I'll call Captain Walker. We'll see how your fancy career goes after that, wife beater."

His jaw dropped. He ran for the door.

Sitting in his pickup, his hands clenched the wheel so hard his knuckles were white. *I need a drink to drown the pain.* He turned the ignition on and shifted gear. At the corner, he hit the brakes. *A drink won't kill the pain—it will give me a blackout.* He turned the corner and drove toward I-15.

~ ~ ~

Because he left in a hurry, he stopped at a grocery store to buy a few items before leaving town; everything else he needed was in his pickup.

Augusta, fifty miles due west, lay at the foothills of the Rocky Mountains. An hour later, Travis arrived in the cow town that resembled a setting for western movies. Catering to the heavy tourist traffic, canyon and mountain outfitting stores had wooden pillars and false fronts. Shingled-balcony roofs sheltered rows of chairs or benches and porch railings were intended for support of boots as much as hands. He stopped at the General Store on Main Street for a quick cup of coffee and realized the tension in his neck had eased. All thoughts of Marion were gone.

He ignored the heavily used Sun River and chose one of the many mountain streams, making camp under a grove of white spruce trees far away from civilization. No bawling Charolais cattle, red-vested hunters shooting anything that moved, or weekend cowboys from the many nearby dude ranches to disturb his peace of mind. He sniffed the air and caught a distant whiff of woodsy smoke, similar to the campfire he soon had going. The crystal-clear creek five feet from his campsite had a small waterfall that would lull him to sleep—accompanied by a singing wolf pack, if he were lucky.

~ ~ ~

When he returned home Sunday night, it was near midnight. Marion was in bed. New clothes draped every piece of furniture in the living room. She had left the clothes and boxes scattered about, as if displayed for spite. In the middle of the floor lay a pile of credit card receipts.

~ ~ ~

The sun already streamed through the treetops when he awoke on Monday; the light filtered through his eyelids. He stretched and eased out of bed, intending to go directly to work. *I can do without the cold cereal Marion considers breakfast, but a cup of coffee would hit the spot.*

In the kitchen, he put water in the Mr. Coffee machine and as he reached for the Maxwell House, his cell phone rang. Dispatch sent him to a homicide and he jotted down the address in his notebook. Grabbing his jacket, he dashed for his pickup.

The homicide was in the newly developed Gore Hill area just past the airport. Other than a few condominium complexes, the swanky neighborhood held only chic, expensive homes. Travis always enjoyed driving to the airport because of the hilltop view. The entire city stretched out before him, the Missouri River looping in and around the town in giant swirls. Today he did not enjoy the view. He felt his stomach roiling, his hands clammy. *This is Monday. Is this another MM victim? He promised to leave new evidence that would convict me of his crimes.*

A sudden thought jolted his memory like an earthquake shockwave. Shit. *I don't have an alibi for the weekend.* His hands began to shake.

~ ~ ~

Arriving at the condo, Travis felt more at ease when Dexter—not Porter—met him at the door. Dexter couldn't be in better hands than learning the ropes from a seasoned pro like Zach. Travis looked into the room and saw a blonde woman duct taped to the floor. Opening his bag, he removed coveralls, polyethylene gloves and paper shoe covers. While he put them on, one thought gave him peace of mind. *I know I didn't kill her—I won't be sick.* He walked over to view the body and a wave of nausea struck him full force. He barely managed to keep down the sausage biscuit he'd snatched at a convenience store. *What the hell is the matter with me? I did not do this.*

Still reeling from the shock of his nausea, Travis swallowed the lump in his throat. *Need to get on with it.* "Dexter, did you get the victim's name?

"Yes, Silvana Aliyev. Poor woman, she just arrived in this country two weeks ago. She's Russian."

"Spell it."

Dexter read from his notes and Travis wrote the name in his notebook. "Who discovered the body?"

"Her next-door neighbor, Louis Burton. He came over when we arrived. Claimed to be only casually acquainted with the victim, but said he heard strange noises coming from her apartment Sunday night. 'Opened my door,' he said, 'and saw a tall, dark-haired man leaving.'" Stated the guy didn't seem in a hurry, and he assumed Aliyev and her boyfriend had a fight. Thought no more of it until the next morning when he noticed her door still ajar. When she didn't respond to his knock, he went in.

Travis's brows drew together. *This isn't MM's typical MO. Maybe it's another copycat job.* "Is Joella on her way, Dexter?"

"She should be here any—here she is now."

Travis pulled Joella to the side, away from the other officers bustling about the room. "Remember," he said in a low voice, "MM threatened to leave another clue. When you find it, try to keep the other guys from seeing it if you can until I see what it is."

"Will do," Joella whispered.

"I'll go next door and interview the neighbor who called this in, but I won't be long—need to be here in case you find something."

~ ~ ~

Travis knocked on Burton's door and waited. When no one answered, he knocked again. Still no answer. About to leave, he stopped when he heard the rattling of a chain lock. The door opened. A bald, white-bearded man in his seventies with a powerful body odor stood halfway behind the door wearing a dirty tank T-shirt. "Whattaya—Christ, it's you."

"What are you talking about?"

"You're the guy I saw leaving Aliyev's apartment Sunday."

Travis felt beads of sweat break out on his brow. *MM left a clue all right. What better than a paid-for eyewitness.* Hesitating, Travis finally got his nerves under control. "I'm Detective Eagle of the Great Falls Police Department."

Burton looked him dead in the eye. "So? That doesn't mean ya didn't do it. I gotta real good gander at your puss when ya came out."

"It wasn't me. Can you describe the man you saw?"

"Sure. How tall are you?"

"Okay, you say he is about my height, around six feet."

"Yeah, and put down your weight too. He had black hair and eyes like yours and the same high cheekbones. No two people could look that much alike. It was you all right."

Travis swallowed hard. "Any identifying scars or tattoos?"

"Nope."

"Can you describe what he was wearing?"

"Nah, I was too busy eyeballing *your* face."

Travis felt his knees grow weak. He handed Burton his card. "Thanks. If you think of anything else, please contact me."

Burton glared, tearing the card in half. "I don't need no damn phone call. It was you."

Outside, Travis leaned against the building gasping for air. *Shit. MM said he was leaving a clue, but I never expected this.* Cold shivers ran through his body, and he zipped his leather jacket closed. It took him a few minutes to gain control of his thoughts. When he returned to the victim's apartment, Joella seemed to be finishing her investigation. She glanced at him, her face beaming. "Fantastic news," she whispered. "I didn't find a single indicator pointing to you. He was bluffing. This crime scene was as clean as the others, the same MO. Few fibers on the body and most consistent with the carpet she's lying on."

"Shit. He wasn't bluffing, Joella. He left the perfect clue."

"Where?" Her eyes darted around the room. What did I miss?"

"The guy who found Aliyev's body. When I knocked on his door, he took one look and said it was me he saw coming out of the victim's apartment. I know I didn't do it. I also don't have an alibi. I went fishing on the weekend."

Joella's eyes glazed over. "Damn, with that story and you not having an alibi... God Almighty, Travis, Montana has the death penalty."

CHAPTER 36

His hovering blondes didn't keep Travis awake that night—Louis Burton did. He tossed and turned, shivering, unable to get warm even after adding a wool blanket to his side of the bed. The incriminating interview with Burton swirled through his brain all night, his tortured mind refusing sleep. At long last, sunshine streamed through the drapes that didn't quite meet and he arose. *Might as well face the music.* He heard Marion grumble as she turned over to check the clock on the nightstand and then pull the blanket over her head to block out the sunlight. *So much for breakfast. Just as well, I couldn't eat anyway.* As soon as he dressed, he left for the office.

~ ~ ~

When Travis pulled into the station parking lot, Joella stood outside waiting at the door. She went to meet him. "My God, you look awful;

didn't you get any sleep?"

"Afraid not. Kept waiting for the phone to ring or a knock on the door."

"I didn't sleep much either. I came in early to see if Burton had phoned, claiming to be a witness. He hasn't. Thought I'd catch you out here so we could talk in private. Why in the hell hasn't he called?"

"I don't know. Are you sure he hasn't?"

"Positive, checked twice."

"Both MM's notes said he wanted me to suffer. Maybe this is his sick way of adding to my torment. If so, he's doing a damn good job of it. Maybe Burton won't call for days."

The questioning expression on Joella's face stopped him. She leaned in closer. "Wouldn't our guys be suspicious if he waits too long to say he is a witness?"

"Not really, he could always claim he didn't want to get involved. Say his conscience finally got the best of him, figured he had to do the right thing."

"What are you going to do about filing your report on the investigation?"

"Well, we've already withheld knowledge of the matchbook, guess one more lie won't get me fired any quicker." Travis sneaked a glance at his watch. "I better get busy and file some kind of report or that *will* seem suspicious. I'll interview the other tenants later. Let's go inside."

Retrieving his notebook from his jacket, Travis laid it on the desk. He gazed at it a long time, finally opening his laptop and filling out the description report from the so-called eyewitness. Because no eyewitness can know the exact height of the person he is describing, he wrote the suspect's height at about six feet and put his own weight of 195 pounds. He completed the portrayal by writing black hair and eyes, high cheekbones and no visible scars or tattoos. No description of clothing. He neglected to mention Burton claimed it was him he'd seen leaving the apartment.

Walking down the hall to turn in his report, Travis felt like he was walking the last mile to the execution chamber. When he handed over the report, his forehead beaded with sweat, and he wiped it with the back of his hand. Back in his office, he sat motionless at his desk, unable to concentrate.

An hour later, Porter stuck his head in the door. "Hey, Geronimo," he snickered, "You got a second career going now? That eyewitness description fits you to a 'T.' Bummer that Great Falls is too cheap to hire a forensic artist—you coulda seen your mug in the paper." He turned and strutted down the hall, his laughter echoing behind him.

His jaw ached from clenched teeth. Almost at his limit of self-control, Travis once again reminded himself of Joella's lecture about anger management. His ringing phone addled his concentration. When he answered, he listened to another blistering call from the mayor. Travis shifted in his chair as the mayor ranted. Only that morning the *Tribune* ran the story of all four of the serial killer's murders again, including pictures and blasting the police for being unable to solve the cases. His name was scattered throughout the article. *Shit. Am I ever going to catch this maniac?*

~ ~ ~

Zach opened his door and saw the epitome of misery plastered across Travis's face. "Joella just told me about the eyewitness on the Aliyev case. What a load of crap. He can't get away with that."

"I wouldn't be too sure," Travis said. "Plenty of innocent people are in jail convicted on faulty eyewitness testimony only—the least dependable evidence of all."

Zach nodded. "You got that right. No one should ever be sentenced to the death penalty on eyewitness testimony alone, but some states keep right on doing it." He sat in the hardback chair by Travis's desk. "I've been going over database MOs again, the ones you thought were similar in Wyoming. I haven't found anything concrete, but you're right; we need to check them out further. Maybe one of us could take some comp time. Go down there and dig around. We don't have anything else to go on."

"That might be a good idea, but let's hold off a couple of days and see if the lab finds anything relevant on the Aliyev case."

~ ~ ~

When Travis opened the door, Ma spotted them and waved as the Unholy Alliance, as Porter called them, walked in. She automatically popped a Coors and poured the wine. Setting the drinks on their usual table she asked, "You having coffee or Coke, Travis?"

"I'll have a Coke and whip me up a BLT too. I haven't eaten all day."

"Sure thing." She walked back to the bar to get an ice-cold soda and a Coors for herself before rejoining them.

Travis excused himself, rose and headed toward the bathroom.

Joella took a sip of wine and then turned toward Ma. "You sure take wonderful care of Travis."

"You bet your boots. He's not only my best friend, he's the son I never had."

Zach flashed a wicked grin emphasizing the cleft in his chin. "How about adopting me, Ma? I could use a few free drinks."

She laughed. "You guzzler, I couldn't afford you."

"If you don't mind my asking," Joella said, "how did you and Travis form such a tight bond?"

"I don't mind at all. He helped me out of a terrible jam years ago when some scoundrel claimed I didn't have legal ownership to Betsy's Bar. He had some trumped-up charges backed with fake paperwork and a real shrewd lawyer. I just about kissed the bar goodbye. Bless his heart, Travis investigated and hired me a first-rate attorney who saved my butt; he paid for the lawyer because I didn't have the money. I eventually paid him back but it took some time. He's always here for me if I need him."

Joella smiled. "I'm glad he has you. He doesn't get much support at home from what he's told me."

"That's for sure. He's miserable in that so-called marriage. His wife is a first-class shrew, but he is so grateful for her working to get through college, that he can't leave her. That and the religious thing. He's too honorable."

When Travis returned, Zach said, "I sure hope one of you found something on Porter, because I didn't. I've gone to Jakes for a beer every night with him when I wasn't with you guys. I watched him fumble more plays than a quarterback. He finally managed to pick up a nice little number one night. And she was blonde, the chemical kind."

Joella looked him in the eye. "And?"

"She still walks among us."

"Oh." For a moment, Joella didn't say anything. "I'm not ruling Porter out yet." In the meantime, we still have the Aliyev case. The lab is checking out the fibers I found on the body and the autopsy tape found a few hairs." She stopped talking to take a sip of wine and then continued. "And you're not going to believe this. I did some more research on Tony. He hadn't been living here long. He also came from Cheyenne. How is that for coincidence? Why are so many clues pointing to Cheyenne?"

~ ~ ~

A few days later, Travis looked up to see Joella coming into his office, her face the epitome of gloom.

"Why so glum, Joella?"

"Oh Lord, I hate to tell you this, but we just lost one of our two remaining suspects."

"Which one found an alibi?"

"Tony. And he doesn't need an alibi—he's dead—killed before MM's fourth victim so we know he was innocent."

"What happened?"

"Seems he was a little too anxious to explain to everyone that he didn't have any connection to the Mafia Gambinos. Turns out, he was a fifty-second cousin or something like that to the main man, but a *nobody* in the organization. That didn't keep him from living the high life in Cheyenne, pretending to be a Mafia Gambino. Grabbed a lot of freebies from kowtowing waiters and hookers on the street who were afraid of him."

"Doesn't sound like he was a very sharp guy," Travis interrupted.

"You're right about that," Joella continued.

"Seems he left Cheyenne in a hurry. My guess would be the Mafia took issue with his little charade, and Tony met with an accident. That would account for why he never came back to Ma's place. He was running scared. And I suspect he later might have recognized me as a cop when I was playing Rita. May have taken the Mafia a while to find him."

Travis frowned. "Damn, that leaves us with Porter. I know he's a bigoted jerk, but I can't bring myself to believe he is sick enough to commit that kind of murder. Come to think of it, the notes sound a little like him, but that sure as hell isn't evidence."

~ ~ ~

Three days later, Travis sat eating the Cornflakes Marion had left on the table along with a bottle of milk. While he was eating, she walked into the kitchen holding an envelope. "Here. I assume this is another love note from your serial killer. I saw it on the floor by the front door."

"Marion, you shouldn't have handled it."

"How the hell am I going to bring it to you without picking it up?"

"You should have...never mind." He grabbed a tissue from the kitchen counter and opened the already contaminated envelope.

Hey flatfoot. Love how the papers are having a field day at your expense. How does it feel to be a celebrity with that perfect description of you in the paper? My guy did a great job, didn't he? What a shame the G.F. cops don't have a forensic artist. Would love to have seen your mug in the paper. Man-oh-man, it makes me feel good to know you are suffering like I have. But this is just the beginning, copper. The best is yet to come, motherfucker. I was gonna grant you one more chance and give you a "freebie" with no clues, but while it's been great fun, I'm bored as hell. Hold onto your hat; another slut coming up—and you are going down. I'm leaving DNA.

Yours!!!!
MM

CHAPTER 37

Travis's heart began to pound. *My DNA? That's impossible. How can he have my DNA?* He jumped up from the table so fast he upset his cereal bowl. *Does he have to get it or does he already have it? If he has it, he must be a regular at Ma's and copped a glass, unless he visited my barber. That sure would clinch a case against me.* When his heart quit pounding, he ran out the door without even saying goodbye to Marion.

~ ~ ~

At the station, he pulled into the parking lot so fast he straddled the line between two spaces, something he cussed out many a rookie for doing. Finding Joella in her office, Travis handed her the note and watched the color recede from her face as she read it. He suspected his complexion might also be a shade or two lighter.

She sat immobile. "Damn, he's moving in for the kill."

Neither said another word, only gawked at one another. After a minute or two Joella's face brightened. "Have you ever had your DNA done?"

"No, I never had a reason to."

"If we had a sample of your DNA, we could compare it, if and when, the lab finds the genetic material the killer has promised to use. The police don't have yours on file, so even if they get what MM plants, it won't point to you. At least not right away."

"That's a fantastic idea. I can go to an independent lab and use a false name, maybe drive to Helena again to be safe."

"Great." She looked him dead in the eye. "But if you go to Helena, no damn camping out on the weekend to rejuvenate your soul. You need an alibi for each and every Sunday until we catch this lunatic."

"I know, I know. After MM said he was setting me up for his crimes, I knew that, especially remembering I had blackouts during the first two murders. Marion and I fight worse on weekends because I'm home more often. The arguments didn't use to last long, but lately they've become appalling." His lips tightened at the memories. "She almost seems to be goading me into fights even when she hasn't been shopping—she rampages on for hours. I can't begin to tell you how I struggled to keep from going to Ma's place." He paused to catch his breath. "I reminded myself of your wise counseling, but if I didn't get out of there

I'd have wound up doing something I'd regret." He grimaced remembering the shame he'd felt hitting Marion. "I always fled. Went fishing. I was so out of control, I never thought about asking Captain Walker to join me. Couldn't think of anything—just getting the hell out of there. That's why I didn't have an alibi for the Randenberg and Aliyev cases."

Joella shook her head, hesitated, and then combed her hair back with her fingers. She paused before speaking again. "Travis, not that we haven't given it our all to find this maniac, but maybe it's time we tell the captain what's going on."

"No," he almost shouted. "I don't want you involved when the shit hits the fan. I'll take full responsibility, tell the captain I found the matchbook and didn't turn it in. You and Zach stay out of it."

"But, Travis..."

"No buts about it. You and Zach know nothing about this. Understand? If the captain finds out, he'll fire me before I can catch this lunatic, and I need to find out why I am so emotionally involved with these victims."

Joella frowned. "Okay, if that's what you want, but I don't like it. Zach and I went into this willingly with our eyes open. We still have time—at least until the next murder. Maybe we'll get lucky. If he's going to use your DNA, he'll have to get a glass you've used, a sample of your hair or something." The words had barely left her mouth, when her eyes flared wider. "Oh my God, if he got that matchbook from Betsy's Bar himself, he could already have a glass you used."

"I know. I thought of that too."

"We need to clue Ma in on the last note, and tell her to watch for anyone trying to swipe a glass," Joella said. "Let's go tonight but not sit together. I'll watch for anything suspicious from people nearby you."

"I'm sorry, but I can't go tonight. I promised to take Marion to some fancy party one of her shopping friends is tossing. I guess I could get out of it, and..."

"No problem, I'll go and clue Ma about his threatening to leave your DNA. If I know Ma, she'll keep her eyes glued to you like a hawk seeking dinner."

~ ~ ~

As in the previous serial killer cases, the lab found no solid evidence on the Aliyev murder. A few unknown fingerprints didn't match anything in the database. The lab still worked on identifying the fibers, but it didn't seem promising. Now that Tony was no longer a person of interest, Travis, Joella and Zach spent every spare moment searching Porter's background for something that might connect him to the crimes. A week went by, but nothing happened. Two murders occurred on the West Side: a domestic bludgeoning and a "floater" from the Sun River but nothing pointed to Porter or had MM's signature. Travis felt utter relief when another detective was designated to handle the floater. Every cop on the force dreaded investigating any decomposed body retrieved from water. The stench was beyond unbearable, worse than a dry decomposing body.

Zach caught Travis in the parking lot at the end of a hectic day. "Have you decided yet if one of us should go down to Cheyenne and look around?"

"No point. The lab is so far behind they said it might be a month before they could get around to finish investigating the Aliyev fibers."

~ ~ ~

Travis became more jumpy every day, lost weight and the dark circles under his eyes seemed almost a permanent feature. Sleep was impossible; his catwalk of blondes dancing to Burton's ugly laughter echoing as though it were background music mocked his efforts. He tried to act natural on the job, but doubted he was successful.

One day when Travis appeared particularly bad, Porter followed Travis into his office. "Hey, Tonto, having problems sleeping? Failure," he said, snickering, "will do that to a guy."

"I told you before, don't call me Tonto."

"Aw, don't get all huffy. Here, some kid delivered this to the station; it's for you. Maybe MM feels sorry for you and is confessing. Seems like the only way you're going to catch him." He laid the envelope on Travis's desk and strutted out.

Travis recognized the printing. Porter and the youngster had contaminated any possible evidence, but Travis still pulled latex gloves from his kit as soon as Porter left. Because a kid delivered the note, Travis was sure there wouldn't be any DNA—just like before, but he'd check anyway.

Hey flatfoot. You sweating yet? Thought I'd make you panic a little longer, even if it won't make up for the years I suffered because of you. Don't worry it's a comin—you just won't know when.

MM

CHAPTER 38

A few days later, the phone woke Travis, his nightmare of buxom blondes disappearing with wakefulness. Rubbing the sleep from his eyes, he heard Zach's animated voice.

"Damn it, buddy, this is it. This victim has MM marked all over it; he might as well have carved his initials on her belly."

Travis threw on his clothes, grabbed his jacket and raced to the scene. He arrived with nerve endings afire, sweat-soaked underarms.

Zach met him at the crime scene tape.

"Do we have a name?"

"Yeah, Jane Simpson. Her roommate found the body." He turned to leave, and said, "Let me know what Joella finds."

Travis had already put on paper shoe covers and gloves when Joella arrived.

"Oh God, Travis. I'm afraid to start," she whispered. "What am I going to find?"

Travis swallowed the lump in his throat. "I don't know." He hesitated a moment, dreading to view the body. Finally, he forced himself to look. As he feared, giant spasms gripped his stomach. Not wanting to vomit, he looked away quickly.

Joella put her hand on his shoulder. "Go interview the companion who discovered the body. I'll take care of this." She put on her protective gear and started her examination.

He needed to question the victim's horrified roommate but his feet felt nailed to the floor. *Dammit, what evidence is he leaving to convict me?* Travis couldn't bring himself to leave. His gut grumbled and he swallowed hard to keep from heaving. He stepped away from the corpse and concentrated on Joella's methodical pace. The distance and not looking at the body eased his nausea.

Her eyes darted back and forth to him. When she finished her task, Joella appeared apprehensive. She glanced at him and began retracing each step of the investigation. Finally, she walked over. "Travis," she said in a soft voice. "The promised clue isn't here. It's the same clean scene as the others and the few fibers I found don't appear promising. He's bluffing. He doesn't have your DNA."

"I'd like to think you're right, but..."

~ ~ ~

Travis had already brought Zach up to date when the Unholy Alliance met at Betsy's that evening more to vent frustrations rather than exploring ways to catch MM. Travis had run out of the 'paths' Gus taught him to use when solving cases. The bar was busier than usual, and Ma sprinted between tables tossing them a wave when she caught Travis's eye.

She joined them several minutes later. "Finally. Couldn't wait to get over here. What was the clue pointing to Travis?"

"Not a blasted thing," he said through clenched teeth. "But then the lab might find something yet—we'll have to wait and see."

Travis stared at the three scowling faces clustered around him. "Let's call it a night."

~ ~ ~

The long wait for the ME's report stressed both Travis and Joella to the point they snapped at everyone. When Joella finally received the report, she downloaded it to her laptop. Her eyes were riveted to the report, the DNA portion standing out like a red exit sign. *Crap, Travis was right; MM was not bluffing. They found something.* Semen.

CHAPTER 39

With trembling hands, Joella opened her briefcase and withdrew the copy of *John Doe's* DNA that Travis gave her after his test. She entered it in the laptop. The waiting moments were excruciating, but the answer was like a hot poker to her gut—100 percent match. She could taste the acidic bile rising from her stomach. Her body shook violently and she collapsed onto a chair. *What kind of monstrous psychopath commits such horrendous crimes and then sends himself letters to convince him someone else is guilty? What a fool I've been.*

She had no idea how long she sat there, lost in a jumbled world of nightmarish thoughts. When the hammering in her chest ceased, she rose. *Time to confront the monster.* She walked down the hall to his office and opened the door, still trembling, her face pale.

Travis looked up from his desk. "Are you

okay?"

She didn't say a word, handing him the test result pages. After a moment's hesitation, she said, "That's the DNA analyses. You were right. This time they found semen. Yours!"

Travis's face turned ashen. He jumped out of his chair. "That's impossible. I'd go along with the lab finding my DNA from hair, a cigarette if I smoked or maybe a glass, but *not* semen. I did not rape that woman. I've never seen her before."

Joella saw the vein in his temple throbbing. She stared straight into his black eyes—the same dark pools of coffee she had found so overwhelmingly attractive before. Now, they reflected a master of death—a monster who kills during blackouts. And now, maybe just for kicks because he'd had no blackouts lately. She straightened her back. "DNA does not lie, Travis. You were once convinced you were the killer. This evidence convinces me." With the words barely out of her mouth, Joella became aware she was talking to a violent serial killer; she shivered and turned to leave.

Travis reached out and grabbed her arm.

"Let me go," she screamed.

He released her arm. "Wait. There has to be some other explanation. I have not had a blackout since the second murder. I know I don't have an alibi for the other cases, but I am not MM." He gazed into space, as if trying to pull an explanation from thin air. All at once, his face brightened. "Wait a minute. This victim was killed Sunday evening, wasn't she?"

"Yes, according to our best estimate."

Travis let out a short, audible breath. "Remember. Sunday you and I were at Betsy's after clocking out. We'd both been called in for a homicide. We were leaving when dispatch sent us on an unrelated case that lasted into late Monday afternoon."

For a few seconds her face remained blank, then, glowed into warm softness. "My God, Travis, you're right. My mind registered such shock reading the DNA results that I forgot. You were with me at the time of the murder." *I should have known he couldn't be that kind of fiend.* She looked down at the floor, her face flushed. "I'm so sorry I suspected you. Can you *ever* forgive me?"

"Understandable under the circumstances. Thank you for believing me now. But if it wasn't me, how in the hell did that maniac get my semen. Is he going through my garbage?"

Joella felt the muscles in her face tighten followed by a plunging sense of guilt. *I have no right to feel jealous.* She peeked at Travis and realized he had noticed her expression.

A vivid blush overshadowed his tawny skin. He hesitated for a brief, awkward moment, his shoulders drooped. "Normally we live like brother and sister, but every three months or so—usually after she's been talking with her priest—she comes home wanting sex. Has to do her duty, I suppose. Believe me, it means absolutely nothing. It's like making love to a corpse. She moves only if she gets the hiccups."

Travis sucked in a long, deep breath before he swallowed hard, his expression pleading for understanding. Joella cringed, feeling utter self-contempt for even thinking about him and his wife having sex. But her mind flipped back to his explanation. *Stop it. They're married.*

Still in disbelief about the entire situation, she watched him pace wall to wall in the small cubicle. "Sit down, Travis. We need to think. There must be an explanation." They both sat wearing the expressions of minds lost in deep thought. All at once, her eyes widened. She looked straight at him. "I've been rehashing everything I've ever read about DNA and it *is* possible for someone else to have your DNA, but there is only one way. Did you by any chance have an identical twin?"

"No, I am an only child."

"I thought that's what you told me. Are you positive?"

"Of course. I didn't have a brother, twin or otherwise."

"Are you really sure? You could have been separated at birth and had one adopted. It happens, you know."

"Yes, I know. It happens, but you did not know my mother. She would have kept the twin if it had Down's, even if it had been a total freak."

"Okay. Fingerprints and hair that supply DNA are a different matter, but in order for semen DNA to be identical, it *must* be from an identical twin. It is the only way possible." She was silent a moment. "Oh my God," Joella said, her voice breaking. "Are the scientific facts as we know them wrong? If they are, no court in the world would believe you." She opened her mouth as if to speak, and then gaped instead. "Holy Christ! If that is true, how many innocent people have been wrongfully jailed and even executed?"

They stared at each other, bewilderment blazing from both faces. Travis jumped out of the chair and began to pace again. She watched him make several laps and snapped, "Sit down, we need to think."

"I am thinking, but I'm not getting any good answers."

Joella was quiet a moment. "Sorry. I'm cantankerous. I just don't know how to solve this."

"Me neither."

Time passed with neither speaking. Then Joella jolted upright. "I know you were not serious when you asked if the killer went through your garbage, but maybe we ought to consider it. I've never heard of it being done in a crime, but it is possible to inject semen." She paused to wet her lips. "The killer would have to freeze it, a complicated procedure, and I don't know how long he'd have to use it after thawing." She looked at Travis's perplexed expression. "It's the only possibility. I'll do some checking on how the procedure works."

"It seems damned far-fetched." He paused a few moments before adding, "but MM isn't your average serial killer."

"That's true, but still…" Finally, Joella said, "I'm glad we didn't tell the captain the entire story when I suggested it. That paid for witness hasn't called the police yet. I checked again this morning. They don't have your DNA on file so we still have time."

"Time for what?"

Her voice was a small whimper, barely audible. "I don't know."

CHAPTER 40

DNA markers floated in and out of Joella's nightmare. She tossed and turned, sweat soaking the sheets in the air-conditioned room. She awoke exhausted. Coffee in hand, she mulled over the situation, and then slapped the cup down so hard it almost broke. *There is no other way. I'm checking out his story of being an 'only child.' But how could he not know.*

~ ~ ~

Joella shared her thoughts with Travis that morning.

"I know I'm an only child," he said. "But if you are determined to explore the possibility, I'll drive to Browning this weekend and talk to Aunt Winona. She's my mother's sister and if anyone would know, she would. If she doesn't, it's a dead end because she's my only relative and I have no idea who the midwife might have been or if there was one. I know I wasn't born

255

in the hospital so there are no records."

"Perfect. In the meantime, I'll research birth certificates. You have one, don't you?"

"Of course."

"I'll check. Maybe I can locate another birth certificate. When and where were you born?" She wrote the information and left saying, "I'll see you when you get back."

CHAPTER 41

Travis didn't ask Marion to accompany him to Browning—it would just be a waste of words. He didn't want her company anyway—he needed to be alone in his anguish and try to think of a possible explanation. Before he left, Travis warned Marion again to be extra careful if she left the house. "Be sure you wear a scarf or hat to cover your hair."

Rain clouds filled the murky sky, matching his mood when he left Saturday morning. The trip passed quickly, his mind reeling with farcical facts breast stroking through his gray matter. The more specifics he considered, the farther away from a solution he felt.

When he arrived in Browning, he drove to the old homestead. Winona had moved into his parents' house after his mother and father died. Arriving, he couldn't help notice how the porch sagged and the house needed a new roof.

Strange I didn't recognize that last time. If I get out of this mess, I'll get someone out here to take care of it.

His aunt sat on the front porch rocking in an old wooden rocker, only a few chips of red paint still visible. Her mouth opened displaying a happy, near toothless grin. "Welcome home, son." She had accepted his new life, but he believed in the back of her mind she hoped he might return to live on the reservation one day.

"Oki, Aunt Winona." Travis smiled, always addressing her with the respectful title.

"Oki, my son. How about some lunch? I just made pemmican. Well, it's almost pemmican. I can't get any good buffalo meat and marrow most of the time and have to substitute tough beef. Plenty of chokecherries in the mountains this year so it tastes good."

"It smells wonderful, Aunt Winona, but I've eaten. I came to ask you some questions you might find bizarre. I'm in a little trouble and need to know something. Did I have a twin brother?" Travis held his breath.

Her brow rose as she squinted at him in the afternoon sunlight. "What a strange question. No, you were an only child."

Travis wasn't surprised. "Are you positive?"

"Of course. I was there."

"You were?"

"Yes, I helped bring you into the world. You wouldn't know, but when your mama got pregnant on the way to the reservation as a new bride, your father became outraged. He beat her—knew a baby would be expensive and cut into his whiskey money. It was just the beginning. He beat her all the time after that, once just before you were born; the blows brought on your mama's labor. We didn't think you'd live because you were so tiny. The ninampskan worked over you for days—he saved your life."

"Yes, I know. Mother had great faith in the medicine man. And I well remember what a raging alcoholic my father was. I still have nightmares about all the times he thrashed Mother just for buying food. Because of his alcoholism, I swore never to drink." He felt his face flush remembering the times he'd broken that vow. He winced. *No need to disillusion her.*

Winona's eyes filled with tears as though remembering the long forgotten nightmares her sister lived through. "Your father was such a dreadful man. I always felt so sorry for your mama. He wouldn't let her buy clothes for you when you were born, said you'd outgrow them too fast. You were dressed in rags and his worn out shirts for months." She paused to wipe away a tear. "Once when you were two-months old, a woman and her newborn baby came from Browning to see your father. Owed him money and came to pay him. She was a nasty woman, laughed and made fun of the rags you wore. Your mama cried. I was there, and I cried too. Her baby was dressed so cute. He looked a little like you, but then all babies look the same—adorable."

Winona had married but remained childless and Travis felt sorry for her because she wanted a baby so badly. They were all beautiful no matter how ugly they might be—and there were some damned ugly ones.

"I wish your mama did have twins, Travis. Then I would have two nice nephews like you."

"Thanks, Aunt Winona. I just wondered." Travis stood and headed for the door, his chest tight and teeth clenched so hard his neck felt stiff. *Damn. Another lead down the tubes.*

"I'm sorry I couldn't help, Travis. Are you in serious trouble?"

"No, not serious," he lied. "Thanks anyway, but it wasn't a wasted trip. It's always good to see you, Aunt Winona. As soon as I get this trouble straightened out, I'm coming back and do something about fixing this place. It needs some work."

~ ~ ~

On the drive back to Great Falls, Travis replayed their conversation repeatedly in his mind. *I am an only child. I am an only child.* But slowly, over the miles, five of Winona's words creeped into his mind, playing over and over like a cracked LP record. *We looked a little alike.* He shook his head as if to clear his mind. *That kid was two months younger—we sure as hell couldn't be twins.* Besides, he agreed with his aunt, all kids look alike.

Out of blue, a few miles later, a long forgotten conversation popped into his mind. Watson, a rookie who recently joined the force, said he thought he'd seen Travis at the Cheyenne rodeo. He had shrugged it off as a look-alike, but now the conversation had new significance. Then another thought crossed his mind: *Those two cold case files I found in Cheyenne had a vague similarity to MM's work.*

All roads in this case seem to lead not to Rome, but to Cheyenne. Why? No, I can't have a twin brother. Winona would know—she was the midwife.

CHAPTER 42

Travis didn't stop to eat on the way home. The miles flew by, his mind filtering every possible idea and scenario into brain pockets for later investigation. *A twin? No! It isn't possible. But it's the only thing we have going other than an even longer shot, Porter.* It was late when he got back to town, and he spotted Joella walking toward her car. He stopped and rolled down the window. "Can you meet me at Ma's?"

"Sure thing and I have news."

"Me too."

"Hope it's good news."

"Not really, but maybe a glimmer of hope."

"Okay, see you there." He watched Joella glance around and figured she didn't want Porter to see them leaving together. Porter had taken to calling her a home wrecker and she'd confessed to wanting to deck the wormy little twerp several times.

~ ~ ~

When Travis entered Ma's, the short-order cook was tending bar, Ma, nowhere in sight. Travis called out, "Hey, Jaxson, bring me a cup of coffee and a Riesling for Joella. Make me a Reuben too." He sat at their usual table just as Joella walked in the front door. She hurried over and sat down breathless. "What's your news?"

"I didn't know it, but Aunt Winona played midwife for my mother. She was there when I came into the world. I *was* an only child." He was surprised she didn't appear disappointed. "Later she told me how sorry she felt for Mama because some white woman from Browning brought her new baby to visit my father and made fun of the clothes I wore. Said the baby looked a little like me, which sent my heart racing. But then she added that all babies looked alike to her, and he was two months younger than me."

As she listened, Joella drummed her fingers on the table.

"What's the matter? You've been fidgeting ever since you sat down."

"I wanted to hear what you had to say first. I have news too. But mine is great news. It's more than a 'glimmer of hope,' Travis. I found him."

"Found who?"

"Your brother."

Travis reared back in his seat, his mouth gaping. "What? It isn't possible. Why would Aunt Winona lie to me? Why would my mother lie to me?"

"Oh, sorry. I didn't actually locate him, but I have proof he might exist."

"How?"

"I discovered it accidentally. Spent a couple of hours playing Trivia Questions with friends the other night. One of the questions asked was how long after the first birth could a twin be delivered. I was shocked. It turns out, the record is almost an unbelievable two months. When I investigated birth certificates before, I checked only the next day or two after your birth and before. I had no idea twins could be born that far apart. So I went back to searching, and Bingo. Someone did register a birth certificate for a Duncan Eagle fifty-eight days after your birth."

Travis's left eyebrow arched. "But, finding his birth certificate doesn't prove this Duncan Eagle is my brother. Eagle happens to be a common Blackfeet name."

"The document didn't list a father, only the mother, so we can't be positive, but at least we now know it is a possibility. What was your mother's name?"

"Kanti."

"That's not the name on the certificate."

"If he is your identical twin, then you were born prematurely and this Duncan came along two months later."

"Unbelievable. But it might be logical. Aunt Winona told me my father beat my mother just before she delivered me. Said she never expected me to live because I was premature and so tiny. Maybe that Browning woman did raise a twin. But if she did, how did she get him? Why didn't my mother tell me? And, why would my brother want to kill me? He doesn't even know me. None of this makes any sense."

"I can't begin to guess, but at least we know a brother is possible," Joella said. They both looked at each other with no idea where to start the search. If the brother were abandoned or given away, no records of any kind would exist.

Travis's lips tightened. "Okay, we know this Duncan exists, but how the devil can we find him? We don't know what his name is for sure. If he is my brother, did he keep the Eagle name, use the last name of the woman who adopted him, or maybe that of a husband if she married later? I doubt it was a legal adoption, but if so, the court always sealed the records in those days. It doesn't sound very hopeful."

Joella reached out and took his hand. "I'm not quitting yet. Doubt I can find any adoption records, but I'll check just in case. Most important, we now know how *your* semen could have been found in the victim. MM did not need to go through the garbage."

I know, and it should be reassuring, but the implausibility of the entire situation is so mind-boggling I just can't believe it.

~ ~ ~

"Here you go, Travis," Jaxson said, placing the Reuben on the table.

The tangy sauerkraut aroma made Joella's mouth water. "Jaxson, please bring me one of those too. Where is Ma tonight?"

Before he could answer the front door

opened, the glow from the streetlight framed Ma's chubby little figure. She spotted them, grinned and waved. "I'll be right over as soon as I get a beer." Moments later, she sat at their table, Coors in hand. "You two look mighty glum. Is it bad news?"

"No," Travis said, "We actually had a bit of excellent news but then we flew headfirst into a brick wall. We're trying to decide where to go from here."

"Tell me about it, Honey. Maybe I can help."

Travis related the entire story. "Because it certainly wasn't a legal adoption, we don't know anything about him—or any idea how to track him down. I'd like to draw him out and get him to brag more and maybe we could trip him up, but he only writes when he wants to gloat. We can't make contact that way."

Ma sipped her beer a moment, her face pensive. After a moment, she looked at Travis, her eyes bright. "Didn't he tell you in the first letter *not* to contact the newspaper or he would quit writing."

"Yes. The newspaper doesn't know anything about the notes. The newspaper *and* the police department," Travis said, grimacing at the reminder he might lose his job.

Ma wore a sly grin. "That's my point. We know he'll be reading the *Tribune* to see if you were listening and if the police are making any progress on the case. Why don't you put an ad in the classified and tell him you know who he is?"

For a nanosecond, Travis's face went blank. Then, he jumped up and kissed Ma on the brow. "Ma, you're a genius. The arrogant bastard might bite on that."

"He might at that," Joella said, "depending on how you word it. What are you going to say?"

"I have no idea. The guy is smart, and he does not want contact. I'll give it some thought tonight. Whatever it is, I'll have to make him mad enough to want to answer."

Joella scowled. "Have you thought of this? If he is mad enough, he might come after you now rather than waiting for the police to catch you."

CHAPTER 43

At home, Travis was thankful Marion had left a post-it note saying she wouldn't be home for dinner. She and Cora were eating out. Without her constant complaining, he'd have time to think about writing the ad. He opened his laptop and gawked at it. His mind was as blank as the screen on the monitor. Later that night, his nightmares offered an abundant selection of thoughts—none suitable for print. He had only an inkling of what to write when he left for work the next morning. Drizzling soggy fog sprayed on the windshield while the steady rhythm of the wipers matched the ideas flipping back and forth in his head. *Hot damn, that might work.*

~ ~ ~

By the time Travis arrived at the police station and parked, the rain had ceased, the sun momentarily peeking through a hole in the clouds. He walked toward the building, dodging the water-filled potholes that reflected dark clouds undulating across the sky. Lost in his thoughts of how to word the ad, he stepped in a deep puddle, luminous with leaked engine oil. He felt the water squish in his shoe. *Shit.* Once inside his office, he hung his damp jacket on a coat rack and feeling his wet sock, he kicked off his shoe. He booted his laptop. While the idea was fresh in his mind, he started to type; once the words began, one followed another rapidly. When he finished, he read it over twice, made a few changes and hit print. He put his wet shoe back on, took the draft to Joella's office and laid the paper in front of her. "What do you think?"

She picked up the sheet and read aloud. "Duncan, I know who you are. You're such a coward you are afraid to talk to your own brother. Why don't you call? The number's in the book. You can buy throwaway phones anywhere, stupid."

Joella laid the note on her desk. "If that doesn't make him angry, nothing can. But will he call you?"

"I don't know, but it's the only thing I can think of. He's too smart to stay on any telephone long. He'll know the phone company can triangulate any calls these days. If he does make contact, he'll use a pay phone—if he can find one—and make it very brief. My only hope is to keep him talking long enough to get a lead of some kind. If I'm lucky, maybe he'll answer a question."

Joella cupped her chin between her thumb

and forefinger, and handed him the note. "It's worth a try."

~ ~ ~

Travis read the ad in the Tribune the next day and every day after for a week. MM didn't call. *Guess he didn't take the bait.* With no other ideas in mind, he was crestfallen. *How the hell do you find someone who doesn't want to be found? Damn, I've got to find him before he strikes again.* Desperate, he sat staring out his office window. Taking the last gulp of coffee from a McDonald's takeout he'd brought with him that morning, he tossed the cup in the trash. It bounced off the rim and, as he leaned over to retrieve it, the glimmer of an idea struck.

Zach stuck his head through the door. "Anything new?"

"I'm working on something now. Might need your help but haven't developed the idea yet. Talk to you later."

After Zach closed the door, Travis's mind returned to the idea that burst into his head when he tossed the McDonald's cup. Everyone goes to a convenience store for gas, coffee and more. All the stores have surveillance cameras and the police often view their tapes. A grimace formed on his face. *I know just who to search for. Me!* Then it dawned on him that he'd most likely find more of 'me' than he would MM. The thought turned his stomach sour. But if he got lucky and spotted MM, maybe he could catch a distinctive piece of clothing, a tattoo or with luck, a car.

Travis used his laptop webcam to take his

picture and printed it. He gazed at the photo, his mind spurting over new thoughts. After a few moments, he shook his head and tore the picture in half. *Which convenience store?* The possibilities were astronomical and he decided to postpone the idea—at least for a while. Any investigation covering that much territory might leak back to Captain Walker. *I can do it later if nothing else arises.*

~ ~ ~

A few days later, Travis prepared to go home after a dreary day of petty crimes. His phone rang. "Detective Eagle," he said. Silence. "Hello, may I help you?" He heard only heavy breathing. His heart raced. *It's him—has to be.* "Talk to me. We're brothers."

A raspy voice snarled, "I don't like phones."

"Okay, so you don't like phones. Just tell me why your consistent, peculiar mutilation?"

The line went dead. Travis rushed down the hall. "Joella," he said, his voice breaking. "He called."

"What did he say?"

"Nothing. He wouldn't talk—claimed he didn't like telephones. I asked him a question, and the line went dead."

"Do you think he'll call again?"

"I doubt it."

"Did his voice sound like that of anyone you may have talked to at Ma's?"

"No. But if we look similar, he has never been in Ma's place. She would have noticed that right away. He must have had someone else get the matchbook."

Travis exchanged glances with Joella and

added, "Yes, the voice did sound a little familiar—like mine."

CHAPTER 44

Travis felt discouraged almost to the point of desperation when he left the office. Driving through his Third Avenue green tunnel had done nothing to relax him. He dreaded facing Marion. Their evenings had disintegrated into episodes of maniacal madness. When he opened the door, he almost tripped over her large brocade suitcase sitting on the floor. She came out of the bedroom carrying a matching overnight case and a tote bag.

"Are you taking a trip?"

"Yes. I can't stand your constant harping or this damn wigwam any longer."

"Are you leaving me?"

A malicious sneer crossed her face. "No, mighty Chief. You're not getting rid of your responsibility to me that easy. I'm going to a health spa in British Columbia. I need to relax, lose a few pounds and get back in shape. Their

273

fitness program is great and builds from week to week."

"'Week to week?' How long are you staying?"

"A month, but I may do a little shopping before I come home."

"How do you expect I can pay for an extended stay in a place like that? How much is it?"

"Don't worry. I received a new credit card last week. The others were maxed out." The words barely out of her mouth, she took her cases and slammed out the door.

Travis sank onto the couch, his jaw clenched, still too distraught about MM to worry about his looming financial disaster. Fighting sleep brought on by a load of mental exhaustion, his mind reverted to some way he might trap the serial killer, dreams again continuing his thought process.

Travis awoke with a start. *What was that?* He listened a moment. *Did Marion come back?* Walking to the front door, a white envelope on the floor caught his eye. He flung the door open and ran into the hall. Empty. Rushing outside into the darkness, he saw no one but his next-door neighbors returning home with bags of groceries. They waved but he didn't return the gesture, hurrying back inside. Picking up the envelope with a tissue, he slit it open. Like the other notes, hand-printed on cheap tablet paper.

Who the hell are you calling stupid, you fucking flatfoot. You haven't even solved the first murder yet, and it sure didn't take a genius to figure out you had a twin even though our dear ol' father got rid of me days after I was born. Sold me to a fucking blonde nymphomaniac to replace the brat she'd just lost. I graduated from sucking milk to sucking her tit and fingering her to a climax two or three times a day. Then she screwed the priest on Sunday, came home, and beat the shit out of me to soothe her guilty conscience. Just because you were born first doesn't give you the damn right to make my life a living hell. I figure it's time you shared the misery. See you in the paper soon, buddy boy—just as soon as the stupid police figure out the DNA is yours. Maybe I need to give them some more help.

MM

Travis collapsed in a chair, his emotions a bubbling cauldron. The note confirmed what Joella suspected, an identical twin brother. *Why didn't my mother tell me?* He couldn't believe she would give him away—not under any circumstances. Baffled by her keeping such a dark secret, he nevertheless felt a glow of optimism. The note also provided a bonus. His ad in the paper had been a total bluff. He didn't know he had a twin; it was only a possibility. *And now, I understand why that particular body mutilation. Joella had guessed right—a sexual psychopath.*

Travis could hardly wait to arrive at the

station to tell Joella about the letter. Her car was in the parking lot and he went straight to her office, bursting through the door. "Great news, Joella. We hit pay dirt with our *Tribune* ad. Not only do we know for sure that I have an identical twin brother, but also why each victim had the same unusual mutilation and why the killings were always on a Sunday.

"How? What on earth happened to confirm so much information?"

"MM delivered a note to my apartment last night; it was full of details." He handed the plastic-enclosed note to her. "Read it."

Joella scanned the letter. "Has a way with words, doesn't he? Getting braver too. Now we know his motive: Anger Excitation. It's usually referred to as sexual sadist, as I suspected. He gains some kind of gratification through his victim's suffering so isn't in any hurry for the woman to die fast." Her brow wrinkled. "They like to spend a considerable amount of time with their prey climaxing again and again before the poor victim dies. I abhor them. All murderers are despicable; but sexual sadists are the most heinous of all." She shivered, goose pimples sprouting across her bare arms.

The vein in Travis's forehead throbbed as he reached for the note.

"I'm sorry; I know how you must feel finding out he is your twin. After living such a horrific life, he stood little chance of not being mentally warped."

"I know, but I can't help feeling guilty."

Joella looked straight into his dark eyes. "Travis, it is not your fault. If anyone is to blame, it is your father and he's dead."

"That doesn't make me feel better. However, the note might solve another long held mystery for me."

"How so?"

"If I have an identical twin, it might account for all those occasions when I had body aches and pains for no reason. Days I limped or my hand hurt and I didn't know why. They've happened all my life. The pain might last a day or two and then go away. Marion always told me I had an over active imagination and needed to see a shrink—there was a time she almost convinced me. And I understand now why I might get nauseous when I see his victims."

Joella glanced at Travis. "Seems hard to believe, but I've read stories claiming the same thing from other identical twins. I don't know much about it other than reading where a few studies proved nothing positive, one way or the other. At least as far as I know."

"You know the thing that really hurts me is how often I begged my mother for a baby brother when I was young. Here I had one and didn't know it. How could a mother keep that from her son?"

"I don't know, Travis. It doesn't seem normal behavior for a mother. Especially one as loving as you've said your mother was."

Travis winced. *His mother was wonderful. But why, why didn't she tell me?*

~ ~ ~

After work Travis, Joella and Zach met at Jakes to discuss their next move. Porter was in

Ulm so they felt safe going to Jakes. Zach had a hot date so the meeting would be brief as far as he was concerned. Travis waited for their drinks to arrive before speaking. "The only thing I can think of is to place a second ad and hope to draw him out before he strikes again."

Joella stirred a packet of Equal into her coffee. "What could you say this time?"

"I have no idea. I'll give it some more thought tonight."

Zach shifted in his chair. "Maybe it's time you bring the captain in on this?"

"What? And get me fired before we even catch MM. Zach, I already told Joella if the worst happens, you and she never knew I withheld evidence from the department. This was all my idea. I'll tell the captain I found the matchbook and didn't report it, and I'll tell him I neglected to state that Burton swore it was me he saw coming out of Aliyev's apartment. I don't want either of you involved in any way. Understand?"

"Okay, if that's what you want," Zach said.

Joella bit her lip and gazed off into the distance.

Travis sat silent for several minutes. "I'll swing by and bring Ma up to date before I go home to try to think of an agenda for the ad tonight—sandwich it in between my bleeding blondes." Hearing the mocking twang in his voice, he laughed. "I'm getting so use to their visits; I think I'd miss the little darlings."

CHAPTER 45

The next morning Travis met Joella in the parking lot and accompanied her inside. "I couldn't think of anything to put in the ad," he said, "other than asking him to meet me face to face."

"That's too damn risky."

"I know, but it's worth a shot, if he won't contact me. What else can we do?" He went to his office and typed: If I'm so dumb, why are you afraid of me? Why don't you meet me, brother to brother? You name the time and place. I'll come alone. Unarmed. Travis printed the note and returned to Joella's office handing her the typed article. "What do you think?"

She read it and dropped the paper. "What are you thinking? That's not only risky, it's downright dangerous. He'll come prepared to kill you."

"Yes, but if I know it, I can take care of myself."

Joella frowned. "If I can't talk you out of this lunacy, I'll follow as backup."

"No, I don't want you involved."

"I am involved, and I don't want to hear anything more about it."

Travis placed the ad at once and sat back to wait. A week went by. MM didn't call. That night when he went home, another note awaited.

You fucking flatfoot. You must think I'm some kind of idiot. Sure, you'll come alone. I'll believe that when pigs fly. Your fucking games are boring me!
MM

Travis felt sick, his saliva acrid. *Oh, shit. He's too mad now. He won't make contact again.* Sleep never came easily anymore, but he lay on the bed to await his floating apparitions. *They are the only dependable things in my life these days.* But his home life was certainly more pleasant with Marion gone. All the peace and quiet also gave him more time to dwell on his catastrophic circumstances.

In the morning, he rose and laughed. While his 'parading blondes' usually gave Travis nightmares—this time they actually gave him an idea. *A good one, I think, but damn it, I'll have to tell the captain everything in order for the plan to work. Hope he'll let me keep my job long enough to put it into action.*

Arriving at work, he stopped at Joella's office. "I'm on my way to tell Captain Walker the entire story including how I withheld evidence from the department."

The distorted expression on Joella's face registered annoyance. "I suggested that earlier but you didn't want to do it. Why now?"

"I received another note from MM." He took the plastic sleeve holding the note from his pocket and laid it on her desk.

She read it quickly. "That didn't go well. Seems like the last ad put him over the edge."

"That's what I'm worried about. I made him too mad. The next victim's death will be on me."

"That's crazy, Travis. You're not responsible for that psychopathic brother of yours. He'd kill again, regardless of what you said to him."

"I know, but I can't help how I feel. I came up with an idea this morning that might bring MM out into the open. If the captain approves, I'll fill you in on the plan."

~ ~ ~

Standing in front of the captain's door, Travis hesitated a moment, then took a deep breath and knocked. *Hope he doesn't fire my ass on the spot.*

"C'mon in," a deep husky voice boomed. No one ever had to ask Walker to repeat anything. He had the voice of a hog calling contestant—a winning contestant.

Travis opened the door and found the captain hunched over his walnut roll-top desk, an antique from the 1800s. He'd inherited the piece from his grandfather years ago. It needed refurbishing badly but Walker refused to have it done. He cherished every scratch and spot, often rubbing his finger over the place as if feeling his grandfather's presence.

Travis sat in a straight-back wooden chair opposite Walker, not saying anything, waiting for the captain to look at him.

When Captain Walker finished shuffling the papers in his hands, he raised he head and smiled, flashing even white teeth. "Hey, Travis. Haven't seen much of you lately. Know you've had your hands full and figured the last thing you needed was me breathing down your neck. The missus has hounded me for weeks to have you and Marion over to dinner. I told her you were busy trying to find our serial killer, and she understands. But let's make it soon."

"That sounds great, but it will have to wait awhile. Marion left for British Columbia. Went to some kind of fancy health and fitness spa where they pamper you with all those idiotic things like mudpacks. Hell, I could have gotten her one of those from the department's parking lot."

Walker grinned, and then turned serious. "Yeah, women. We'll do it when she gets back, and in the meantime, let's go fishing."

"I'd like that—as soon as I nab this serial killer. That's what I came to talk about."

"You'll get him."

"Thanks for the vote of confidence, I need it. I know the mayor is having fits. He about burned the wires up with his last call to me—know he's been on your back too."

"Don't worry about the mayor. I can handle him. Our serial killer must be one sharp guy to kill four women and leave no clues."

Travis felt the flush creeping onto his face,

the sweat beading on his temple. "Afraid that's not quite true, Captain. He has left clues. I didn't report them."

The captain's face turned crimson, his eyes bulging. "What the hell are you talking about?"

Travis took a deep breath and poured out the entire story: his blackouts and fear he might be the killer, his visiting blondes, the notes he'd been receiving from MM, his ads in the *Tribune*, Betsy's matchbook, the paid-for eyewitness and that the last victim had semen. His. When he came to the identical twin part of the story, the captain's jaw dropped. Walker seemed stunned, unable to speak for a moment.

Once the captain gathered his wits, he barked out his words. "Is that all?"

"Yes, everything except my plan to catch him."

"To hell with your plan," he bellowed. "You've been withholding evidence. What the shit is the matter with you; I can have your badge for that."

Travis shifted in his chair, and waited a moment until the captain's complexion began to return to its normal ruddy glow. Walker never stayed angry long. "I know I was wrong, Captain, but if you'll give me a minute to tell you my idea, I think you'll agree it's our best chance of nabbing this guy—my brother."

When Travis said 'brother,' the captain appeared to calm somewhat. "You're in a hell of a situation, aren't you?"

"Not really, sir. My brother is a sexual psychopath and I intend to stop him."

"Okay, let's hear your idea. But know this, if it doesn't work, your job is in jeopardy and you could be prosecuted."

Travis forced down the golf ball sized lump in his throat and laid out the entire plan.

Walker's face softened. "That sounds like a workable idea. I'll agree to it, but now you'll be putting your life on the line as well as your job."

"Yes, sir, I know. Thank you again, Captain. Appreciate your understanding. I'll get on it right away."

~ ~ ~

Travis stopped at Joella's office, his heart still flip flopping.

She sat staring into space as she had when he left. "How did it go?"

"Better than I thought—or deserve. The captain is going out on a limb for me. Now I must catch MM. I'll be back after I write something; I'll bring it over for you to read."

~ ~ ~

Travis sat gawking at his laptop willing his fingers to write words of wisdom. No words appeared. Rain beat a steady rhythm on his window as chain lightning illuminated the sky into what seemed like constant flickering daylight; he could see the lilac bushes across the street, the illegally parked cars. Another bolt struck, rattled the windowpanes and startled him from his trance, the weather mimicking his torturous thoughts. *I must word the newspaper article just right or MM will never bite.* Travis brooded over his computer for what seemed like hours, the gloom outside doing nothing to inspire him. Finally, he stood and gazed out the window, his mind still in a daze. *Damn. I need to focus. This piece isn't going to write itself. Time is running out.*

He returned to his desk and sifted through the mountain of notes and files on MM, searching out the many details he had withheld from the newspaper. Organizing his notes, he began typing. He described his role in the investigation, making him sound like a Ned Buntline turn-of-the-century dime-store novel hero. He elaborated about the killer's many personal letters to Detective Eagle. *Seeing this story in print with all the details may push him into action.*

When Travis reread the description of his own involvement, self-loathing for the boasting, conceited tone of his role burned through his veins. He needed to make his brother even angrier, outraged enough to commit one specially selected murder—Detective Eagle's wife. *He'll want revenge for the article. She is the logical victim for his twisted mind.* Finally finishing the article, he read it over a couple of times. *That ought to do it.* Then he added the final sentence: Detective Eagle is anxious to solve these crimes because he has a beautiful blonde wife to protect. Travis hit print.

Removing the paper from the printer, he went to Joella's office and handed it to her. "What do you think?"

She turned her laptop off and nodded occasionally as she read. "This might work." Then she apparently read the last sentence because her mouth fell agape. "You can't say that. It's like painting a target on your wife's forehead."

"That's the idea."

"Yes, but how will Marion respond to being a decoy? I don't think she'll like it one damn bit."

"You're right, she'd blow a gasket. But that isn't a problem; she won't know anything about it. She left for a month's stay at a fancy spa in British Columbia. Her timing couldn't be better. If she hadn't, this plan wouldn't have worked. Fortunately, she won't see it in the newspaper or know anything about it not that she ever reads anything more than the sales anyway. What do you think of the article?"

"I think it's damn dangerous—but if you're determined, it might be worth a try."

"I don't know how else to draw this maniac out before he strikes again."

"When this article hits the street and he's ready to make his move, he'll check out your apartment and there *must* be a wife there or he won't show. He's never seen Marion. I'll put on a blonde wig and be the decoy."

"No you won't. No point you risking your life too."

"You need a woman there, and it is going to be me. I won't hear anything more about it. Understand?"

Travis lowered his head. "Okay. Guess you're right. But I don't like it."

"When do you think this will go down?"

"Who knows? The newspaper will be thrilled with the new details and are sure to run the article Friday. He could make his move any time after that, but I expect he'll stay true to his MO and strike Sunday. His motive for killing that day is powerful, and those similar cases on the ViCAP were all murdered on a Sunday too."

"Okay. I'll come over as soon as I can."

"I have only one bedroom; you can use it and I'll sleep on the couch."

"Fine. Run it by the captain to see if he will approve of me acting as the decoy."

"Will do. He agreed to my plan, and the only new part is your participation. I'm sure he'll be okay with it because it's our best chance of snagging my brother." A deep frown furrowed his brow. "Damn, I hate saying that word. I begged my Mother for years for a brother and now that I have him, I'm trying to put him on death row."

"Better him than you."

CHAPTER 46

Travis went to bed early, almost eager to see the return of his nightly procession rather than suffer the turmoil that gripped his brain. Awaking after only a few hours of sleep, he lay staring into the darkness. Tossing and turning, he unscrambled the covers but was unable to go back to sleep. He glanced out the window, the inky blackness of night seeping past the drape edges.

Finally, he rose, went to the kitchen and started the coffee maker. After downing three cups of coffee, he heard the newspaper boy in the hall. He grabbed the *Tribune* and opened it. The article stared at him from the front page in large print. *MM can't miss I have a blonde wife. He hates me so what better victim than the woman I love.* Travis laughed to himself. *The woman I love, what a farce.* He felt more confident than he had in months, but he had a strange ache in the depths of his gut. *If we had only been raised together...*

~ ~ ~

At the police station, he stopped at Joella's office. He noticed a large suitcase by the door. "Are you coming over tonight?"

"No. I'm going now. It isn't Sunday, but this is bound to be special for him. Who can say he'll wait for Sunday or night. He might even stake out the apartment. Some of his crimes were possibly done during the day, and he might change his MO to get your wife."

"Okay, I'll go with you."

"You can't. You're supposed to be at work. He doesn't know me."

"I'm not going to let you be there by yourself."

"Don't intend to. I talked to Zach last night and he's arranged to be in the vacant apartment across the hall listening to the bug he's planting in your apartment as we speak. We spoke to the captain and he's agreed with this part of the plan too. He's sending Watson with Zach. The captain has already sent our stakeout guys to case the neighborhood, get familiar with the streets. They're in place and most likely bored, sick of cold coffee and stale doughnuts by now."

"Sounds like you've given this a lot of thought and put it into action before I even got here."

"Zach and I thought of the idea last night after work and talked to the captain early this morning. I got your address from the personnel department."

"Okay, but I still don't like your being involved." He fished in his pocket, removing a key from a key ring. "Here, get a copy made on your way to the apartment. Watson can slip away and bring it to me at the station. If MM is watching already, it would seem suspicious if I had to knock on my own door to get in. Keep the door locked."

"That doesn't make sense. We're trying to give him every opportunity, not lock him out."

"Remember the door was locked at all the victim's homes," Travis said. "Lock it."

"Okay, okay, stop worrying. You know I can take care of myself and Zach's an excellent cop; he won't let anything happen to me."

Travis caught Zach in the hall as he was leaving. "Joella told me about the plan you both hatched. Are you sure you want to go along with this?"

"Of course, partner. What kind of a friend would I be if I didn't? This is certainly not the right occasion to tell you this but hard to find the proper time these days." He wore a silly grin, his eyes crinkling. "I know how you hate wearing a monkey suit, but since I acted as best man at your wedding, I think you should return the favor."

Travis's face broke into a twisted grin. "You're kidding. Mr. Big Time Bachelor going down in flames. Cynthia, I presume."

"Who else? We've been keeping steady company ever since she strutted into Betsy's in that purple eye buster as you called it."

"My congratulations," Travis said, slapping Zach on the back. "I look forward getting to know her. She must be quite a gal to have captured a love 'em and leave 'em guy like you. When is the big day?"

"We haven't set the actual date yet. We both wanted to wait until this nightmare with MM is over. Didn't want our day ruined by the best man running off to catch a serial killer."

~ ~ ~

Travis returned to his office, but he might as well have gone home for all the good it did. He paced, twitched, looked out the window and then gazed at his blank computer screen accomplishing little. Every few minutes he glared at the wall clock as if willing it to move, then double-checking the time with his watch to see if the clock had stopped. *Where is Watson with the damn key?* He called Zach and learned Watson had left two hours earlier. *Something must be wrong. I'm going home, key or no key.*

Opening the door of his pickup, Travis spied Watson pull into the parking lot. Watson stepped out, strolled over while drinking a cup of coffee, and handed Travis the key.

"Damn it, you almost missed me."

"Chill out, dude, I'm here now."

"What took you so long? Zach said you left two hours ago."

Watson winked. "The tiny, cute waitress at McDonald's was mighty hot. Couldn't leave until I got her crib address."

Travis clenched his teeth and glared at the pleased-with-himself expression on Watson's face. "What's the hell is the matter with you? You're on duty. You aren't going to be a cop long being this irresponsible."

Watson only shrugged and sauntered back toward his vehicle. Travis shook his head and turned on the ignition.

~ ~ ~

Anxiety made it difficult for Travis to stay within the speed limit. He didn't take his usual green tunnel route but drove home the shortest way. Entering the building, he stopped to check his mailbox in case MM left a note there instead of under the door. The box had only his normal mail: junk and bills. At his front door, he put the key in the lock and opened it. He stiffened as a blonde Joella flew into his arms almost knocking him over and planting a kiss on his lips.

"Hi, Honey, you're home early. Great, we can have a drink before dinner." Whispering in his ear, she said, "Thought I'd make it look good."

Travis grinned. "I like that idea."

When he entered the apartment, the aroma of pork chops filled his nostrils. Not only had the place been tidied, the table held a bright yellow linen cloth and unlit candles. "Hey, I sure enjoy this 'making it look good,' but you shouldn't have gone to all this trouble."

"Didn't have anything to do so decided I might as well give us an enjoyable wait."

"It'll be 'enjoyable' all right. Pork chops are my favorite food."

"Perfect. We have all the trimmings and chocolate cake for dessert. Know you don't drink anymore, so the 'drink before dinner' was for show. I brought my espresso maker over, and we can have a cup after dessert."

"Sounds great. Did Zach get that bug working?"

"Yes. He called me some time ago to say the system worked fine."

"Great. I saw our backup parked across the street when I came home. Unmarked car and plainclothesmen. Captain Walker sent Conway and Sidney, both good men. Like I said, I'm sure he'll come Sunday but can't depend on it so we need to take every precaution available."

~ ~ ~

Normally Travis had a decent appetite, but he ate to the point where he would have loosened his belt a notch under different circumstances. "That was a fine dinner, Joella. I don't know how you found enough in this kitchen to fix anything. Marion is a defroster, not a cook."

She laughed. "The cupboard was pretty bare so I did a little shopping. Let's have our espresso in the living room."

"Great idea."

She poured two cups and took the steaming mugs into the living room where Travis had put on a CD turned very low. "If you'd rather watch TV, we can."

"Not really. There's isn't anything worth watching these days."

"Have to agree with you there. I don't watch much except the news and sports."

Travis sat on the couch and Joella joined him. "This is very good espresso. Thanks for bringing your machine over. I always liked espresso. Wanted to buy Marion a maker, but she claimed they were too much bother." Travis drained his cup and Joella took the dishes back to the kitchen. He watched her trim figure sashay across the living room. *Damn nice hip action.*

The vision was still fresh in his mind when Joella came running out of the kitchen, her eyes opened wide. "I saw someone outside the window."

CHAPTER 47

Travis grabbed his Glock from his polymer hip holster on the table. When he checked the unmarked car across the street, Sidney gave him a thumbs-up and Travis went back inside. "Everything is okay in front." Joella's white face exaggerated the green eyes, the usual blue glints flashing like traffic signals. "I'll check the backyard, you wait here." In the kitchen, he grabbed the garbage bag and went out the back door.

"Be careful."

Travis didn't answer, but as he left, he noticed her start to pace. He was back in a few minutes. "I didn't see anything unusual or out of place in the backyard. Maybe it was a neighbor."

Joella's frozen facial muscles relaxed and her shoulders dropped.

"We better get some sleep," Travis said. "Do

you want the first shift or the second?"

"Doubt I can sleep, but I'll give it a try. Wake me when it's my turn."

"Will do."

She walked toward the bedroom door. Turning around, she winked and blew him a kiss. "See you in the morning, Chief." Her eyes twinkled with mischief.

Travis laughed. "Yeah, Minnehaha. See you tomorrow." He put his hip holster on the table next to the Lazy Boy. Sitting, he didn't raise the footrest, recline the back or take his shoes off. But, he wasn't sure if his decision to remain fully dressed was prompted by the possible appearance of MM or him weakening and flying to the bedroom like a homing pigeon.

CHAPTER 48

When she shut the door, Joella glanced around the bedroom and pulled the drapes closer together; they were too small and left a gap between them. *You'd think Marion would have noticed that and bought some the right size.* Disgusted with herself for criticizing a lady she'd never met, she slipped out of her shoes placing them beside the bed. She laid her weapon on the nightstand and lay down fully clothed. Joella closed her eyes, but as expected, she tossed and turned, gazed at the ceiling, went to look out the window, blew her nose and finally dozed off when it was nearly time to change shifts. She slept fitfully. Suddenly her eyes flew open. *What was that sound?*

She snatched her Glock and ran out of the bedroom. "Travis?" He wasn't there. Sweat beaded her forehead and her skin crawled.

"Travis," she screamed running to the kitchen.

The room was empty. Joella was about to yell for Zach when she heard a sound at the door and saw the doorknob turning as slowly as the minute hand on her watch. Adrenalin coursed through her veins and she raised her Glock, pointing it at the door.

Travis opened the door and her arm went limp.

"Shit. You scared the hell out of me. Where have you been?"

"I went outside to look around."

"Don't you ever do that again unless you tell me." She inhaled a small gasp of air and wiped her brow. "It's your turn. Go get some sleep."

"There's no way I can sleep. I'll just sit with you."

He needed sleep, but Joella knew it was an argument she couldn't win. He sat in the Lazy Boy, again not kicking back. Joella laid her weapon on the coffee table. They said little and as the hours crawled by, he yawned, his eyelids heavy and closing, then jerking open.

I know he hasn't slept good in weeks. He's exhausted. "Travis, raise your feet and lie back. At least be comfortable. I'm right here." *Maybe he'll doze off.* He did as she suggested and soon his head nodded, a soft snore emanating from his throat. She had pretended to read a novel without noticing she held it upside down. After he fell asleep, she discovered the upside down book and turned it around, still no words entered her brain. The hours crept by as slowly as the ticking clock. Near dawn she went to the kitchen and put the coffee maker on before returning to the couch. The nutty aroma of coffee roused him.

"Damn, I fell asleep. Joella, you should have woken me. Anything happen?"

CHAPTER 49

"Not a thing." Joella answered Travis. "You needed a nap and I was awake, no need for both of us to lose sleep. I'll scramble some eggs for breakfast and then you can go to work."

After eating, Travis went to the station to give the illusion of normalcy. With a serial killer on the loose, working on Saturday would be natural. He worked a few hours, but worry consumed him. He couldn't stay away from the apartment and went back to eat lunch with Joella, which would seem like an ordinary thing to do with his wife.

When Travis returned to work, even the petty criminals seemed to be taking a holiday and dispatch remained silent. He would have preferred to be busy. Too nervous to work, he went to the firing range. He'd lived with guns all his life, was an excellent shot and had qualified for all the weapons he used on the force. *Maybe a little extra practice will come in handy before this day is over.*

~ ~ ~

Joella greeted him at the door when Travis returned to the apartment. "Dinner is almost ready." She knew anxiety most likely filled his mind leaving little room for hunger urges. He'd lost weight lately so she made a big dinner hoping to tempt him. "Do you like New England style pot roast with a lot of vegetables?"

"I love any kind of pot roast. It smells scrumptious. Anything suspicious happen?"

"No, it's been quiet as a cemetery. Other than Sidney and Conway checking in, the only ghost I've talked to is Zach; he's called a couple of times. He can smell dinner cooking and is complaining. Said all they have to eat are energy bars and cold pizza he took with him yesterday. I'd enjoy taking them a home-cooked meal but I don't dare. MM may not be watching, but that would be a dead give-away if he is."

Travis managed to polish off a plate full of food. After dinner, he complimented the cook as she started to clear the table. "No, you cooked dinner; I'll take care of the dishes and cleaning up. Make yourself comfortable in the living room." He loaded the dishwasher and puttered about the kitchen a long time, before joining her on the couch. "You look nice tonight."

"Thanks. It's a new outfit. Knowing what a stylish clothes freak Marion is, thought I'd better look the part."

He grinned. "You didn't need to do that; you

always look nice." After a moment, he turned somber. "Joella, after this mess is over, I don't know what's going to happen. I could go to jail. I'll most likely lose my job. I know the captain will do everything he can to help me, but I will not have him jeopardize his career for me."

Joella felt her complexion blanch as she thought of the consequences.

Travis quickly added, "Guess I could always become another PI. That seems to be what most disgraced cops do these days. Whatever happens, you and Zach are in the clear. As you know, I told the captain I found the matchbook and didn't report it or the paid-for witness who it seems was only a scare tactic anyway. Also told him about having my DNA done, but he does not know *you* saw the results. They have no way of connecting either you or Zach to this case." Joella opened her mouth but before she could speak he added, "And that's the way it is going to stay."

"If that's what you want, but I went into this willingly as did Zach."

"Doesn't matter. I don't want either of you involved."

He stared at the ceiling a moment and then shifted his eyes back to her. "I also want to thank you, again. You've been such a good influence on me. I haven't had a drink since the blackout after MM's second murder and I owe it all to you. Gave a lot of serious thought to our conversations. Your wise counseling about my considering the source and changing the way I respond to others hit the bulls-eye. The shrink was right too. I am an alcoholic. I know that first drink will be my downfall, so there won't be any more 'first drinks.'"

She grinned to make light of the situation. "I didn't do anything special. Just repeated some of the smarts I learned during my months of therapy. See, that's two cures for the price of one," she said with a half-hearted laugh. "You'd have eventually come to the same conclusion. I know your character is too commanding to remain a drunk."

"I don't know about that. My father was a raging alcoholic, which means I inherited the predisposition for alcoholism. I don't know if you're aware of it or not, but Indians have the largest percentage of alcoholics than any other ethnic group."

Joella noticed his shoulders droop and assumed he was remembering those dark days of childhood whippings.

A moment later, he straightened. "That's why I was so determined not to drink and I didn't. But when Marion quit her job to begin a career of shopping, I let my anger get the best of me. Talking to you made me see the light. I can brush Porter off easier too. Marion and I still argue over money, but I don't run to Ma's."

"That's wonderful. I'm proud of you." Joella sat forward, shifting the pillow behind her back. "I want to thank you as well. If it hadn't been for you, I'd still be at odds with my family."

"I didn't do anything."

"Your conversation about needing family and recommending I get in touch with mine to reestablish contact was the motivation I needed. The entire family is tight-knit now. It changed my life. I'm more grounded."

"Glad I could help." Once again, Travis put on a CD turned low so they could hear any strange sounds. He sat next to her on the couch and they waited... But like last night, MM didn't show.

The evening grew late, and Joella said, "Maybe that line about your blonde wife didn't register."

"I doubt it. He is too sharp to miss that. He's waiting for Sunday. His motive for killing that day is powerful; according to his note, that was the day his mother beat the shit out of him after having had sex with the priest." Travis checked his watch. "Do you want the first or second shift tonight?"

"Doesn't matter. I'm too unstrung to sleep anyway."

Travis checked in with Sidney and Conway.

When he closed his phone, Joella said, "Did they have news?"

"No, just the regular routine: boredom and tired of cold coffee."

Having discussed all the important points of pertinent information, their dialogue began to lag, the air now filling with a different kind of tension. Travis stood. Then he inspected the windows and the door. He fidgeted with the pillows and the CDs stacked by the player before he sat again. Joella brushed her hair back several times and tugged at her blouse. She smoothed her skirt a second time and he flinched when he caught her eyeing his bulging crotch. Joella felt her face flush. She tilted her chin upward and locked eyes with his.

Hesitating only a moment, Travis leaned over and kissed her lightly, and then abruptly backed away. He stared deeply into her eyes and then planted a savage kiss on her lips. She responded with an intensity to match, her fingers tugging at the buttons on his shirt. They tore at each other's garments as they made for the bedroom, shedding the blonde wig and their clothing helter-skelter across the floor. Their exploding passion overcame all police training and common sense, leaving no room for words.

~ ~ ~

Afterward, Travis said, "I'm sorry, Joclla. I didn't mean for that to happen, but I've wanted you for so long. I just had to kiss you one time."

She knew his guilt most likely ate away any feeling of ecstasy he might have felt. "Please don't apologize—I wanted you too."

"Yes, but I'm married. It isn't fair to you."

"Let me worry about that."

He brushed the hair back from her brow. His eyes wandered to the soft curve of her breast and he kissed each nipple lightly. He ran his hands down her thigh, and she felt the muscles in her leg tighten, Her hips arched in response to his touch. He was about to mount her again when his cell rang.

"What the hell," he said, snatching the phone. "Detective Eagle."

Zach's laughter boomed across the line. "I knew you two had the hots for one another, but will you pa-lease take pity on me. I'm horny as hell just listening to you two—and *I* don't have any female company."

Travis closed his eyes. "Shit."

Joella rose up on her elbows, the sheet falling away and exposing her breasts, nipples standing at attention. "What's the matter?"

"Zach bugged my apartment, remember?"

Joella's face flushed. "Oh my God."

"It's a damn good thing MM didn't strike tonight." Zach interrupted. "He'd have had a front row seat to the best show in town, and you two wouldn't have heard the curtain come down."

In spite of how their loss of control could have gotten them killed, Joella felt herself glow with unadulterated contentment. She closed her eyes. *But...that cannot happen again—at least while we're on duty.*

Before he dressed, Travis checked with Sidney and Conrad again. Everything remained quiet; he sat on the bed and planted a light kiss on her brow, quickly backing away. "You sleep and I'll stand watch."

She brushed his hair back and wrapped her arms around him. I'm so strung out. Hold me a minute or two before you go. Maybe then I can sleep."

CHAPTER 50

Cocooned under a satiny down coverlet that cuddled every curve of her body, Joella stirred. Still half-asleep, sweet memories of last night drifted through her mind and made her smile. *That was fantastic—did I really see fireworks?* She felt his arm draped tenderly across her hip and a warm fuzzy glow flowed through her body.

The rasping rumble of a distant garbage truck hurtled her brain into consciousness. *Oh my God. We fell asleep.* Now fully vigilant, she heard a strange and unfamiliar sound outside. She carefully lifted Travis's arm and slid out of bed. He didn't awaken. Not bothering to dress, Joella grabbed her weapon from the nightstand and ran out to the living room window. She saw nothing suspicious, but checked in with Conway and Sidney who reported all was quiet. Then the dreadful actuality seeped in. *This is*

Sunday.

Joella looked at her watch. Only three o'clock. She gathered her and Travis's clothes spread across the living room floor. After she dressed, she took his clothes and quietly laid them in the chair near the bed. He still slept soundly. He'd been fatigued for weeks and she decided to let him sleep.

In the kitchen, the coffee pot held one cup of yesterday's brew. She warmed the stale coffee in the microwave and put on a new pot. Her nerves on edge, she dashed to the windows and door listening for any microscopic sound. Peering out the kitchen window, Joella caught the first pale beams of sunlight breaking the horizon. The rich rays streamed through the windowpane. Pink, blue and green shafts of light danced about the kitchen as the sun glinted off the crystal prisms hanging in the window. The room was alive with dazzling color contrasting the angst in the pit of her stomach.

Joella poured a cup of fresh coffee and sat at the kitchen table lost in anxious stress. Absentmindedly she took a gulp of coffee almost dropping the cup. Her throat was on fire, scorching away all thoughts of ecstasy as the ugly door of reality blasted opened. *Good God. The captain will fire us both.* She sat a long time staring into the unknown. *What can we do? Zach isn't a gossip—our secret is safe with him but what about the recording?* Travis was too proud to ask Zach to help. *Damn it,* he won't—but I will. I'll talk to him as soon as I can. He'd do anything for Travis, maybe "accidentally" losing some of the evidence. Been* *done before by more powerful people than cops.* With the seed of a plan now blossoming, she returned to the present, but one thought kept battering her brain. *This is Sunday.*

CHAPTER 51

When the aroma of fresh, strong coffee found his nostrils, Travis opened his eyes, a silly grin pasted on his face. For the first time in months, the lovely Joella had negated his prancing blondes. He reached for her but she was gone, the sheets cold where the soft impression from her body remained, the scent of her green apple shampoo lingered on the pillowcase. Still half-asleep, he remembered comforting her last night. He stretched lazily, the vision of last night whispering through his mind, the feel of her soft lips on his. The tantalizing aroma of bacon and eggs jarred him alert and his mouth watered. Flipping the sheet back, he dressed and went to the kitchen. "Good morning. Did you get any sleep?"

She looked up, her eyes bright, a faint smile on her lips as though the magic of last night filled her memory. "I sure did, Chief. But under the circumstances it *cannot* happen again."

His facial muscles turned flaccid as if he already had designs for a repeat performance. "What are you talking about?"

"We both fell asleep."

"Shit. When I woke up, I thought you had decided to take the other shift."

"No, I awoke early and dressed. We could have both gotten our throats slit last night which is what I meant, it cannot happen again. We were on duty."

Travis started to speak but quickly closed his mouth. After a moment, he added, "It sure as hell will not happen again."

In spite of her angst, a small giggle escaped her lips. "I'll take a rain check though."

The light blush of her complexion caught his eye and a Cheshire grin spread across his face. "I think that can be arranged."

Joella beamed a warm smile, but quickly turned serious. "Today is the day. It's Sunday." She shivered. "I thought we'd eat in here this morning. This yellow kitchen is so cheery, and I desperately need a reminder that life can be uplifting, even in the midst of such enormous evil. I will be here all day, but I think you'd better go to the station for a few hours or anywhere else."

"I'd planned to spend the day with you. It's Sunday and he won't expect me to be gone."

"Can't take a chance. He wants Marion and he might not come if you're here. We need to give him plenty of time to find her alone."

"I don't like leaving you by yourself."

"I'm not. Sidney and Conway are across the street, and Zach and Watson are only a few feet away listening to everything that goes on in here. Remember?" This time, she laughed without blushing.

~ ~ ~

The moment Travis finished eating, Joella shoved him toward the door, winking. "Zach is right, we were lucky MM didn't change his MO and come Saturday night. We'd both be modeling a bit of duct tape." For their possible audience of one, Joella put on a good show handing him a long grocery list and kissing him on the cheek. He nodded when she raised her voice louder than normal and said, "Take your time, honey. I'm not in a hurry."

"Okay, I'll go," he whispered. "I'll check for a thumbs-up from Sidney and Conway on the way."

CHAPTER 52

Joella had put on a brave front while Travis kept her company, but after he left, her skin crawled—every little sound a threat. She returned to the kitchen tidying the room to keep busy. Pouring another cup of coffee, she tried to relax but kept imaging a noise outside and made several trips to the window to check. The open curtains revealed nothing. She carried her cup to the living room and sat on the couch. *What was that?* Joella jumped to her feet, grabbed her Glock and ran to the window. Out of the corner of her eye, she swore she'd seen a movement rounding the corner of the building. The stakeout car was in place. Other than the residents' parked cars, the street seemed empty and silent. Numbing silence, yet a symphony of creaks, clicks, snaps and cracks played a concerto in her mind. *Get a grip on it—you're not going to be of any use this way.* She forced herself to sit and watch television without realizing what filled the screen. Finally, she shut off the TV and went to the kitchen. *Another cup of coffee...*

CHAPTER 53

Travis stopped to check the mailbox just in case. He found Saturday's mail he'd forgotten and flipped through each piece with the tip of his fingernail. One white envelope stood out, a statement from a new credit card company. "Shit." He jammed the mail back in the box scraping his knuckles.

On the porch, he shaded his eyes looking at the sky as if checking the weather. For two days he'd parked his truck across the street from the apartment to have an excuse to walk by the unmarked police car. As he passed, Conrad tilted his coffee cup in salute; Travis didn't break stride.

Travis almost ran through the grocery aisles flinging items into the basket. He arrived back at the apartment breathless. "Nothing?"

"Not a thing."

~ ~ ~

After lunch, Joella told him she would love to have a glass of wine with dinner and sent him to a package store on the far side of town. "It's the only place that carries that brand," she lied.

"I'll go, but I don't like being gone from here so much. Before opening the door, he said, "Have you talked to Zach lately?"

"Yes, while you were buying groceries." She laughed. "He's tired of cold pizza. Wants you to bring him back a brew and a bimbo—not necessarily in that order. Otherwise everything is a go."

At the door she gave him a lingering kiss and whispered in his ear. "This one is 'not for show.'"

Travis closed the front door and locked it.

A minute or two later, Joella heard the latch rattle. *That duplicate key must not work very well.* The door opened. "What did you forget?" Travis stood in the door wearing polyethylene gloves and canvas coveralls. Stunned, she staggered backward. *Holy Christ. He is MM!*

CHAPTER 54

Icy shivers shot through Joella's body. Her lungs constricted. Fusillading thoughts raced through her mind. *He's wearing his "working" clothes. I'm not a blonde. Did seeing me in a blonde wig for three days unhinge him?*

Trying to gain control, she gasped for air, her throat burning. She looked at his face again. *That's peculiar.* His expression seemed different somehow, but it would if he had a split personality. Then her eyes riveted on those black pools of coffee she so loved. "You're not Travis!"

She jumped back and screamed Zach's name while reaching for her gun. The shock of seeing the Travis's look-alike so unnerved her that the thought of using karate couldn't break through her panic. MM crossed the room in a blur of motion, punching her in the face; she crumpled like a rag doll, her phone flying across the room. She struggled to get up, blood spilling from her nose and lip. Looking at him, she spied *two* MMs—and two of everything else.

"Stay where you are or I'll slit your fucking throat right now. And you might as well take off that stupid wig, you're not his wife."

"What are you talking about? I'm Marion."

"What kind of an idiot do you think I am? His wife left town days ago."

Sweat beaded her forehead. "You've been watching the apartment that long?"

"Shit. I've been watching for weeks. And I know all about that cop next door. He won't be bothering us so don't get your hopes up."

He thinks there's only one. "My God, did you kill him?"

"I sure as hell wouldn't leave him alive to come after me. The jerk made it easy—he was pretending to listen to the transmission from the bug your guy planted, but eyeballing a silenced porno flick on his cell phone while jerking off. The flatfoot didn't even see it *coming*—he was already *doing* just that," he said, grinning as if replaying the scene from memory. MM's mouth twisted into a leer. "Had to admire his taste in educational film."

Her mind reeling, tears formed in her eyes. *Is it Zach or Watson?* Now sorry she'd sent Travis to the far end of town, Joella could only hope he had ignored her request and went to a closer liquor store. *Stall for time. Keep him talking.* "How did you get a key to Travis's apartment?"

"Don't need no damn key."

Her eyes glistened with fear and confusion. "What do you mean? How did you get into your victim's homes without breaking and entering? Did they let you in?"

"Shit, you are one dumb broad for a cop. Anybody can take an online locksmith course, no questions asked. I learned how to open doors early in their program—didn't bother finishing. Got so good I could open a lock almost as fast as using a key. A credit card use to work but now most of the damn bimbos have deadbolts. Have to use these handy-dandy little gadgets that locksmiths utilize," he said, taking the slender tensioner and a pick from his pocket and showing them to her. "The sluts didn't even hear me."

Joella glanced at MM and realized she no longer had double vision. She tried to rise.

"Stay where you are, bitch."

She sat, winching from the pain in her face. *I think he broke my nose.* Her lip had ceased bleeding but the blood from her nose ran toward her mouth and she tilted her head, wiping the blood with the back of her hand. *Keep him talking. Whatever you do, keep him talking.* "I'm curious. Why did you kill all your victims in the living room?"

His laughter had a creepy, menacing tone, reminding her of the old movie when Richard Widmark pushed granny's wheelchair down the stairs—with her in it. MM's twisted sneer boded pure evil. "Seemed logical. If you're going to *die*, what better place than the *living* room."

Joella used the edge of the coffee table attempting to get on her feet.

"Bitch, I told you to stay down." He bent over and punched her again, knocking her unconscious.

~ ~ ~

Rolling her over, he withdrew a knife from a leg holster and slit her clothes down the middle letting them fall on both sides of her body. "Don't need to wash the damn clothes this time, baby. You're both going down," he said as if she were awake, the words giving him exotic pleasure.

He retrieved the rucksack he'd dropped at the door and unpacked a roll of duct tape from a Ziploc bag. *No fibers on this baby for the cops to track.* Withdrawing the tape, he put two strips across her mouth, bound her ankles and wrists in front of her and picked up her immobile body, placing her on an upholstered armchair. He laid the tape on the floor by her feet and reached into the bag again. MM laid a scalpel next to the tape.

~ ~ ~

When Joella came to, she felt the coolness across her skin, the tautness on her mouth and around her limbs. Lowering her eyes, she detected the tape binding her naked body. An icy chill swept through her when she noticed the scalpel. *Hurry, Travis. Where are you? At least I'm not taped to the floor—yet.*

MM glared at her. "Good you're awake. Now all I have to do is sit back and wait for my fucking brother. You may not be his wife, but he's sure got the hots for you—that was quite a show you two put on last night. I had a great view through a gap in the drapes, just enough brightness from the nightlight to see. Too bad you gotta die baby—you got a hot little figure there and some mighty juicy looking tits." His mouth twisted into a sneer. "Shit, all this yakking is making me damn thirsty." He strode toward the kitchen.

Joella heard the refrigerator door open and slam shut; cupboard doors slammed too. She struggled with her hands trying to loosen the tape, but it wouldn't budge.

When MM came back, his face contorted in a sneer. "Fuck, that stupid flatfoot doesn't have a drink in the house. What a loser."

Joella's breath came in quick gasps. *Stay calm, Travis should be back soon. God help me. How can I warn him?*

CHAPTER 55

Travis had thought it wouldn't take long to get Joella's wine, but he couldn't find the brand she wanted on the shelf. When he asked the clerk, the man told him he'd sold the last bottle minutes earlier.

"I'll open another case in the backroom. Be right back." He limped around the counter dragging his stiff leg behind him.

Travis drummed his fingers on the counter and checked his watch again. When the man returned, Travis flung a twenty-dollar bill on the counter and snatched the bottle without waiting for change. His gut churning, he ran toward the door, hearing Gus's soft whisper in his mind: *"Hurry man—the path's ended."*

Travis slapped his emergency flasher on the roof, clamped it and hit the gas pedal. *I should have never let Joella talk me into going to the liquor store.* Two blocks away from his apartment, he turned off his light. At his building, he parked and ran to the entrance glancing at the stakeout car across the street. *Where the hell are Conway and Sidney? Did they get MM?*

He darted into the building and stopped at his door. All seemed quiet. Drawing his Glock, he pointed it at the floor. With his other hand, he withdrew the key from his pocket and put it in the latch. The door opened. He froze in mid-step at the horror before him.

MM stood behind Joella's chair, a large knife at her throat. She was naked, her clothes lying on the floor where they had fallen. Blood trickled from her nose, strangled mumbles coming from deep in her throat. "Drop the gun, buddy boy, or she gets it right now."

"You son-of-a-bitch. If you hurt her, I'll kill you myself."

MM's laughter would have wakened the dead. "Now just how do you plan to do that asshole? I'm in control. Not you. Now drop it and kick it over here."

His training forbid giving up his weapon, but one look at Joella and he slowly stooped over, laying his gun on the floor. He used his boot to skid the Glock toward MM.

"Now, cuff yourself."

"I don't have them."

"That's a crock." Grabbing Joella's hair, MM snatched her head back further and nicked her neck with his knife. A spot of blood appeared.

"Stop! I'll do it."

"Put 'em on. I want you alive—at least for now."

Travis pushed his jacket aside, removed the

cuffs from his belt and put them on his wrists.

"They should be behind your back but ain't taking a chance you'd be stupid and try to jump me. Hold up your hands."

"Okay, there on. See?" he said, jerking his wrists apart. *Gus is right. Even the smartest criminals eventually make a mistake. Before he had only one victim, now he has two, and he's enjoying himself so much, he isn't thinking. That's mistake number one.*

"Now plant your ass in that chair on the far side of the room. You so much as twitch, she gets it."

Travis walked across the room and sat. Checking Joella's tightly bound wrists and feet, he noticed MM hadn't tethered her to the chair. *Mistake number two, MM. But what the hell good will it do me now?*

Never removing the knife from Joella's throat, MM stretched out his leg and drew the Glock closer with his foot. He picked it up and finding no handy place to put the weapon, he laid it on top of the thick upholstered chair back. "Shit, you're lucky, buddy boy, I could have killed her a long time ago. But I've been waiting for you, sucker. The cops were too stupid to pin my crimes on you even after I furnished them your DNA."

"They aren't 'stupid.' My DNA isn't on file. They had nothing to compare your sample with. Why didn't you have your paid-for-eye-witness go to the police?"

MM grinned, exposing yellowed teeth, one missing on the right side. "That's was a nice touch, ain't it? I was saving him for the final nail in your coffin. But this shit's gone on too long. Figured you'd suffered enough and decided to give myself the pure pleasure of taking you out. I wanted to watch you fry in the chair, but the damn state changed the law—only do injections now. I gotta live with that but there is a bonus. Like Wrigley's gum, I get to double my pleasure watching you suffer while she dies. Then, you get yours." He snickered, "Think I'll hack your cock off—maybe a little slicing and dicing before the main event."

Travis's rage simmered at the explosion point. *If I ever needed to control my anger, it is now or we won't stand a chance. Maybe I can get the drop on him if I keep him talking long enough. Where the hell are Zach and Watson? One of them should be here. Unless...I need to keep him talking until I can catch him off guard.* "Why do you hate me—I've never done anything to you? I didn't even know I had a brother until recently."

"Cause you're stupid, flatfoot. I've known about you all my life."

"How could you when I didn't? Aunt Winona said I was an only child, and she was the midwife for my birth."

"That old crow—she wouldn't know a damn thing because our ever-loving father sold me to that blonde nymphomaniac only days after I was born. Dear ol' Dad got a hundred bucks for me, sight unseen. If Pa wasn't dead drunk, he was some fucking stud. He was humping both Ma and that so called adopted mother of mine, so I heard everything about you."

"Okay, but why didn't Mother tell me about you?"

"Cause the ol' man threatened to kill you if she did. The bastard knew he'd go to jail for getting rid of me, and Ma damn well knew he meant what he said. He *had* to keep you because Winona was there when you kicked so hard to get out. But when Ma had me, they were holed up in an abandoned prairie shack near Sweet Grass."

Travis leaned forward in his chair seeking a moment when MM might be distracted.

"Guess Pa was doing a little rustling and driving cattle across the Alberta border to sell. He didn't know about me—probably shit his pants when I came out. Didn't even bother with a damn birth certificate. He hid Ma out in that shack until he found the bleached bitch who bought me. She'd just lost a brat so was easy to pawn me off as hers." He paused, a grimace on his lips. "The damn nymph told me all about it when I was only a kid—thought it was funny as hell. She later visited Pa to give him the last of the money she owed for me. Ma brought you outside and the bitch laughed at the rags you were dressed in. Told me later, 'See how lucky you are.' I'd have gladly worn rags. Hell, I'd have gone buck naked to be in your shoes."

"I'm sorry you've had it so rough, but it wasn't my fault."

"The fuck it wasn't. If you hadn't kicked so hard to get out first, it would have been you sucking the bitch's tit."

"That is not true. I was born premature

because Father beat our mother so severely she went into early labor. I don't know why you weren't born at the same time, but you weren't." Travis gritted his teeth. "Wish I had known about you. I always wanted a brother. Here I find I have one and don't even know your name," he lied. "What is it? I called you MM because I hated the Merry Murderer nickname the Tribune attached to you after the second killing."

"You weren't the only one who wanted a brother, buddy boy. I did too."

Travis cocked his left eyebrow. *Is this guy a little human after all?* "Really, you longed for a brother?"

"Sure thing. I wanted one bad, real bad—one to share the sucking duties," he grimaced as if reliving the distasteful chore. "Hey, I'm famous, buddy boy, the whole world knows the Merry Murderer. My real name, not that it makes a damn bit of difference, is Duncan. That bitch named me after the priest she screwed on Sundays. Can't tell you the number of times I wanted to *dunk* her until she quit breathing. I ran away from home every chance I got, but the slut always called the cops. When they found me, they took me back. I was thinking of ways to kill the bitch, 'ways' I could get away with when she upped and died on me. I was thirteen."

"What did you do then?"

"Dear ol' Ma left me quite an inheritance—fourteen bucks. Didn't own the house where we lived and no life insurance. I swabbed out bars in Browning, sleeping in a corner most nights. I hustled for every nickel. Went hungry a lot. I wanted to get as far away from that fucking reservation as I could. Hitched a ride to Cheyenne with a trucker. The only decent guy I ever met. He actually gave me twenty bucks until I could find a job."

"Don't imagine that carried you far. What did you do then?"

"You got that right. Washed damned cars and swabbed out more bars for a few years. One night a dandified drunk was flashing a wad in the bar I was working at. When he left, I rolled him in the alley. Couldn't believe my luck. The dumb ass had $8,900 in his wallet. That kept me until I was sixteen.

"Before the dough ran out, I gave myself a nice little birthday present with my last few bucks. Picked up a blonde floozy in a bar. After some damn unfulfilling sex, she whined about my not using protection and bawled like an abandoned calf. The bitch was married and petrified she might get pregnant. She wailed and wailed. I knew it was only a matter of time before she'd go to the cops yelling rape—just in case. So I killed her. What an electrifying jolt. Hotter climax than with the bimbo."

"Was she your first victim?"

"Yeah, but after a sonic surge like that, I knew she wouldn't be the last. Stayed in Cheyenne a few years rolling drunks and slicing up a few sluts along the way. Got disgusted with my shitty life and decided it was time for a little justice. Make *you* pay." He rolled his eyes and released a long ominous snicker. "The cops in Cheyenne are dumb as those in Great Falls. They haven't solved the three cases I left them yet."

"I'm sorry, Duncan. But like I said, it isn't my fault. Had I known you existed maybe things would have been different. I could have helped you. When you know all the facts, I can see how your life took the path it did." He felt sick to his stomach at his false justification.

"Yeah, yeah sure. You think you can just erase the thirteen years of hell you put me through."

Travis turned away to hide his disgust. "How were you able to commit so many crimes without leaving evidence?"

"That's where I was smart. When I first located where you were and learned you were a cop, it gave me a great idea. I entered the Police Academy. Didn't wanna be no damn cop but figured what better way to learn how to commit a clean crime than study the mistakes others made. I'd already spent hours on the Internet reading detectives and cops' bragging websites. Damn educational." Pausing, a twisted grin spread across his face as if remembering his cleverness. "What I didn't learn there, I did at the academy—kind of like a Swiss finishing school. Learned all the tricks of the trade.

"How did you get into the academy? You have to be a high school graduate."

"Naw, they'll take you with a GED too. But I had to take that stupid damn test three times before I guessed enough right answers to pass. When I got out of the academy, I took an online locksmith course—no breaking and entering. Bet that left the pigs mystified. Wouldn't make the mistakes the other dumb dudes did. Killing lousy bitches and getting away with it became easy. Never left a clue."

"Like I said, Duncan, I could have helped if you had contacted me."

"Shut your damn face. My arm is getting tired. Time to get on with it." He switched the knife to his other hand and reached for Travis's Glock sitting on the armchair; he rammed it into his bag. Then MM pulled a revolver from his rucksack. He placed the barrel against Joella's temple. "Time for a little extra fun."

Travis gawked at the gun. *Silencers do not work on revolvers—but that is a silencer.*

"How do you like this heat, buddy boy? I had to roll a bunch of drunks to get enough dough to buy this baby. I had planned the 'extra fun' for you and figured I'd need a silencer. This dandy fits the bill: a Russian Nagant for a little Russian roulette," he said with a menacing sneer. "They quit making these babies in 1945, but you can still find them at gun shows, ammo too."

Travis felt the hair on the back of his neck stand on end. He saw Joella pupils dilate with fear and tried to ease her panic. "That antique couldn't kill a mouse."

"Hey, this baby has more power than a 22; besides, it doesn't need to be powerful. After I saw how hot you were for this chick, I decided to use it on her first. I hope she's lucky. Killing with a gun ain't my style—you know that. Carving is no fun if she's dead."

Travis glared at his brother. "Leave her out of this. Your quarrel is with me."

330

MM snickered. "Nice try." He laid the knife on the floor by the tape and scalpel. "You know how it works, flatfoot. I've already emptied the chamber except for one bullet." He gave the cylinder a spin and placed the barrel back on Joella's temple. "Let's see how lucky she is." His eyes were on Travis as he pulled the trigger.

The fall of the hammer on an empty cylinder sounded like dynamite in Travis's ear.

Joella recoiled, her face pasty white, sweat pouring from every pore.

Immediately, after pulling the trigger, MM swung around and pointed the Nagant at Travis who had jumped to his feet, as though MM had known he would.

"Plant your ass back in that chair. Well, whatta ya know. First timer's luck. Let's try this sucker again. Bang," he said, snorting. Joella jerked and after a moment tried to stand but Duncan cuffed her in the head, knocking her back onto the chair, her nose and lip fresh with new blood.

Travis jumped again.

"Try that again—one more time—and she's dead."

Rivulets of sweat rolled down his neck, Travis's shirt already clinging to his body. He swallowed the acrid tasting saliva in his mouth. *What in the hell can I do. Think man. Think...I have no choice. My odds aren't good, but I have to jump him and pray he misses me.*

Before he could rise, MM pointed the Nagant at Joella again and pulled the trigger. Travis felt his heart stop. Joella's eyes rolled back and she fainted. Duncan sneered eyeballing her. "Doesn't have much stamina for a cop, does she? It don't matter—you're the entertainment I wanted anyway. Wonder if you'll be as lucky as the bitch? Let's find out." A clatter at the door startled them. All eyes swiveled toward the door that burst open.

"What the hell," Duncan stormed. "You're not supposed to be here until after ten."

"I know. That was hours ago."

"Ten o'clock p.m. stupid—not a.m."

CHAPTER 56

Travis froze, eyes opening even wider. "Run! He's the serial killer."

Marion didn't move.

"Run," he yelled again. *Why is she standing there? Is she in shock seeing two of me?* "What are you doing here? You're supposed to be in Canada."

She laughed. "That was only a cover story. I never left town. Been holed up in a hotel going nuts because Duncan said I couldn't be seen anywhere."

"What?" Travis's mouth hung open, a gasp escaping. "How the shit did you know about my brother when I didn't?"

"Pure luck. The last time I was in Buford, I went shopping in Cheyenne and ran into him on the street."

"Yeah," said MM interrupting. "She thought I was you following her. A rabid raccoon couldn't have been madder; she was almost frothing at the mouth. Took me a long time to convince her I wasn't you. Afterward, we had a nice long chat over drinks. It didn't take long to realize we both wanted the same thing—you on a marble slab."

Travis glared at Marion. "You knew he was murdering all those poor women and didn't do a damn thing about it?"

"I didn't know. Not then. He just promised to make me a grieving widow. Claimed he felt sorry for me. After the second killing, he contacted me and said I had to get you to go fishing or drinking on a specific Sunday. I couldn't understand why." She stared at the floor for a moment. "That's when I suspected he might be the serial killer. I told him I didn't want to get involved, but he refused to kill you unless I helped. I'd been fantasizing about being a rich widow for weeks. I simply couldn't give up my dream—I was downright desperate. Anyway, he swore he'd never killed any decent women—only cheap, lousy sluts who deserved it."

Travis's highbrows shot up. "And that made it all right? You idiot. The only reason he came to town was to kill me."

"Well, how was I supposed to know that?"

"How the hell could you go along with him? You said you loved me."

"Loved you? Shit, I only married you after I learned I'd get your pension if you were killed. That and the hefty insurance policy I insisted you take out would make me a rich and merry widow. I figured with your holier-than-thou attitude and your ever-lasting determination to put those wife-beating husbands in jail that you'd get knocked off within a year or two. Never dreamt it would drag out for thirteen long and boring years. I couldn't take it any longer."

His wife's confession left Travis horrified, with a hard knot in his stomach. There'd been nasty remarks about his sanity in the past, and once he was convinced she wanted to get him committed, but he'd never realized she was capable of this.

For the first time Marion looked across the room at Joella. "Who the hell is that woman? Why is she naked?" Her eyes scanned the area around Joella. She took in the duct tape, scalpel and knife lying on the floor by her feet. Her face turned ashen, eyes shining with fear. I—I did everything you asked. I gave you all the information you wanted—the Sundays Travis didn't have an alibi." She sucked in a gasping breath. "I worked hard, hours sometimes, goading him into fights so he'd run to Ma's. But I didn't sign on for killing anyone while I was here."

MM's eyes were a glassy glower.

Marion began easing backward toward the door, her eyes locked on MM.

As Travis watched, he heard the Nagant emit a soft-sounding thud. Marion fell to the floor, a neat hole spurting blood between her eyes.

Travis stared at Marion's body, numb with the reality of the situation. When he refocused, he caught a glimpse of Duncan using the back of the chair to jam a shell into the Nagant. *Shit. He's had time to reload at least two.*

MM put the gun down and picked up the knife again. "Fun times over, kiddies. Let's get down to business." He gave Travis a glaring look. "You move that chair over in the corner. If you wiggle your ears, she gets it."

His eyes gleamed in high expectation. "Time to get this package ready." A twisted grin spread across MM's face as he started around Joella's chair. His eyes were riveted on Travis, and he caught his foot in her clothes lying on the floor. He lurched forward, dropping the knife.

Travis shot out of the chair like a loosed arrow. Before MM regained his balance, Travis grabbed him from behind, spreading his fingers around his brother's neck. Teeth clenched, Travis squeezed the jugular and larynx.

Duncan tried to pry Travis's fingers from his neck but he couldn't get leverage. His arms flailed, legs kicking back wildly. Travis's grip tightened like a predatory python.

Unable to see MM's face, Travis knew his eyes would be bulging, his complexion turning pallid. MM stopped moving within twenty seconds and sagged to the floor, seemingly unconscious. But in their current situation, Travis dared not allow him to recover and quickly knelt, continuing to compress his brother's neck. The voice he heard burning in his brain was not Gus's. It was his voice. *I'm killing my brother.*

Travis continued squeezing knowing it took two to four minutes for death by strangulation. When he was positive MM was dead, he ran to Joella. She winced as he slowly pulled the tape from her mouth.

She worked her mouth up and down. "Oh God, Travis. I was so sca—scared."

"Me too," Travis said as he carefully slid MM's knife between Joella's wrists, cutting the tape and then peeling it back to free her hands, wrists red and bruised from her struggles. "Reach in my jacket pocket for the cuff key." In moments, Travis was free.

"Oh, Lord, I tried to warn you but I couldn't

get loose." Her lips trembling she had difficulty speaking, but finally said, "I'm okay. Run next door. He killed either Zach or Watson; one of them must have been out. Go! I'll call the captain and the ambulance."

Travis grabbed his Glock from inside MM's rucksack. Finding no pulse on Marion's or Duncan's bodies, he ran to the apartment across the hall. When he opened the door, he spotted Watson, sprawled on the floor, cell phone still lying atop his relaxed hand, a neat hole in the center of his forehead and a path of dried blood. Travis checked for a pulse, crossed his hands over his chest and said a quick prayer to *Naató'si*. He no sooner finished when Zach burst through the door, his arm in a sling and his head bandaged.

Zach scanned the room, taking in the situation. His face turned pale. "Damn it, buddy, I'm sorry. This is my fault. Why was I so stupid to leave Watson alone? But he was driving me nuts with his constant bitching about stakeout boredom, his chicks and playing video games. He pigged out on our supplies so I went for takeout." He stared at Watson's body. "I should have sent him, but he is so irresponsible I was afraid he might not come back."

"We all make mistakes."

"Yeah, but my stupidity could have gotten you and Joella killed. Hope you can forgive me."

Remembering how it had taken Watson two hours to bring him his apartment key, Travis said, "You didn't have much choice. He didn't deserve to die, but Watson was not a good cop." Nodding at his arm sling, Travis said, "What the hell happened to you?"

"A drunk driver slammed into me and I spun into a telephone pole. Blacked out. My head was bandaged and my arm in a sling when I came to. The medics insisted I go to the hospital, but I ran to the patrol car leaving them yelling after me. When I got here, I called in an Officers Down."

"What are you talking about? Sidney and Conway?"

"Yeah. MM must have gotten them on his way in to your place. A double tap behind the head."

Travis frowned. "I didn't see them when I came from the wine store. They probably were slumped in their seats. Shit. Sidney had three little kids."

Travis ran back to the apartment to see Joella standing over MM wearing Marion's blue velvet robe she must have retrieved from the bedroom. "The ambulance is on its way."

Now free from paralyzing fear, Travis had a chance to scrutinize Duncan's face. His mouth fell open. He was looking in a mirror: there were his high cheekbones, craggy face and the now lifeless black eyes. *No wonder Watson swore he'd seen me at the Cheyenne rodeo.*

Travis felt pure revulsion glaring at the dead monster, but deep in his soul his emotions were conflicted, his face a picture of questioning misery. *Here lies the brother I always wanted.*

Joella stepped in by his side, taking his hand in hers. "I'm sorry Travis; but I'm glad he's dead. Dead before he got *his* revenge."

"He won't be killing any more blondes natural or otherwise. Guess we were alike in more ways than looks. We both were attracted to blondes: I married one—he killed them."

Joella squeezed his hand. "His death should bring an end to your platinum parade at night."

"They ended last night—thanks to you. And now I can finally tell Gus I found the right path."

Travis eyed MM again. *Duncan—my brother. What a waste.* He slowly raised his eyes heavenward, and addressed *Naató'si* with a different expression. This time, he did not cross his hands over his chest, the Blackfeet symbol of acceptance and thanks.

Joella looked surprised. "I haven't heard those words before. What does that mean, Travis?"

"There but for the grace of God, go I."

Feedback is essential for Indie Authors such as myself. If you've enjoyed THE GREEN TUNNEL, please leave me a review on Amazon. However, if you bought this book from the author, you must state that fact in the review or Amazon will not post it because they didn't sell the item. I would appreciate hearing from you.

ABOUT THE AUTHOR

Born in Great Falls, Montana, Dorothy Courtnage Wilson developed a passion for writing at an early age. Twenty-five years later she married a service man stationed at Malmstrom AFB. A gypsy's life commenced as the happy couple relocated from  Montana to California, Texas, Georgia, Louisiana, and Florida where she retired from the Civil Service. Her husband was never stationed abroad, so now Dorothy travels extensively.

Her interest in writing began at school with her love for poetry, which soon developed into self-pleasure writing: short stories, a novella, and a biography. Her second book, The Green Tunnel, is her first published work.

11593348R10210